Embracing My Submission

The Doms of Genesis, Book 1

Jenna Jacob

Embracing My Submission
The Doms of Genesis, Book 1
Jenna Jacob

Published by Jenna Jacob

Copyright 2012 Jenna Jacob
Edited by Chloe Vale
ISBN 978-0-9885445-1-2

DEDICATION

For Sean, Amy, Chris, Eric, Jessie, Tyler and Jack: You fill my life with joy and complete me. I love you with all my heart, forever and a day, no matter what.

For Shelley: I wouldn't be living my dream, if not for you. Two little words can't begin to convey what is in my heart, but...Thank You!

For Pearl: You talk me off the ledges and raise your pom-poms over and again. Thank you for sharing your heart of gold!

For Mom, Julie, and Cindy: Your unconditional love has made me a better woman.

For Sophie: Thank you for opening the door that started the wheels turning.

To Chloe Vale: I'm so glad you have the patience of a Saint. Thank you for your editing magic.

To my family and friends: Thank you all for your love and encouragement but most of all, for believing in me.

Take a peek at the end of this story for other Jenna Jacob titles soon to be released.

CHAPTER ONE

"Good evening Master George." I smiled uncomfortably as the Dom gazed into my eyes. Quickly turning my attention to Dahlia, his submissive, I relaxed. I didn't have to worry about saying the wrong thing or breaching protocol with a fellow submissive. Okay so maybe I'm a bit of a coward, but self-preservation is the key. Besides, the last thing I wanted was a Dominant reprimanding me for an unintentional breech of etiquette.

"Oh, Dahlia, I love your corset. Is it new?" I cringed inside as she remained silent and lowered her eyes. *Oh, hell!* I'd failed to ask Master George's permission to speak to his sub, thus breaching protocol. *Open mouth, insert foot...again. Priceless.*

"My apologies Master George." I swallowed tightly. "May I please have permission to speak to Dahlia, Sir?" My cheeks burned in embarrassment.

Daddy Drake, my protector and mentor, a muscle-bound, Leather-Daddy Dominant standing next to me, chidingly cleared his throat. I could feel his eyes boring into the side of my head like a frickin' laser beam while palpable displeasure rolled off his massive, tattooed body in waves.

A slight smirk curled on Master George's lips as I cringed and lowered my eyes. Staring down at the marred wooden podium inside the lobby of Genesis, a private BDSM club where I donated my time processing the patrons for a night of wicked pleasures, I hoped Drake wouldn't chastise me right then and there. I'd die a thousand deaths of embarrassment if he did.

Humiliation was a trigger for some submissives, but definitely not for me. Being taken to task in front of an audience might plummet some straight to their "submissive place," but it only served to piss *me* off. Not a stellar reaction for a submissive, to say the least. Hopefully Drake would wait until the members mingling in the lobby were processed and inside the club before he took me to task. I could hope anyway.

"Any other time I would grant your wish, Emerald. My girl thanks you for your compliment. And may I say you look quite ravishing as well."

I raised my eyes, smiling shyly then softly thanked him for his words of praise.

"Dahlia treasures your friendship, as do I. However, my girl has atonements to make this evening. If she repents to my satisfaction, perhaps later, before we leave, I will allow her to seek you out so you two may visit."

"Thank you, Sir," I whispered and lowered my eyes.

Master George issued a stern look at Dahlia. I wondered what she'd done to warrant his punishment. I didn't dare ask—I simply sent her a quick smile of reassurance, a small show of support to bolster her confidence for whatever reprimand awaited her. When she surreptitiously flashed me a quick smile and a subtle wink, I almost choked. The little vixen wasn't the least bit rueful. She'd obviously manipulated Master George in some fashion, coerced him into dispensing a punishment for *her* pleasure. An unacceptable ploy submissives sometimes pulled known as "topping from the bottom." I hoped she knew what the hell she was doing.

That type of subterfuge usually came back to bite a sub on the ass. I'd seen it happen time and again. Master George was a strict Dom and smart too. Dahlia's fate could be anything from a physical punishment to sitting in a corner the rest of the night alone. Being sequestered was a heinous punishment for any sub who ached to be used by their Dom. While some Dominants enjoyed a sub with a bit of sass, trying to force your owner to give you what you want versus asking for it was a dangerous game, indeed. Maybe Dahlia was just trying to keep Master George on his toes. *Yeah, good luck with that.* I painfully bit my lips together as I tried not to burst out laughing at Dahlia's manipulation. I'd be hard-pressed to come up with a plausible explanation to Drake or George if I allowed the tiniest giggle to escape.

"Drake. A pleasure as always." Master George smiled and shook my mentor's hand. "Where is your boy tonight?"

Drake issued a heavy sigh. "Trevor's inside the club. Sammie's keeping an eye on him for me. I've leashed him to the bar naked. Seems we both have some discipline to dispense this evening. I have every intention of firing his insolent ass up proper." A sadistic sparkle flashed across Drake's eyes.

I smiled tightly, envious of what awaited Dahlia and Trevor and longed to experience anything close to what they would receive. Unfortunately, I was missing one vital key...a Dominant. I would definitely need one to experience pleasure or pain. Knowing my fellow subs would be handing over their power to their Doms only served to reinforce the abysmal fear that I would never find the "yin" to my "yang," never get to experience the joys of submitting to my "one."

It didn't stop me from yearning. No, I was relentless when it came to envisioning a strong man to take my power, coalesce it with his own, and forge me on a fantastic submissive journey. My fixation to find a Dominant was a steady, all-consuming desire that seemed to morph into an edgy, where-the-fuck-is-he demand burning inside me. I fantasized—constantly—about being collared and living happily ever after in a Dom/sub relationship, always wondering when that day, if ever, would come. Maybe I wasn't meant to find an owner? Maybe I was destined to blow smoke up my own ass the rest of my life. Maybe there was no hope of assuaging the frustration plaguing my soul. Or maybe he was right around the corner.

You would think after pouring myself into the lifestyle, absorbing everything humanly possible about the dynamics of a Dom/sub power exchange, I would find one. Nope. Nada. I was still un-owned, still searching for that elusive "one." Kind of like a needle in a haystack. With my luck, I could probably plop my unfulfilled ass in a needle factory and still not find him. Yet I couldn't give up hope. It was all I had. And I was learning volumes about submission and the lifestyle as a whole, but it wasn't doing me a damn bit of good.

Scanning the group of members assembled in the lobby, I realized every submissive waiting to be checked in had a Master or Mistress. How utterly depressing. There were times, like now, that the overwhelming hopelessness of being un-owned stirred ugly, jealous feelings toward Dahlia, Trevor, and all the other owned subs. I felt shameful, as if I wore a scarlet letter.

Shaking my head to chase the negative thoughts from my brain, I focused instead on my blessings. I wasn't adrift in an ocean, flailing without a safety line. Drake had taken me under his wing as my protector and mentor. He was good to me and for me. He was held in high esteem in the community, but sometimes he was far too strict. I often wondered if his imposing size and reputation kept the available Dominants at bay. Were they unwilling to cross Drake's path? Or was it all me? Was I lacking in some basic submissive way? Like a quart low on submissive pixie dust or something? I had no clue. Exhaling softly, I knew I needed to steer my negative thoughts in a more positive direction. Start a mental gratitude list. That usually worked.

Drake did his best to see that my needs were met. Over the years, we had formed a close bond, both in and out of the club. I loved him like a brother, and he knew me better than I knew myself. He always tenaciously forced me to analyze my motives and actions, even when I didn't want to, and he never once gave up on me. I had to look at the big picture. Being protected by Drake made me a very lucky woman, even if I could still feel his eyes burning into my skull. Watching and waiting as George and Dahlia parted the heavy velvet curtains and entered the club, I turned and faced Drake. Arching my brow, I held up my palms to stave off his lecture.

"I know. I know."

"If you knew, then why did you?"

Dissuading him with a look of innocence, I shrugged. "I always talk to Dahlia and Master George. It's part of my job to be friendly and welcoming. It's what I do." Batting my lashes at him in feigned innocence, I grinned.

Obviously seeing through my veil of finely crafted bullshit, he shook his head, sighing in disgust. "If I owned you, I'd whip your ass."

"You still can!" I smiled, winking mischievously.

"No, sweetheart. You'd enjoy that way too much. Where would the lesson be?" His lips curled in a tight condescending smirk as more members filtered through the door.

The lobby filled quickly, but that was normal for a Friday night.

8

Drake and I hastily checked them in at the podium. I smiled at the familiar faces as they laughed and talked. It warmed my heart that so many had grown to be valued friends over the years. We were like a family of sorts. An extremely kinky family, but a family all the same.

Scanning the crowd, my eyes leveled upon...*him*. Tall and handsome, with rugged features. A broad frame with scrumptiously wide shoulders, like a football player. The man had a thick neck and a narrow waist. My heart thundered in my chest as my mouth began to water. Sandy-blond hair carelessly framed the most incredible ocean-blue eyes I'd ever seen. A shiver ran down my spine and my nipples pebbled.

The stranger was dressed in black slacks with a tight-fitting black T-shirt that molded and outlined his rippling biceps and pecs. I swallowed the lump in my throat as he smiled, chatting with the people around him. His dazzling smile could light the sun. My stomach flip-flopped as a needful throb centered between my legs. I nervously licked my lips and stared like a doe in the headlights at the gorgeous man.

He certainly wasn't the one I was expecting. He was nothing like the man I hoped would someday walk through the door. But then only a fool would continue searching faces in the crowd for some vaporous apparition from a reoccurring dream. No sane person would waste their time looking for a ghost. Especially not the hunky ghost that haunted me nightly, or the equally mysterious she-ghost who always appeared first, begging me to *"find him."* I had no idea who the two specters were or what they wanted, but without fail, they tandemly invaded my dreams nearly every damn night. Over time, I'd grown to expect them before I drifted off to sleep. I'd even given them names. He was "Sir Drool." The dude was drop-dead gorgeous and had an aura of Dominance that nearly brought me to my knees. And I'd dubbed her "Fanny-Frustration." The woman persistently pestered me to find the elusive Sir Drool. Most mornings I woke up exhausted from running down endless halls brimming with closed doors in an attempt to locate the phantom Dom. Obviously there was more symbolism in my stupid dream than I cared to dissect. Hell, I'd given my nightly visitors names, thus proving I was a few French fries short of a kid's meal.

9

Fanny-Frustration always appeared first. The woman bore an uncanny resemblance to me, but for reasons I couldn't explain, I knew she wasn't me. Fanny was an elegant gossamer apparition with a voice like an angel. She was soft and sure, continually drilling me to *"find him—find my 'one.'"*

Was she on crack? Didn't she know I'd spent the better part of four years trying to find *any* Dom, let alone the mouthwatering hunk she summoned night after night? As if that weren't torture enough, she had to ratchet my frustration level by conjuring images of the melt-your-panties-in-a-puddle Dom over and again.

Sir Drool was so decadently captivating, I would often wake to find my covers tangled around my feet and my fingers plunged deep inside my slick, quivering sex. Broad shoulders with thick, roped muscles bulging beneath his milk-chocolate flesh alone was incentive for my fingers to dance beneath the covers. But it was his liquid amber eyes that fueled powerful sleeping orgasms. Sir Drool always appeared with an obscure, mischievous twinkle in his shimmering butterscotch eyes. A girl could get lost in those eyes. Lost and never want to find her way home.

Oh, but it didn't stop there. His one stunning feature that drew me like a moth to a flame was his lips, or rather his bottom lip. It was thick and full and so damn inviting. A deep, ripe, sensual peach color so enticing I longed to reach out and skim my finger over the full brim. I wanted to slide my tongue across its plumpness and capture it between my teeth.

As far as dreams went, I couldn't complain with such toe-curling eye candy. But the unsettling part was Fanny's crushing, frantic, stubborn demand that I find him, amplifying my dissatisfaction with being un-owned.

In all my days at the club, I'd never glimpsed anyone who looked remotely close to Sir Drool. Every bald, light-skinned African American male that walked through the door caused my neck to snap and my belly to tighten in anticipation. Yet none turned out to be *him*. As ludicrous as it seemed, I found myself falling a little in love with the dream man. Yeah, there had to be a straightjacket out there with my name on it somewhere.

The striking blond man standing in the lobby wasn't remotely close to Sir Drool, yet I felt particularly drawn toward him with an unsettling chemistry of sorts. I felt like a vapid sophomore drooling over the star quarterback. I couldn't look away. Was there such a thing as lust at first sight? Maybe. Or maybe I was just too horny for my own damn good.

There was no denying the man made my blood pump, my knees weak, and my needy pussy shamelessly respond. My palms were sweaty, and butterflies were having a free-for-all in my belly. Not to mention I was dripping wet. I stood staring at the man silently praying he was a Dominant...an un-attached Dominant. Not that I was desperate or anything. *Yeah. Right.*

I leaned to whisper to Drake, asking if he knew the man. He shrugged his beefy shoulders and shook his head no. That was odd. Drake knew every member of the club. Evidently, the sexy mystery man was new. I focused, well somewhat focused, on checking in the members while trying not to blatantly stare.

I jerked, gasping as Drake tugged my hair. "It's not polite to stare, girl," he whispered tersely in my ear.

"I'm trying not to," I murmured as tiny contractions rippled through my drenched core.

"Try harder," he growled.

"Yes, Sir," I whispered then closed my eyes for a moment, willing my sensitive nipples to cease throbbing. That didn't work either. As the stranger made his way to the podium, anxiety blossomed like a spring flower. My body lit up like a Christmas tree.

"Good evening." His deep voice reverberated in my chest, and a flurry of goose bumps peppered my arms. His stunning smile sent my blood pressure to near stroke level while my knees shook like baby saplings in a hurricane. I wanted to groan as my nipples pebbled painfully beneath my corset.

Unable to resist, I stared at the tiny lines gathered at the corners of his hypnotic blue eyes.

"This is my first visit to Genesis. My name is Sir Jordon, and you are?"

That voice. *Oh sweet mercy!* He was pulling me under in a swirling, churning ocean of debauchery. Images of him thrusting deep inside, driving me into sexual oblivion, or gazing up at me between splayed thighs while he feasted on my slick and ungodly swollen folds filled my mind. I swallowed tightly, trying to chase

11

away the vivid imagery. Protocol dictated I lower my gaze...but beat my ass crimson, there was no way in hell I could look away.

"I'm Emerald, Sir Jordan." The breathless tone of my voice sounded like a starving sex kitten.

A wolfish smile tugged at his mouth as his eyes flickered then settled on me with a smoldering gaze.

"Welcome to Genesis. We're pleased to have you join us this evening." I managed to force out the words with a little more confidence.

His eyes held mine. Captivating. Entrancing. And his lips curled into an even more alluring smile. "Emerald. What a lovely young thing. You are simply breathtaking, pet. Your Master or Mistress must be immensely proud of such a fine, succulent sub."

My stomach flip-flopped in fear as I flashed an edgy and cautious look at Drake. *Master? Mistress? If you only knew, pal.* The trifling thought careened through my brain as I stood frozen like a granite statue.

"Good evening, Jordon. My name is Drake."

Bless Daddy for breaking the awkward silence as he extended his hand. "Welcome to Genesis. It's a pleasure to meet you."

Somehow, I peeled my eyes off the tantalizing newcomer and cast them downward, thankful that Drake did not reveal my discreditable, un-owned status.

"I believe Mistress Ivory is your tour guide this evening. If you'd care to follow me, I'll be happy to make the introductions." Drake stepped behind me, swatting my ass as he began to escort Jordon into the club. "Behave."

I shot him a scowl. I'd not done anything bad...yet.

"I look forward to seeing you inside, shimmering Emerald." The beguiling smile that spread over Jordon's lips curled my toes. My throat was dry and constricted. I glanced into his gorgeous eyes and issued a nervous nod, then immediately dropped my gaze.

Trembling as I peeked from beneath my lashes, I watched the muscular pair of Doms walk away. I greedily admired Jordon's tight ass, broad muscle-defined shoulders, and long, thick legs. The man made me melt like a candle.

You bet your hot ass you'll be seeing me later, Sir. I'll make damn sure of that, I silently promised as I tried to control my trembling hands. Exhaling deeply, I gathered my wits and focused on checking in the remaining members in line.

Trying to herd them through as quickly as possible, my mind wasn't on task. It was focused beyond the thick velvet drapes. I wondered what Jordon was doing, who he was talking to, what he thought about Genesis, and if he was serious about wanting to see me inside the dungeon. What if an available sub had already set her sights on him and was trying to woo him? Anxiety stabbed my chest. I had no claim on the man, but I didn't want to be shot out of the water before I had a chance to launch.

In less than thirty minutes, the lobby had cleared. Of course to me, it felt like hours. I smiled a bit too anxiously at James and Tony, the security personnel working the main door.

"It's ten o'clock. Time to lock up, Emerald." James pulled a ring of keys from his pocket and locked the heavy wooden doors. "Ready to go join the fun?"

"Always. Are you two working the dungeon or the private rooms tonight?" I asked, stacking up the pages listing the names of members in attendance for the evening. My job would be complete once I dropped the papers off to Mistress Sammie, the club's bartender.

"Tony and I are working both. Will we get a chance to watch you scene tonight?"

"I wish." A skeptical chuckle rolled from my throat. "Don't hold your breath. That's not even remotely in the cards for me tonight. I'll be watching and wanting."

"Damn! I was hoping we'd get to see Mistress Sammie help you relieve some stress," James teased with a sly wink.

"In your dreams and mine." Blowing a heavy sigh of frustration from my lips, I shrugged. "Drake's got me on big O-denial. I swear I think that man secretly wishes my hymen would grow back or something."

"Ah, yes. Orgasm denial. Effective little tool." James smirked.

"Oh, like you suffer from that. Don't even go there. You're a switch. All you have to do is issue your own command, and poof, you're off that restriction," I teased.

"Sort of." He laughed.

"How's your girl?" I asked as I followed him to the thick velvet curtain.

"Arianna is not my girl. She's a switch like me. We just work well together." He grinned.

Having seen James submit only a handful of times, he always seemed more like a Dom than a sub to me. There was no doubt he had the best of both worlds. He could dominate or submit, and having a partner do the same would ensure every clawing desire would be met. *Lucky bastard!*

I never could wrap my head around dominating another person. It wasn't in my DNA. But then again, if I didn't find a Dom soon, I might have to reconstruct my DNA just to get the orgasms I craved. Pondering that thought, I tried to find a downside, and at the moment there was none. But dominating another? No. It didn't float my boat in the least. If I held the Dominant power, I'd only give myself permission to come, and once that was done, I'd probably still feel empty and hollow inside. Toss that notion to the curb.

Looping my elbows through the men's thick, muscular arms, I sashayed through the opened curtain. The dungeon was full. Practically all fifty stations lining the walls were in use, and every table in the center of the room where guests could watch and visit was occupied. Yes, Genesis was packed tonight.

The sound of cracking whips and slapping paddles, accompanied by various octaves of pleasure-filled moans and cries of pain, echoed throughout the room. The air was heavy with the rich, musky scent of sex. Members seated at the tables talked in low murmurs, but their voices were drowned out by the copious sounds of play.

I found Dahlia naked on her knees, her mouth working furiously upon George's glistening hard shaft. In his hand, snapping robustly upon Dahlia's exposed ass, was a wicked black buggy whip. Her eyes were glassy as she looked up at him with a loving expression. Her body jerked at each well-aimed strike of the whip. George caressed her hollowed cheeks with his other hand as his lips moved in private conversation, no doubt praising the girl for accepting his punishment.

Filled with longing, I watched their exchange. I was happy she was able to fulfill her submission but secretly wished I could be Dahlia for an hour or two. Lost in fantasy, I failed to notice that

14

James and Tony had abandoned me. They'd veered off in different directions to help monitor the dungeon's activities. Feeling alone and a little vulnerable, I made my way toward the bar.

Skimming my eyes over the crowd in hopes of catching a glimpse of Jordon, I paused, taking in all the sights. Submissive bodies were stretched taut and secure against numerous St. Andrew's Crosses. Others were tethered to wooden suspension frames, kneeling on the carpet, or laid out on long, padded tables. Their Doms and Domme's administered everything from soothing cupping to wicked, stinging whips. They all looked spectacular in their submission.

So many vibrations hummed through the air, it was hard to absorb them all. The low static crackle of violet wands interspersed with laughter and cries of pain. Being surrounded by like-minded people who shared the same desires comforted and soothed me.

A grateful smile spread across my lips as Mistress Sammie placed a soda on the bar. I smoothed down my billowing corset skirt and slid onto a padded barstool. Handing her the guest list, I took a long drink. "Thank you, Mistress."

Sammie, a petite blonde Domme with shimmering pale blue eyes and ample breasts that barely remained harnessed beneath a black leather corset, smiled and nodded. Her thin legs were firmly sheathed within glossy red leather pants, and how she managed to walk, let alone work in her trademark five-inch stilettos, constantly blew my mind.

"It's busy tonight. Do you need any help behind the bar?"

"No, honey. You go enjoy yourself. You've already worked the door. Get out there and mingle. I've got it all under control." Refilling my cup, she smiled broadly, her bright red lips glistening beneath the recessed lighting above the bar.

"I think I'll do that. Have you seen Daddy Drake?"

Pointing across the room to a large St. Andrew's Cross, she issued a wicked laugh. "Poor Trevor is getting his ass fired up. He was tied here all night, worrying his nut-sack about what Drake had in store. I wish I wasn't working. I'd offer to help out." The anxiousness in her voice made me shiver.

"I think you big bad Dom's just live and breathe to gang up on us poor innocent subs," I teased with a low giggle.

15

"The day you're innocent is the day I'm a virgin." Sammie laughed heartily. "Trust me, girl, it wouldn't take much for a few of us big bad Dom's to gang up on you. You just keep claiming innocence and see what happens." She gave me an evil grin.

"Yikes!" A nervous giggle escaped my lips as I jumped up from the barstool.

Sammie was the only Dominant Drake ever allowed to play with me. The two had been friends for years, and Sammie was his valued confidant. That trust made it easy for me to submit to her. She was always tender yet firm. Everything she introduced me to was through physical sensation and not mental control. From the soft tickle of a feather to the stinging bite of a Dragon's Tongue, she gleaned great pleasure in slowly ratcheting up my repressed orgasms. Amplifying every sensation until she reduced me to pitifully begging through my tears, she'd keep me suspended on the cusp of release. It always amazed me how she could coax so many earth-shattering orgasms from me.

At first, I was nervous about having a woman touch me. But I soon grew to love her feminine Dominance. She was like leather and lace: rough and demanding in a devilish but delicate way.

Watching all the Doms and subs, I once again began to feel bitter. Determined to nip it in the bud, I reminded myself to count my blessings.

Turning my attention to the cross Trevor was cuffed to, I watched, captivated, as Drake's whip trailed wicked red welts upon Trevor's already reddened and striped butt cheeks. Trevor's back arched, and he choked out a tormented cry as Drake intently watched his slave and lover accept his castigation. His focus was fixed, and he was attuned to his slender, ivory-skinned slave boy cuffed to the wooden frame. As Trevor's body slumped forward, his head and shoulders drooped between the deep *V* at the top of the cross. His shoulder blades nearly touched as his arms bore the weight of his body and his desperate cries of pain filled the dungeon. My heart clutched in helplessness.

Trevor wasn't just a submissive brother, he was my closest friend. I ached to help him, but there was nothing I could do. Clueless to what dreadful transgression he'd committed to warrant Drake's vicious punishment, all I could do was watch and cringe.

I drew in a quivering breath as Drake lowered the whip and stepped forward, gripping a handful of Trevor's long blond hair in his paw-like hand. Pulling his slave's head back, Drake murmured something into the wailing man's ear then languidly swiped his tongue up Trevor's neck. Stopping briefly to nibble his ear, Drake began seducing away the pain from his sobbing boy. I watched him lick Trevor's lips, which opened readily, and the two men shared a sweltering, erotic kiss that brought a tender smile to my lips. I was awed at the control in which Drake brought his lover down from the edge with tenderness, compassion, and love. Trevor gave his all without reservation. With total acceptance. With absolute devotion. Unconditional love. In my eyes, Trevor was submission personified.

A tear of admiration blurred my vision. As soon as Trevor regained his composure, Drake stepped back and began arching the whip high into the air.

Engrossed in the tantalizing scene, I took two steps forward and promptly ran tits-first into Sir Jordon. His massive, hard chest was like a wall. The soda in my cup slopped like a tiny cresting wave, spilling over my hand and onto the floor.

CHAPTER TWO

"Whoa. Hold on a minute. Where are you going in such a hurry, beauty?"

Electricity raced through my body as Jordon's erotic voice rumbled from his massive chest, vibrating against my tender nipples. I wobbled precariously on my high heels as his strong fingers clutched my waist. His touch was firm and unrelenting as he continued to hold me in place not only with his hands, but also with his hypnotic eyes. My mind filled with images of those strong, capable hands gripping my shoulders while his shaft thrust deep into my weeping sex. Oh, God! Not only did I drench him with my soda, I just drenched my panties, too. Damn.

"Oh!" I gasped in embarrassment. "I'm so sorry, Sir. I didn't...I wasn't watching where I was...did I spill any on you?" Mortified, I shook the wet soda off my hand.

"No, sweet girl, you didn't. Are you all right? Can I get you a napkin?" His alluring eyes sparkled with invitation.

My nipples screamed painfully as another rush of cream saturated the small strip of cloth between my legs. Granny panties couldn't have captured the torrent gushing from my barren pussy, let alone the scant G-string I wore.

"No, Sir. I'm so sorry," I whispered as my face burned in a combination of arousal and embarrassment.

"Nothing to be sorry for, girl. No damage done." Looking at the cup in my hand, he frowned. "I think you need to get your owner another drink, though."

"Oh no, Sir...it's not for...it's mine," I stammered, nibbling on my bottom lip and casting my eyes to the floor. Damn it. Why did he continue to assume I had an owner? I couldn't very well blurt out that I was the odd sub out. I'd made a big enough fool of myself.

"Raise your eyes, girl. Tell me, where is your owner?"

Following his instructions, I pensively gazed into his erotic, cerulean eyes, certain he'd heard me swallow the basketball-sized

18

lump lodged in my throat. Hell, even Drake, clear across the dungeon, cracking his whip, could have heard it. *Gawd, can you make a bigger fool of yourself?* Suddenly the soda slipped through my wet fingers and landed with a heavy thud on the floor.

"Oh shit!" I gasped. Great. Just great. I cussed in his face loud and clear. Could I fuck this up any more than I already had? Obviously I could because I just did. Tears burned my eyes as I lowered my head. I couldn't look at him. Terrified repugnance at my foul mouth and clumsy incompetence would be reflecting in his eyes. I did the only thing I could do. I turned and ran to the bar.

"Mistress Sammie. I spilled my soda." I wiped away the tears cresting over my lashes before they spilled down my cheeks.

"Emerald? Why on earth would spilling your drink make you cry?" Sammie's eyes narrowed in concern as she instructed Joe, her bar helper, to get the mop and towels. With so many members wearing high-heeled stilettos, it was paramount the spill get cleaned and dried immediately. "Where is the spill, honey?"

"There!" I pointed toward the tiled section of the floor where I'd made an absolute fool of myself. I couldn't look up. I didn't want to see Jordon running for the front door screaming in horror at my totally un-submissive first impression.

"I got it," Joe called as he rounded the bar.

"Do you want another drink?" Sammie asked in a combination of confusion and concern.

"No, Ma'am."

"So why the tears? It's just a spilled soda, and Joe's getting it taken care of. It's no big deal. Why has that upset you so much?"

"I don't know. I'm being stupid." I sniffed and dabbed my eyes with a bar napkin. "Can I please have Daddy's key? I want to go back and set up for Trevor's aftercare."

"Sure honey. Do you need to talk about anything?" Sammie pressed as she handed me the key.

"No, Ma'am." I shook my head as I accepted it. "Thank you."

Confessing my *faux pas*, even to Sammie, was humiliating and infuriating. I could feel my anger bubbling inside like a superfluous volcano. I needed time to try and cool off. Without looking back, I raced toward the private rooms. The narrow hallway was empty, void even of security staff. My fingers trembled as I plunged the key into the lock. Opening the door, I flipped on the light. The familiar surroundings of Drake's private room began to soothe my agitation.

Folding down the heavy spread from the king-sized bed, I shook my head. "Damn it! I finally find a Dom that intrigues me and I go and make a total ass out of myself. Priceless! God, I'm such an idiot." I sighed heavily, pulling down the soft cotton sheets, talking to myself like a mad woman.

"He probably thinks I'm a ditz. A certifiable loon. And why shouldn't he? I've just confirmed the obvious...I'm worthless. No wonder I can't find a fucking Dom."

Fighting back tears, I set Drake's favorite lube and a six-pack of condoms on top of a towel next to the bed. "And if I don't stop acting like a dork, I'll never find a Dom. Like there's a chance in hell of that in the first place. I'm so stupid. Shit."

I exhaled a heavy sigh as my shoulder sagged in defeat. "And swearing in front of him, now that's ripe."

The more I chastised myself, the angrier I got. Setting four squares of milk chocolate next to the towel, I grabbed a silver ice bucket from the shelf. Tossing in bottles of juice and water, I stomped toward the door, intending to fill the bucket with ice from the machine at the end of the hall. Looking down, I once again slammed into Sir Jordon. The bucket slipped from my hand and crashed to the floor.

"Oh for shit's sake!" I whined in frustration as I crouched and righted the bucket, shoving the plastic bottles back inside. My face burned in embarrassment, and I longed to melt into the thick ivory carpet, to vanish from view.

"Having a bit of trouble with slippery fingers tonight girl?" Sir Jordon chuckled softly.

"Evidently." I sighed. "I'm sorry, Sir. I'm usually not quite so clumsy."

"Think nothing of it," he whispered. "However, I do have a slight bone to pick with your owner." Suddenly his tone changed from a carefree timbre to a stern, acrimonious tone.

"What have I done, Sir?" I jumped to my feet and gazed into his incensed eyes as a tremor passed through my body.

"Twice now I have asked you one simple question, and twice now you've failed to answer me. I've come to the conclusion that either *a*, you are being rudely disrespectful to me on purpose, or *b*, you're embarrassed to reveal who your owner is." He titled his head slightly, a scolding yet erotic fire blazing in his eyes.

"Or *c*, Sir. You obviously didn't think about option *c*." I didn't plan for my voice to project such a sarcastic tone, but he'd backed me into a corner. I had no other option than to miserably confess I was un-owned.

"What is option *c*?" He pursed his decadent lips, his focus on me so intense, I felt like he was piercing my soul.

"I don't have one!" I could hear the anger in my voice.

"You don't have an option *c*?" One eyebrow arched and his handsome face reflected complete confusion.

"No!" I snapped. "I'm un-owned, goddammit!"

Convinced that my fate had been sealed, it didn't seem to matter that my voice was bellicose and condescending. I was a lost cause. No sense trying to hide the obvious. He knew it, and I knew it.

Pushing past him, I ran to the ice machine, all the while hoping he would go back to the dungeon and leave me to my self-loathing anger. Furiously shoveling ice into the bucket, I didn't dare look back at Drake's doorway. *Please let him leave. Just make him go away.*

When I turned to find him leaning nonchalantly against the doorframe, his thick arms crossed over his broad chest and watching me through narrowed eyes, my feet issued a slight stuttered step. Damn, but he was gorgeous. Even wearing that ferocious, pissed off expression, he was handsome to a disturbing degree.

Casting my eyes toward the floor, I stormed back into the room, shoulders slumped. A hint of musk and sandalwood carried in the air as I breezed by. He smelled virile and erotic. My stomach swirled as I inhaled deeply, wanting to imprint his exquisite scent to memory, to etch it to my soul and balefully merge him with the other unattainable Dominants long past. My face burned in shame, commensurate to the fiery sexual hunger blazing in my veins.

"Why not?" he asked as he followed me into the room.

Placing the ice bucket on the nightstand with a heavy thud, I turned and in a bold un-submissive move, I glared into his eyes. I'd already inflicted all the damage I could ever do to the whole situation. I had nothing left to lose. "Why not what, Sir?" The tone of my voice was fraught with impatience and disgust.

"Why no owner, girl? Besides your recalcitrant mouth, which alone proves you need a strong Dominant to keep you under his thumb. You intrigue me, Emerald." Standing much too close, his warm breath wafting over my lips, shards of lightning ignited up my spine. "Tell me why you have no owner, girl?"

"I...I...." I was attempting to find a reason as Drake entered the room carrying Trevor in his massive, bulging arms.

"Emerald?" His voice held a tone of concern.

Feeling like a teen caught by a father necking with her date on the front porch, I stepped away from Jordon. "Everything's ready, Sir." I nodded and swallowed tightly as I followed Drake to the bed.

"Are you all right?" Drake asked as he laid Trevor upon the mattress. His boy's back and ass were covered in a patchwork of wicked, red welts. Trevor whimpered as he curled into a fetal position.

"Yes, Sir. I'm fine." I nodded, though I had no idea where my sudden bravery came from. Maybe it was simply having Drake in the room, knowing the imposing Daddy Dom was there and had my back. For whatever reason, I felt a wave of relief wash over me.

"May I please comfort?"

"You may." Drake nodded solemnly then turned his attention toward Jordon.

I turned and climbed onto the bed. Peeking over my shoulder, I saw a look of unease settle upon Drake's face.

"Is there something I can help you with Jordon?" His tone was strangely reminiscent of a reprimanding father. I smiled.

"No. I was simply talking to Emerald while she prepared for your arrival." That calm and carefree demeanor had returned. He flipped it on and off like a light switch, which I thought was strange. I suspected it was probably some bizarre form of Dom posturing.

"Ahhh, I see. You're more than welcome to watch her comfort my boy if you'd like," Drake invited.

"Thank you. I'd enjoy that very much."

I sensed the two men approaching as I crawled alongside Trevor. Holding a bottle of water and a piece of chocolate in hand, I knelt next to him. Softly caressing his peaceful face, I smiled. He was flying high in his subspace. I'd never experienced it before, but

22

an ache to be floating right alongside him filled me. Swallowing back the tightness in my throat, I opened the water.

"Take a drink sweetheart," I whispered in Trevor's ear. His pathetic whimper brought a smile to my lips. "Shhh. It's just me baby. Let me help you. Come on honey, take a drink."

Placing my arm behind his neck, I eased his head until his lips met the bottle's rim. Softly murmuring, I coaxed as he guzzled the water. A quick nod of his head indicated he'd had enough. Sealing up the water, I placed a piece of chocolate against his lips. "Here's some sweet."

Trevor moaned as he savored the milky brown square. "Thank you," he whispered.

I smiled and lightly threaded my fingers through his sweaty, tangled hair. Leaning forward, I peppered the side of his face with gentle kisses. He groaned and turned for a kiss on the lips. Suddenly, Drake's firm hand was gripped in my auburn curls, and with a brutal yank, he pulled me away from Trevor's mouth.

My nipples shriveled, my juices flowed, and my clit screamed. Tiny whimpers filled the room...my whimpers. Involuntary tremors wracked my body as it responded the way it always did when someone pulled my hair. Quaking and quivering uncontrollably, my hips writhed from side to side. My swollen folds teased my turgid clit. I needed to come and come hard.

"I love watching your reaction to this, Emerald," Drake praised in a loving tone. "Are your nipples hard, girl?"

"Y...yes, S...Sir," I whimpered, my tunnel contracting with a vicious squeeze.

"Is your pussy wet?" Drake's tone was feral yet taunting.

"Y...yesss, Sirrr." I groaned in a combination of excitement and embarrassment, knowing Jordon watched the exchange.

"Yes, pet. I know it is. I can smell you. If I were hetro, I'd fuck you so hard you wouldn't walk for days," Drake growled, lightly nipping his teeth upon the sensitive column of my neck, further fueling the intensity of my hunger.

My tunnel convulsed tightly as I gasped in big gulps of air.

"Mistress Sammie discovered this little trigger during a scene with Emerald. It was quite erotic," Drake explained to Jordon. "You came hard that night didn't you, sweet girl?"

23

I whimpered affirmatively as I continued to quake.

"Yes. Your screams filled the dungeon as you shattered on the cross. Every Dom in the club, straight and gay, sported painful erections watching you come undone."

"What an amazing trigger," Jordon praised in a slight sigh. "Such an exceptional girl."

"Yes. She's beyond treasure. She's a once-in-a-lifetime find."

"And yet...she's not owned. Pity," Jordon whispered.

"You won't kiss my boy's mouth tonight, girl. Do you understand me?" Drake's directive was savage. "He's not earned your treat. He'll have to suffer without his sister's compassion."

I moaned louder as Drake tugged, reinforcing his instruction. "Yes, Sir. I...I under...understand you." I gasped, praying he'd release my hair before the mounting orgasm consumed me in front of Jordon.

"You act like you need to come, girl. Do you?" Drake growled, tugging once again.

"Yes, Sir." I whimpered in a pathetic plea. "I mean, no Sir."

My mind was a jumbled mass of confusion. I desperately wanted...*needed* to come, but I felt awkward and confused. Surely Drake didn't mean to muster my orgasm, did he? He'd always relegated that task to Mistress Sammie. And never before had he provoked me in such an intimate manner. Ever.

"Not by you. You don't like vaginas." I knew I was making little sense.

A low rumble of laughter rolled from deep in his throat. "You're right, sweetheart. I don't like vaginas. They're messy little caverns, always leaking and puddling. I'm strictly a cock man. Your panting and vicious trembling tells me you want to come, just not by my hand. Is that correct?"

"Yes, Sir."

"But would you like to come by Jordon's hands?"

His words enticed me in a teasing, taunting tone. My mind was screaming. *Yes! Yes, yes, a thousand times yes. I need to come. I want to feel his hands on my bare flesh. I want to taste his mouth, his tongue, his cock, to feel him drive deep inside me, and I want it, now!* But the desperate plea lodged in my throat. All I could do was cry in a pitiful moan.

24

"You don't know anything about him, girl. He's a stranger. Would you really want to come for a stranger? Let him fondle you. Stroke you. Urge your release?" Drake's whispered words were laced with enticing subjugation.

"I don't know." I gasped in confusion. I was torn between the onslaught of demand scraping for freedom and the fear of a total stranger setting it free.

"Of course you do. You want to come, don't you pet?" he whispered lovingly in my ear as he firmly tugged my mane.

A soft mewl floated from my lips.

"Don't worry, precious, I will be here with you. Nothing will happen that I don't approve of. You know I'll take good care of you."

"Trevor," I blurted out in a frantic whisper. I was struck with the sudden fear of leaving him unattended. Or was it the fear of failing once again in whatever escapade Drake had cooked up? A glance down found Trevor serene and sleeping.

"He's soaring on a big dose of endorphins. We'll just let him float, love. He's earned it. And wouldn't it be wonderful to be sexually sated, curled up next to your brother?"

Emotions whirled through me like a tornado on the prairie. Drake's bedeviling fostered a blistering torrent within my womb, coupled with cold winds of fear at the thought of fragmenting beneath Jordon's hands. Conflicting passions swirled me senseless.

Whimpering in undecided frustration, my mounting orgasm threatened to break through and devour me. Every nerve ending in my body was electrified. Sizzling. Throbbing. Howling in need.

"Pull your breasts free, pet," Drake instructed, effectively taking the decision from me.

With trembling fingers, I reached beneath my corset and eased each breast from beneath the silk brocade. My nipples were drawn tight. Sensitive. Even the ultralight brush of my fingertips over the turgid peaks almost had me coming undone.

Drake directed me from the bed by my hair. "Up, girl. Stand. Don't move. You're going to come for Sir Jordon. You're going to let him touch you while I hold you against me. Do you understand what I want you to do for me, pet?" He emphasized the words with a swipe of his tongue over my neck.

"Yes, Sir." I whimpered as Drake's body heat and buttery-soft leather vest caressed my back.

"Jordon, would you mind locking the door, please? Then by all means, put this poor girl out of her misery," Drake asked in a formal manner.

"It would be my honor." Jordon's lips curled in a wicked smile.

I was in a carnal fog. My body hummed. My hips, as if possessed, rocked from side to side in an effort to alleviate the frenzied throbbing of my clit.

"You haven't come since the last time you scened with Mistress Sammie, have you?"

"No, Sir." I gasped.

"Poor pet," Drake tsked. "That's been at least two months. I would say you're past due. Wouldn't you?"

"Yes. Yes, Sir."

I watched Jordon's luscious muscles ripple and bunch as he closed and locked the door. When he turned to walk toward me, the massive bulge in his trousers nearly cast me over the edge. His erection was huge, straining in mouthwatering invitation. I wanted to drop to my knees, open my mouth, and suck down every swollen inch of him.

"I think this sweet slut is in serious need of relief." Drake chuckled. "Please. Help yourself."

"I'd love to." Jordon's expression was animalistic.

His wicked smile and twinkling eyes sent a ripple of excitement spinning down my spine. I thought he might attack me without preamble. I was surprised as his gentle hand brushed an errant curl from my face. His touch was soft, yet I felt the blistering heat of his fingers, fingers I prayed would find their way to my core and fly me headlong over the edge to blessed relief. Breathing in his delicious scent, I closed my eyes, allowing his alluring fragrance to fill me.

"Give me your lips, girl. I want to taste you. Then I'm going to make you scream for me...eventually."

My mind was trying to process his growling promise when his mouth brushed mine then pressed firmer in demand. His lips were electrified velvet, supple yet commanding, possessing me with soul-shocking conviction. His tongue traced the seam of my lips in unequivocal petition. I opened for him, greedily accepting his hot, slick tongue on a blissful moan.

His body pressed ardently against mine, with the heat of his plentiful cock nudging my belly. He was as enormous as I'd imagined. The room spun, flinging me like a carnival ride as I fought the urge to devour him whole. I was filled with the need to suck him so deep inside my hungry mouth that he would fill the aching void in my soul. I melted against him and fed upon his glorious tongue, sucking and biting like a ravenous animal.

Roughly pulling his mouth from mine, he pinched my nipples, tugging soundly on my embedded silver rings.

"Did you forget who's in control here, girl?" The command of his voice made me whimper. "You're not going to get flippant with me again, are you?" Tilting his head, he raised a brow in question as a slow, teasing smile spread across his swollen lips.

"No, Sir, I promise," I mewled, writhing against him. I leaned in, hungry to feel his mouth once more upon mine, aching for his hot, slick tongue to entice me even higher.

"What did you say, Jordon?" Drake's thunderous tone resonated in dismay.

My body grew rigid in dread. *Drake.*

"Emerald was flippant with you? When?" he asked angrily.

"I'm sure she meant no disrespect, Drake. I suspect the poor girl just had a bad night is all." Jordon smiled and winked at me.

"That's no excuse," Drake bellowed. Spinning me around to face him, he roughly cupped my chin up, forcing me to look into his stormy eyes. "Were you disrespectful to Jordon, girl?"

I exhaled heavily and closed my eyes, nodding as a rebellious avalanche of despair consumed me. Drake's sigh blasted over my face as he released my hair with a harsh snap of his wrist.

"Look at me, Emerald," he hissed between clenched teeth, pinching my jaw soundly.

Hesitant but obeying, I opened my eyes and was met with far too much clarity. The gut-wrenching degree of Drake's anger blazed in his gray eyes. Guilt inducing disappointment was carved on his face.

"Cover yourself and leave immediately. Go sit at the bar. Do not speak to a soul. I'll be out to talk to you shortly. I am thoroughly ashamed of you at the moment."

His scornful look coupled with his harsh words crushed me. I wanted to scream but instead I cast my eyes toward the floor, stuffed my breasts back into my corset, and ran from the room.

Fighting back tears of humiliation, I snuck behind the bar and grabbed my purse, thankful that Mistress Sammie was busy and oblivious to my presence. Trying not to draw attention to myself, I kept my eyes cast downward and walked steadfast toward the exit. Snagging my coat, I jammed my arms through the sleeves and raced out of the building.

CHAPTER THREE

Embarrassed.

Humiliated.

Crushed.

The entire night was a complete debacle, and now I was paying the ultimate price. I'd been sentenced to submissive "time-out." Drake had no right to punish me like that. Damn him...He'd wheedled and promised blissful release and because of one ill-timed comment from Jordon, he'd taken it all away.

"I'm not a yo-yo!" I felt like I'd been manipulated to the nth degree as I pulled out of the parking lot.

Hungry hormones raced through my body, while humiliation, like black tar, pumped thick through my veins. Drake was going to be pissed to the gills when he realized I'd run off. I'd never disobeyed him before. Guilt expanded like a murky cloak of despair, glazing over my throbbing frustration.

"Why does something like this always happen to me?" Pondering all the ways I'd messed up in the past, I pulled into the parking lot of Maurizio's, a quaint little Italian restaurant and bar. I needed a drink to soothe my frazzled nerves and attempt to sort out all that had transpired. Somehow I'd find a way to make amends with Drake, later...much, much later.

Sliding up to the bar, I fastened the top button of my trench coat. It wasn't raining, in fact the night was warm, but I was wearing fetish wear in a vanilla restaurant. I had no desire to be ogled like some high-priced call girl.

"Shot of Crown," I demanded. Scotty the bartender quirked one brow high on his forehead, then without saying a word, filled the small glass.

I couldn't begin to count the number of times Drake, Trevor, and I had sat at this bar laughing and telling bad jokes with Scotty. But tonight it was just me and my thorny emotions.

Tipping back the amber liquid, I welcomed the burn as it warmed my throat and stomach. Tapping the rim, I nodded for another. Scotty's brows drew together as he pursed his lips then refilled the glass. I slammed the shot and damn near choked.

"Rough night?" Scotty asked in a slightly dry, sarcastic tone.

I nodded and tapped the rim.

"Where's Drake?" Studying me through narrow eyes, he hesitated then filled the glass.

Tossing back the shot, my eyes watered from the acrid liquor. "Back at the club," I croaked out in a hoarse whisper then impatiently tapped my glass once again.

"You driving tonight honey?"

I simply nodded.

"Last one, then I take your keys."

"I don't need a babysitter, Scotty. A few shots won't *impair* me."

"I think tonight, you do." He flashed a lazy grin then winked. "Don't worry, I don't charge by the hour. Let's talk."

"No," I replied in a sullen mumble.

"Suit yourself. But I've got strong shoulders and a big ear." With a gentle pat on my hand, he filled the shot glass.

"Thanks." I nodded as a wave of anger flooded my veins. He patted my hand in pity. I loathed pity. Biting my tongue and the urge to snatch my hand back, I tipped the glass, cringing as the fiery burn skulked toward my stomach.

It had been a disastrous night, one I hoped never to repeat again. I needed to resign myself to the fact that I wasn't meant to have an owner. I sure as hell didn't deserve one, not the way I'd behaved. But how could I let go of my desires? Was there a way to slough off the basic nature of my being?

"Shit!" I cursed beneath my breath. "One more, Scotty."

"No." The bartender adamantly shook his head.

I wrapped my hand around his and forced him to lift the bottle. Pouring a double shot into the glass, I looked at him in defiance.

"I thought you were a submissive. Aren't you supposed to do as you're told?" Scotty whispered low.

"On a good day." I lifted the glass to my lips and gulped every drop from the glass. "Guess this isn't one of them."

"Hell!" Scotty growled and walked away, taking the bottle with him.

I couldn't scrub Drake's angry disappointment from my mind. I'd never seen him so mad, not even at Trevor for some of the antics he'd pulled over the years. No, I was in for a thorough ass chewing, at the very least, when Drake got his hands on me.

"Hey sweetcakes. Can I buy you a drink?"

I looked up and tried not to roll my eyes in revulsion. A man stood before me, with a sexually confident gleam in his eyes. Not only did he look like a throwback from the seventies, he was old enough to be my dad. His jet-black dyed hair was slicked back with some ungodly gooey gel, and he wore a dizzying print silk shirt unbuttoned to his navel. And if that weren't bad enough, sprouting forth with unabashed pride was a thick gray carpet of chest hair. I wanted to retch. He was quite a package, but it was undoubtedly the gold Mr. *T* chains that thoroughly iced the whole revolting cake.

"Go away." I turned my back to him, hoping the Bee Gees wannabe would take my not-so-subtle hint.

"You don't have to be a bitch about it, you fucking whore." Disco Dip Shit spat and then took his leave.

Gritting my teeth to keep the caustic comeback from rolling off my tongue, I was vaguely aware of Scotty talking on the phone. Raising my eyes, I glared at him. A guilty expression flashed across his face as he realized I was listening to the conversation.

"She's had five, and I won't give her anymore, not without confiscating her keys."

"Is that Drake?" I demanded.

Scotty frowned and curtly nodded.

"I am outta here!" I tossed two twenties on the bar. As I stood and turned, I heard Scotty relay my departure to Drake. I knew he wasn't being a snitch to hurt me and was no doubt disturbed by my unusual solo visit, but I couldn't help but feel betrayed. Hell, I'd been betrayed by just about everyone I'd ever allowed inside my walls. All except Trevor. He'd never betrayed me.

I reached my car and pulled out of the parking lot. Rage bolstered my wits and sobriety until I was safely home. Once inside my familiar four walls, the floodgates burst open like a crumbling dam. Blubbering like a fool, I stumbled to my bedroom and stripped off my fetish wear. Even naked I couldn't peel off the feeling that I was destined to wear a neon sign flashing "Loser" for the rest of my life.

Humiliation and rejection laminated my every pore. There was absolutely no way I could ever face Jordon again. I wasn't even sure I could face Drake again. Humiliation settled in the pit of my stomach.

I paced my room, thinking about all the years I'd dedicated to the lifestyle and the club, and wondering what the hell I was going to do. Hours upon hours learning, and even more spent teaching new subs, donating my time to greet guests, working behind the bar, and cleaning equipment. Hell, every free moment of my time had been spent trying to make Genesis a comfortable home, not just for me, but for everyone. And now what was I left with besides a heavy cloak of shame and a dark, ugly hollowness scoring my heart? Nothing. Not a goddamn thing.

Feeling numb, I stepped into a hot shower and sat on the floor. The stinging water bit my face while I cried in self-pity, self-loathing, self-destruction.

It was a long time before the tears stopped. The hot water had long turned cold, but it didn't matter...I was numb inside and out. Turning off the shower, I stepped out and roughed a towel over my cold flesh, sniffed, and then turned to face the mirror.

The image staring back at me was stark. Haunted. Lifeless. No light twinkled in my eyes. I was met with a dull, flat reflection. My nose was red and my eyes were swollen. My cheeks were blotched, red, and ugly.

"Whatever possessed you to think you were a sub?" I sniffed, questioning my own reflection. It was a discussion I'd had with myself numerous times. Needing to know the reason, or at least an excuse for my submissive desires, I stared at myself, waiting for an epiphany...one that never came.

There was no enlightened recollection of some pivotal moment or Freudian-type trauma in my life that would explain why every fiber of my being ached to please a Dom. There was no defining line around my eyes or lips that could pinpoint the elusive reason.

As I climbed into bed, hopelessness settled deep in my bones. I *was* hopeless. Hopelessly jaded and envious as night after night I watched other subs fulfill their dreams. Hopelessly empty, alone, and tired of battling the arresting desires constantly raging within.

I wanted to be rid of the relentless frustration, exorcise it from my being. There was never going to be a Dominant who would take a chance with me. I was inexperienced and a total embarrassment. Thankfully my night with Jordon was over, but with it went any chance of finding my contentment. I always managed to screw things up, never consciously, but still...I ended up sabotaging every potential opportunity, like tonight.

I'd overheard Nick, a regular at the club, discussing me with Drake once, but he was quickly ushered away. Was I an embarrassment even to Drake? What if I'd *wanted* to be used by Nick? He was an incredibly handsome Dominant. Gentle. Patient. But now, after so much time, even Nick had a submissive. I would have loved an opportunity back then to at least try to get to know the Native American man on a submissive level. But Drake didn't even discuss it with me. And why would he? I'm only the submissive. It's not like I get to call the shots. He did...err, used to...or might still? Oh, hell...I had no clue where I stood with Drake anymore.

I had to let it go, stop thinking about it. I was only going in circles, and I was getting nowhere fast. I needed to shut off my brain and go to sleep.

Expelling a heavy sigh, I closed my eyes, promising to analyze my submissive-suicidal behavior in the morning. Maybe then I'd find some answers. Maybe I'd wake up and find the entire night was simply a bad dream. Well, I could wish anyway.

Tossing and turning, I was still unable to switch off my brain. The clock on my nightstand, with its eerie green glow, revealed two o'clock.

Suddenly there she was...Fanny-Frustration, wearing a smile so warm and loving, I couldn't help but smile back. Graceful and floating with an ethereal white light, she was breathtaking. So glorious and beautiful. *"Stop doubting. You're only making this harder on yourself. You're close. Closer than you've ever been. Don't be afraid! He'll reveal himself to you, but you must be strong. You have to be brave. You'll have to pay a terrible price, but he's worth it. I promise!"*

I was suddenly afraid. She had never spoken such an ominous warning in my dreams before. As I opened my mouth to demand she explain the cryptic message, she brushed a slender hand over my cheek and smiled. Then with the wave of her other hand, the image of the gorgeous black man appeared. His eyes sparkled and that mischievous half-smile curled on his sensual mouth.

"He may not be ready, but you are. Never doubt what you are. He'll eventually find his way, too. But you must be confident in your quest. Don't falter and don't hide. You'll have to be willing to risk it all to find happiness. Don't be afraid. You both need each other so desperately." Her soft lips caressed my forehead, and she vanished as she always did, but this time Sir Drool's image remained.

I couldn't stop myself. I reached out and brushed my fingertips over his full bottom lip. He blinked as if he could see me, too. His eyes grew wide in an expression of shock.

"You're here. I've been waiting so long for you," he whispered. *"I never thought...You have no idea how much I want you."* His eyes were filled with love.

"Me?" I asked in stunned surprise. Just touching his warm, exotic lip infused a potent ache that stung me to the bone. He felt so real. So alive. His warm breath caressed the pads of my fingers as I stood before him, trembling.

"Yes, you." He nodded, swiping his tongue over my fingers, his saliva slick and hot. *"If only I could touch you like this, I'd shower you with all the magic you deserve, and I'd never let you go."*

"Please...I need...I want. Take me, I'm yours," I begged.

"I can't." And with a pained expression, he evaporated.

~*~

Waking with a start, I sat upright in bed. My mind felt fuzzy, thick with fog from my dream. My heart squeezed bittersweet. He'd felt so real. Then the memory of his parting words and the misery reflected in his eyes crushed my soul. Without pause, the ghost woman's words filtered through my head.

"What horrible price do I have to pay? What the hell is she talking about? He may not be ready. That's the story of my life." I exhaled a deep sigh, wondering if the damn dreams meant anything or if they were my inner desires manifesting in my sleep.

Glancing at the clock, I saw it was six thirty in the morning. It was far too early to try and analyze something that probably didn't mean a damn thing, except that I was a certifiable basket case and should seek professional help.

Maybe I should make an appointment with Master Tony. He was a Dominant and a shrink, I bet he could figure out what the hell was wrong with me. I dismissed the option as quickly as it fluttered through my brain. I had no intention of spilling my guts to anyone about my abnormal dreams. I'd somehow figure it out, hopefully.

By ten o'clock, I was on my fifth cup of coffee and my second set of aspirin. My phone seemed to ring non-stop, and I had vowed no more shots of Crown the rest of my natural born days.

Clients irate over pestering notices from the IRS kept me busy. While I loved being a CPA, there were days like today that I wondered why I'd not chosen the carefree occupation of a garbage collector.

This is why you make the big bucks, baby!

The phone rang again. I snatched it up, bracing myself for another IRS crisis.

"Lunch. Maurizio's. Noon. I'm buying. Don't be late." Without waiting for my reply, Drake hung up.

"Son of a bitch!" Squeezing the bridge of my nose between my finger and my thumb, I groaned. This was not going to be fun. And I *really* didn't want to deal with Drake today. Glancing at the clock, I saw it was already eleven thirty. I slung my purse over my shoulder and raced out the door.

~*~

The scowl on Drake's face, accompanied with dull, unreadable eyes, told me I was in deep shit. It didn't take a rocket scientist to determine he was not happy to see me, not in the least. It was time to pay the piper, or in this case, a very pissed off Dom. I glanced over and nodded to Scotty, who was once again behind the bar. He flashed a bright, happy smile and nodded back.

Two heaping plates of lasagna sat untouched at the table, and my stomach rolled. Before I was even seated, Drake's eyes leveled on me. "Do you want me to rescind my protection? If you do, just say the word." His brows were drawn together in a menacing scowl, and there was no doubt he was in full, badass Dom mode.

35

"No!" I protested with a soft shiver and then plopped down across from him in the booth. "Why would you ask such a thing?"

"Your behavior screams otherwise." His lips were a tight line as his steel-gray eyes ruthlessly drilled into mine.

"Look, I'm sorry I ran out last night. I couldn't handle everything that happened. I needed air and time to think. I couldn't get that at the club."

"I'm listening," he growled impatiently.

"I kept screwing up everything with Jordon. You may not believe me but I tried to make a good impression. Honest to God I did. He's...there's something about him. I wanted to explore the possibility that maybe...Fuck. Why couldn't things be different?" I struggled to put my feelings into words. Most times I had no trouble whatsoever blurting out every little emotion or thought, but today I couldn't seem to make heads or tails of my choking chaos.

Drake stared at me, not saying a word.

"Damn it, Drake. Stop it. Stop looking at me like you're going to explode. Let me try to explain how I feel, would you please?" I begged quietly.

"Take all the time you need. *I* don't plan on running away unlike someone *else* I know."

Now he was acting like a patronizing parent. "That's not fair," I huffed. "Last night was a disaster. No matter how hard I tried, everything I did just kept turning to shit. I kept stepping out on the wrong foot the entire night. And the molehill I made soon became a goddamn mountain. First, I spilled my drink, almost drenching him. Then he followed me back to your room and berated me for not answering his question like I was some newbie playing games with him. It pissed me off."

Drake sat listening to me with an unreadable expression as I flailed my explanation.

"I...I accidently snapped at him, that was all. I wasn't trying to be *recalcitrant*, like he accused me of. There was no way I could confess to him that I had no owner. It would have made me look more pathetic than I already am. But I ended up telling him anyway, reaffirming my pathetic ineptness." Swallowing the lump in my throat, I gritted my teeth to keep from breaking down and bawling like a baby in the restaurant.

"Suffering from feelings of inadequacy still, girl?" He arched his brows.

Trying not to scream in frustration, I inhaled deeply. Not only was he pissed off, he was pissing me off as well. He was hitting below the belt by slinging my insecurities back in my face.

I took another deep breath, and tried to curb my seething anger. "Nearly every sub at that club has a Dom or Domme, except me. You have no idea what it's like to be pitied by them and how belittling it feels to catch their patronizing glances." Placing my hand over my heart, I slathered my words in mock sarcasm. "'Oh, poor Emerald. The girl tries and tries but can't find one who'll take her. There must be something horribly wrong with her, bless her little heart.'" I slapped my hand on the table as I leaned in, scowling right back at Drake. "Do you have any idea how pathetic that makes me feel? No. You couldn't possibly know." As tears once again stung my eyes, I tried to hold them back, but my control was quickly unraveling like a tattered thread. I took a deep breath.

"You have no idea how shameful it was to confess to a Dom who made my stomach flutter and my heart pound like a lovesick school girl that I don't have an owner. And then *you*. You taunted me. Promised me that I could...well you know." I took a nervous glance around the nearby tables, praying my voice wasn't carrying over the entire restaurant. "You lured me into believing I could relieve some sexual frustration, and in a matter of seconds, you had me looking like an even bigger fucking failure. You dangled that orgasm in front of my face like a damn carrot only to snatch it back. It hurt Drake. You humiliated me in front of Jordon, and you hurt my feelings." Tears brimmed my eyes as I hung my head in defeat.

There was a long pause, as if Drake were gathering his thoughts. I didn't look up at him partly out of embarrassment, partly out of fear. Finally he spoke, low and soft.

"First of all, I'm sorry I hurt your feelings. That was never my intent. I know how you feel about humiliation, and I vowed long ago not to push that button with you. It serves no positive purpose. That's more than obvious right now. But think of how *I* felt hearing you'd been disrespectful to a guest. First impressions count for a hell of a lot in our lifestyle, not to mention I've trained you better than that." His tone was hushed but laced with displeasure. "Do you honestly believe *anyone* at the club thinks there's something wrong with you, let alone makes the kind of comments you imagine they do?"

Without waiting for me to answer, he continued. "If there were something that made you remotely undesirable, I'd damn well correct it. I may not own you, but I *am* responsible for your actions and those involving you. If you're too goddamn mouthy, which you are, it's *my* obligation to correct it. If you're too goddamn hardheaded, which you are, it's *my* obligation to correct that, too. The only problem keeping you from finding a Dominant is reining in your fucking pride."

"I'm not giving that up, Drake. I may be a submissive, but I'll be damned if I ever lose myself again. I've been there, done that, and by God, I *won't* do it again. I refuse to be some asshole's doormat. If losing my pride and self-respect is the only way I can be a good sub then fuck it, I'm done."

"I'm not asking you to do that, and you damn well know it. Submission doesn't mean doormat, and you know that, too." He closed his eyes and sucked in a deep breath. "You have to knock down the walls you hide behind in order to fully submit. You have to release your pride. *Release it,* not lose it. Sometimes you have to take a chance, yeah, a big fucking chance, that a *real* Dominant will find you. And that he'll cherish your gifts and *not* fuck you over. It's called gaining and earning trust. You can't automatically judge every damn Dom based on one bad experience. Especially when you *now* know you were partially to blame."

His words stung like a fat slap across the face. It took every ounce of willpower I possessed not to storm out of the restaurant. And I would have if he'd not unequivocally hit the nail on the head. He was right. I was hiding behind my walls, ensconced in a heavy cloak of pride. Expecting the worst and at least on some obscure, unconscious level, sabotaging any real chance to achieve what I longed for the most.

Sometimes self-realization was a butt-ugly bitch.

"Do you understand what I'm saying to you?"

"I'm not stupid." Of course I understood, but it didn't mean I had to like it.

"No, you're not stupid." He flashed a scowl. "And since you

don't want to rescind my protection, and since I *am* the one you've designated to correct your rueful behavior, I fully intend to do that tonight." His eyes narrowed and his nostrils flared as he struggled to keep his voice low and controlled.

"You will come to the club dressed for a session. You will arrive at exactly seven o'clock, and you will wait for me in my private room. Alone. Trevor will not be allowed to visit you. He'll work your shift at the front door and you, my dear, will make amends to me. However *I* see fit. Is that understood? Unless, of course, you want me to release you from my care." An evil glimmer reflected in his eyes.

I swallowed tightly. "I've told you, I don't want that. I will meet you tonight at seven o'clock in your room." Trepidation replaced my fury.

"And?"

"I will accept your punishment."

His brows rose in silent question.

"Sir."

"And?" he asked in a perturbed tone.

"And...and I don't want to give up your protection, Daddy." I whispered in shame.

"And?"

"I don't know what else you want me to say...Sir." I lowered my head as my brain raced, clueless as to what requisite of his I'd not fulfilled.

"And you will *never, ever* run from me or my instruction again. Or trust me, girl, I *will* release you to the wolves."

"Oh. No, Sir. I won't do that again. I promise."

"Good. Now let's eat," he said with a broad smile.

Eat? Was he kidding? My stomach was swirling like a Tilt-A-Whirl, pitching and rolling in a riotous swell. Fixated on what he'd planned to do to me, an assortment of painful scenarios flashed in my mind as my heart drummed solidly.

"Is it going to be painful, Daddy?"

"Indeed." He nodded with an evil smirk.

I scowled, desperate to push the fearsome thoughts from my mind. I'd never been punished before. I'd never crossed a line so vehemently that I'd needed to bear a punishment. Guilt and fear consumed me as tears burned in my eyes.

"I'm sorry." My voice cracked as I looked up at Drake.

"I believe you are, girl." His expression was somber. "You're still going to be punished."

"Yes, Sir." I nodded, clutching my fork. The sauce-covered noodles blurred as I blinked back the tears pooling in my eyes.

"You know I love you." Drake's tone softened as he reached across the table and caressed my hand.

Tears spilled over my lashes as I nodded. Fighting back the sob burning in the back of my throat, I looked into his eyes. "I don't deserve you or your love."

"No. You deserve someone far better than me."

I slowly shook my head as tears streamed down my cheeks.

"Yes, you do honey. I knew you longed for a Dominant, but I hadn't realized you felt so unfulfilled without one. I know I can't give you everything you crave. We discussed the limits of our arrangement when I first offered to be your protector and mentor. I'm sorry for not being able to provide all you need." He squeezed my hand as a deep sorrow filled his eyes.

"I should have told you how bad the void inside me had gotten." I sniffed, wiping away my tears.

"Yes, you should have. And it shows I've been entirely too lax."

"I don't know what you mean."

"I've taken for granted the expectation that you'd communicate with me. Obviously I'm not properly caring for you because you're hiding emotions from me." Dipping his head, he raised his brows. His gray eyes penetrated, emphasizing his point. "Tell me about your feelings toward Jordon. Why him? What makes you want to give him your power? He's an unknown Dom of the club. Unknown to me and to you."

"I don't know. He's beyond gorgeous. And you're right, none of us knows a thing about him." I swallowed tightly. Without reason, I was nervous voicing my desires to Drake. "He stirs something inside me. I don't know if its lust or submission, but I wanted to find out. That's a moot point now. I'm sure he thinks I'm a basket case and has totally written me off." Raking my fingers through my hair, I issued a sigh of exasperation.

Drake steepled his fingers and lightly tapped them on his lips.

"What if he hasn't written you off? What would you do? Would you still be interested in him?"

"Of course." My heart clutched with a flutter of hope. "But I'm not a fool, Drake. The chances of that happening are slim to none. He's not going to want to have a thing to do with me."

"For conversation's sake, pretend it was possible. Tell me *why* you want this man, aside from the fact that he's a fucking hot mass of man candy." A devilish grin curled on his lips.

I grinned. Even Drake appreciated Jordon's luscious physique. "He is that." Pausing, I attempted to gather my reasons. "The minute he walked into the club, I was drawn to him. He carries a commanding aura that I can almost feel." Goosebumps prickled my skin just thinking about him. "Of course I have no idea what type of Dominant he is. He could be loving or sadistic. I don't know. But neither extreme scares me. I just want the chance to get to know him. I know our first encounter didn't bode well with him. I wish I could rewind time and change *everything* about last night." Nibbling on my bottom lip, I looked into Drake's compassion-filled eyes. "Is it going to hurt a lot, Drake?"

"Oh, stop fretting. You know I'll never give you more than you can handle. But you will feel the reminder of your station, get reacquainted with your submissive place, *and* have no question as to where your mind and mouth should be focused. Just think of it as my gift of love to you." A broad, sly smile spread across his lips.

I trembled as I worried about how much pain was in store for me.

CHAPTER FOUR

At seven o'clock on the dot, I knelt on the soft carpet in Drake's private room. Nervous and trembling, my heart thundered in my chest. All afternoon I'd paced, cried, and worried about what he had in store for me. That is, when I wasn't mooning over hopeless fantasies of Jordon.

Thoughts of the handsome Dom filled my head almost more than fretting about my punishment. Trying to keep Jordon in perspective, I reminded myself that I'd screwed up far beyond repair and shouldn't hold on to foolish hope.

Craning my neck, I looked at the clock on the nightstand behind me and trembled in anticipation-laced fear.

7:05. *Okay Drake, I'm as ready as I'll ever be. Let's get this over with.*

7:10. *What is taking him so long?*

7:15. *You're doing this to fuck with me. I know it!*

7:20. *Damn it, Drake, I'm going to waltz my ass back home if you don't get here soon. The anticipation is driving me insane!*

The snick of the lock disengaging had me quaking with fear. Keeping my eyes glued to the floor, I trembled in silence.

"You're as beautiful as sunset splayed out in your submissive pose," Drake praised, and I smiled. "Stand and present." His voice thundered as goose pimples erupted across my flesh.

My knees wobbled as I stood. With my face still shrouded, I thrust out my arms and pressed my wrists together. The scent of leather filled my nostrils as he bound the soft, fleece-lined leather restraints around my wrists.

"I hope this isn't a new gown, girl," he growled in a low voice. The tone in his next breath was harsh as he instructed me not to move. Withdrawing a sparkling silver knife, he slid the blade into the silk material between my breasts. I gasped and tried not to shudder as the knife sliced through the fabric. My gossamer gown silently slithered to the floor and pooled at my feet.

42

"Thank you for not wearing panties that I'd have to ruin as well," he whispered close to my ear. "Close your eyes, my sweet. I'd hate for you to see what I have planned for you."

A violent shudder shook my body as he placed a blindfold over my eyes, plunging me into total darkness. My mouth was so dry that I couldn't have spoken even if I'd known what the hell to say.

Drake led me from the room toward what I assumed was the dungeon. The temperature in the hallway was much cooler than his room and my nipples pebbled painfully.

"It's time for you to show me just how sorry you are, girl. I have no doubt you'll make me proud."

With Drake's hand firmly wrapped around my elbow, he ushered me down the hall. I could hear soft muffled voices that suddenly silenced. I could smell the distinguished scent of leather, disinfectant, and the subtle fragrance of sex mingling with sweet vanilla from the candles adorning the tables.

I was in the dungeon.

I listened closely for the sounds of play: the crack of a whip, the slap of a paddle, a moan or whimper from my fellow submissives. But there was nothing. Nothing but unnerving silence. It was a Saturday night. Genesis had to be packed with members. Had everyone stopped their scenes to watch me? It was intimidating to think I might be the only sub on display. Anxiety blossomed in the pit of my stomach and crawled over my skin.

Gripping the cuffs, Drake stopped and wrapped a burly arm around my waist, pulling me against his soft leather vest. His broad chest warmed my back as I strained to hear any discernible sound. There was nothing but an anxious vibration buzzing in my ears. I detected the sound of breathing, but the tremulous whisper was faint, then gone. Maybe I'd imagined it.

I wondered if there were people watching, gazing upon my naked, cuffed, and blindfolded body. Were there unknown witnesses leering or silently watching with sympathetic eyes? I faintly whimpered as my body continued to tremble in fear.

"Do I need to get a ball gag, girl?" Drake asked in a thunderous, aggravated tone.

I quickly shook my head no.

"Answer me!" he demanded.

43

"No, Daddy." My voice was hoarse, my mouth dry.

After what seemed like an infinite pause, Drake cleared his throat. "I would like to thank you all for volunteering to help Emerald find her place."

A new wave of panic crashed down on me. Lowering my head, I bit back a whimper of terror. He'd invited others to punish me! Who were they? What were they going to do? My mind raced. My limbs tingled as adrenalin exploded and oscillated through my veins.

I wanted to peel my body from his warm, leather chest and run. Run away. Far away. Far from the terror of the unknown. *Easy. Calm down.*

My heart hammered a frantic rhythm in my chest, and I tried to quell my unmitigated fear. If I ran again, he'd never take me back. I knew he'd never harm me emotionally or physically. It was time to buck up and be brave. If I hadn't run from him in the first place, I wouldn't be in this fucking mess right now. I was going to have to take it like a big girl and stop being such a wimp. I was always so damn envious of my fellow subs. Now I was getting exactly what I'd always wanted. So why was I so damn scared?

Nervous, I licked my lips and tried to gain some semblance of control over the panic vibrating inside me.

"Over the past four years, Emerald has brought much joy to my life and to many of you here, as well. Through her own actions, she has forced this punishment which I shall implement with a heavy heart. This is my girl's first punishment. I pray its incentive enough to be her last." The silent void was broken by numerous murmurs as I tried to swallow my fear.

"Is there anything you wish to say before we begin, pet?" Drake whispered in my ear.

"I'm sorry, Daddy Drake, for causing embarrassment to you and to myself. In the future, I will strive to better represent you in all ways." My voice cracked and my tears were absorbed by the satin blindfold.

"I believe you girl," he said in a deep sorrowful tone. "Turn around."

He pulled away, taking with him the warmth and security of his body. I felt his broad calloused hands grip my shoulders as he led me forward. Trembling like a leaf, Drake pressed against the small of

44

my back, guiding my breasts and stomach against the cold wooden frame of a St. Andrew's Cross. I gasped as the icy wood met my flesh and chills shook my already trembling body.

Without warning, an unknown pair of hands stretched my arms and feet, busily binding me to the wooden frame. My mind filled with images of some B-horror flick I saw as a child. The one where a circle of people dressed in black hooded cloaks tethered an innocent virgin to a sacrificial altar.

I really needed to get a grip. I was a far cry from an innocent virgin, and Drake would never allow anyone but a trusted friend to put their hands on me. The only thing being sacrificed tonight was my lily-white ass. I sucked in a deep breath then the busy hands disappeared.

"You will not be rewarded with a warm up," Drake announced as the crack of his whip split the silence.

I was crying in fear before the first bite of the single tail landed on my ass cheeks. Fiery pain exploded from the primary blow. I knew if I was going to survive his punishment, I needed to process the pain quickly. Between clenched teeth, I inhaled slow, deep breaths. The fire from the blow swelled outward, crawling up my spine and through my arms before washing down my legs just as another wicked stroke detonated across my ass.

In quick succession, Drake landed half a dozen lashes. Biting back a cry of pain, I attempted to allow the blistering all-consuming flames to flow through me. Fighting the urge to scream, I focused on breathing as my limbs shook uncontrollably against the cross.

Suddenly two small, warm hands began caressing my burning butt cheeks, and I moaned in delight. A small, soft mouth claimed my lips. I knew by her taste it was Mistress Sammie, and I sighed in gratitude. Her slick, gentle tongue slid past my lips. I groaned and suckled it. Fingernails danced and tickled my spine as I whimpered inside her mouth. Her small hand clutched my curls, pulling my head back and away from her. I cried out as my pussy contracted solidly.

"You don't cry out from the whip but you cry out from this?" she whispered, tugging on my mane. "You're an amazing girl, Emerald." Her breath was warm against my ear.

Rolling my hips as hot nectar coated my folds, I pitifully whimpered, exalting in the lightning bolts of pleasure racing down my spine. Welcoming the throbbing ache pooling deep inside my womb, I rocked my pelvis in need.

"Are you doing all right, precious?" she whispered, dancing her tongue over my ear as her fingers plucked my distended nipples.

"Yes, Mistress." I gasped.

"Good girl," she praised lovingly and then sank her teeth into the soft column of my throat. I yelped, melting against the cross as her sensual tongue licked the love bite.

"You're so beautiful, baby!" she praised.

The radiating pain in my ass eased as Sammie administered sensual caresses. It was a glorious combination of heaven and hell. Then just as suddenly as she'd appeared, Mistress was gone.

"Thank you, Mistress." I sighed in gratitude, unsure if she heard my words.

Instantly another succession of painful lashes bit into my flesh. The agonizing surge of white-hot fire consumed me, only this time I couldn't contain the pain, couldn't compartmentalize it. It was far too overwhelming.

Unable to ride the waves as they crashed through me, I threw my head back. An animalistic scream tore from my throat. My knees dissolved. Slack and spineless, my tethered wrists bore the full weight of my body, and as I slumped against the frame, mournful pleas for mercy strained my throat.

Strong, thick hands clutched my waist and pulled me upward, forcing me back on my feet. Drake's leather vest was hot against my back. Heat radiated from his body in a fevered pitch. It was too much. Too intense. I was burning alive.

"You've taken your punishment well, my love." His voice was low as he praised me. "But I'm not done with you yet."

A low mewl of anguish reverberated in my throat.

The whip snapped in the air with a deafening crack. I jerked, terrified of having to endure more. I couldn't take anymore. Panic wrapped its icy hands around my throat, and I began pulling against my restraints. Fighting for freedom, crying and whimpering for mercy, I fought to free myself from the cuffs like a trapped animal.

"Emerald!"

At the sound of Drake's thunderous voice, I froze.

"Relax, pet," Nuzzling my head toward the warmth of his

breath, he caressed the shell of my ear with his lips. I whimpered, needing Drake's reassurance as I tried to do as he ordered and relax. "Your pain is over. Let me shower you with pleasure, sweet girl."

The warmth of his body disappeared, and I moaned in delight as light, wispy kisses from the soft-tipped popper of the whip danced over my ass. Drake wielded the single tail with envied skill. His ability was so perfected and honed that he could flay open, wickedly welt, or lovingly coax caresses over flesh from the innocuous leather toy.

My body relaxed against the wooden cross as I began to soar. There was no conscious thought in my head. Every kiss of the whip was confined to a tiny pinprick of light centered deep inside my brain.

I was flying.

Sailing in a crystal white, gossamer light of subspace.

I was finally experiencing that place of serenity, the place I'd always yearned to be. It was the most euphoric escape I'd ever known.

Heartfelt thanks murmured from my lips replaced my tears of fear and pain. Soaring higher and higher, it was as if I'd left my body. The residual pain throbbed and spread like liquid lava through my limbs, propelling me further into the dreamy, ethereal subspace. Even knowing this euphoric state existed, I never in my wildest dreams imagined it would feel like this. Every nerve ending sizzled as my mind, like thick honey, slid into another dimension. I was being reunited with my submission.

I was vaguely aware that Drake had stopped feathering the whip over my skin. Then unknown hands were upon me. They were large, calloused, and rough, and I knew by the touch it was not Drake. The anonymous fingertips raked down my back then wedged beneath my aching nipples to pluck and pinch the turgid tips. Whimpers of delight and gasps of carnal arousal seeped from my lips as the stranger's tongue and teeth imbibed the heated flesh of my throat.

Feeling the restraints loosen, I moaned in despair. I didn't want the session to end, couldn't fathom retreating from the blissful serenity encapsulating me. Wanting, no needing, more time to languish as the endorphins flowed through me, I begged, "No."

"You're not done yet, sweet slut," Drake whispered as his thick, strong hands encased my shoulder, turning me around. I was grateful for his support since my legs were the consistency of Jell-O. Shots of Crown had nothing on subspace.

He pressed my back against the wooden cross, and I cried out in pain as my raw ass met the smooth, polished wood. It was almost too much to bear, but Drake's warm breath wafted across my shoulder as his fingers plucked a nipple. Someone secured the cuffs to my wrists and ankles once more.

"You please me, Emerald." His praise sent my heart soaring. "I want you to come hard for me, sweet pet."

As his thick fingers anchored into my mass of curls, he yanked. His instruction permeated through my rapturous fog.

"Oh, God," I mewled, arching on my tiptoes and thrusting my pussy forward in a silent bid for attention.

"You can cry out to him soon enough." Drake chuckled.

"You may begin when ready," he instructed the unknown abettor.

I whimpered as the stranger's hands, lips, and teeth swarmed my naked flesh, not with the tenderness shown before, but assaulting in feral, hungry, desperate zeal. Shuddering in arousal with my limbs solidly fixed to the cross, I was helpless to do more than rock my hips and wantonly moan. Drake's hand remained steadfast, occasionally tugging my head back, exposing more flesh on my throat to be suckled and nipped.

A masculine tongue invaded my mouth as the rings adorning my nipples were tugged and twisted. I felt the heat of his mouth ebb down my body and his warm, slick lips caressed my hips, belly, and thighs as a steady stream of honey spilled from my cunt. I desperately needed his fingers, his cock, or a dildo to be shoved into my empty channel to release the sweltering orgasm swirling within me.

It was then I caught the familiar scent. The essence I'd branded to memory...Jordon was the unknown man feasting on me. His were the deliciously torturing hands and mouth devouring my flesh.

"Yes. Yes. Thank you." I groaned as warm, controlling hands encased my face.

"Yes. Yes. Thank you for what, beautiful Emerald?" His deep, erotic voice sent electric pulses flaring through my body. Even as my heart pounded in my ears, I could still hear the warmth and compassion laced in his words.

"Please!" I begged in a mournful wail.

"Please what? You do not want to ignore my questions again, girl," he warned ferociously.

"Please kiss me," I answered without hesitation.

"Kiss me, who? Who do you want to kiss you?"

"You! Kiss me, Sir Jordon. Please."

His warm lips slanted over mine as he plunged and swept his tongue deep. Hot and slick, he caressed my mouth, leaving no curve or crevice untouched. I waited for what seemed an eternity, testing my restraint before I began to suckle his tongue. A low growl thundered in his chest and reverberated in my mouth.

Drake clinched his fist as I moaned against Jordon's tongue. My pussy released a torrent of cream as I ground my crotch unabashedly upon his steely erection. Releasing my tongue, he captured my bottom lip between his teeth, pulling and sucking the meaty flesh into his mouth. His lips moved lower, along the column of my throat, licking, nibbling, and nipping the sensitized flesh. Gasping and whimpering, I barely contained my scream of need.

"Do you want to come, sweet slut?" Jordon whispered in my ear.

"Please, Sir. Please. Oh please."

"Perhaps I should take pity on you and let you shatter, but there are conditions, sweet girl. This will be mine," he growled, plunging his fingers into my mouth, circling them over my tongue and teeth. "These will be mine," he snarled, biting the lobe of my ear while tugging the silver rings embedded beneath my nipples. "And this will be mine," he grunted, palming my dripping cunt. "I long to own you someday, someday very soon. Now that you know my intentions, do you want *me* to let you come, precious?"

I was lost in a sublime dream. He wanted me. After making a total fool of myself, he still wanted to pursue me. Not only that, he wanted to claim me. Own me. There was nothing on earth I wanted more. "Yes, Sir. Please. Please."

"Fuck. I love the way you beg."

He plunged two fingers deep inside me, burnishing my G-spot with savage decree. I cried out as I began to plummet over.

49

"Now, girl. Come for me. Come loud and hard."

Fear clutched my heart for one brief second before my brain acknowledged his shout of permission. Jordon's mouth enveloped my nipple, and he sucked hard as Drake yanked my hair. I surrendered, screaming to the heavens as the powerful wave consumed me. Swirling in a vortex of spasming, quivering euphoria, my contracting tunnel gripped his fingers, locking them deep within my clutching core.

"You're so fucking beautiful," Jordon whispered before his lips claimed mine, drinking in my cries of abandon.

~*~

Sated and still flying on a rush of endorphins, I opened my eyes. The blindfold was gone, and I found myself in Drake's private room lying on his soft bed. Jordon's warm, strong arms encased me. His arousal, thick and hot beneath his trousers, nuzzled against my throbbing ass. His deep, velvet voice whispered loving praises in my ear. I spied Drake seated at the edge of the bed, a smile filled with love poised on his lips.

"Drink girl. I'm extremely proud of you," Drake instructed as Trevor appeared and slid his hand behind my head, offering a bottle to my lips. I drank in needful gulps and nodded.

"Don't you ever get into trouble again," Trevor admonished in a quiet but terse tone. "It just about killed me watching you take all that." His warm hand caressed my cheek as I smiled in a dreamlike state.

"It was heaven," I whispered.

"Oh hell, sister. Daddy, you've created a monster!" He snickered. "May I comfort her, Sirs?"

"You may," Jordon whispered in my ear as Drake's stern voice granted his boy permission.

Trevor's warm lips pressed softly against mine. I moaned and returned his loving kiss. Jordon's fingers tugged on my nipple rings. Whimpering, I arched my back and opened my mouth, searching for my brother's warm, slick tongue.

"Greedy little minx." Jordon softly chuckled. "You act as if you're still needy. Do you want more, sweet slut?"

All I could do was groan and nod my head as I ended Trevor's kiss.

"It had been a while since she'd had a release. I'm sure there's probably another orgasm or two hovering beneath the surface. But she'll have to wait till another day for that pleasure. I've been quite generous, and she damn well knows it." I could hear the joy in Drake's voice, sense the loving smile curl on his lips. I was proud to have pleased him.

"My boy and I will leave now so that you can get to know this lovely treasure. The door will remain unlocked," Drake announced in a firm tone as he pried Trevor off the bed by his hair.

The door will remain unlocked. Drake's meaning registered in my still-sluggish mind. He would allow Jordon to take over the reins of my aftercare, but he wasn't granting him power over me yet.

"She will be in safe hands, Drake. I assure you," Jordon promised. "Thank you for allowing me time to get to know her."

A shiver raced down my spine as I began to feel more naked, more open and vulnerable in the hands of a virtual stranger, a stranger I yearned to give my submission to. A stranger I wanted to please and hoped would want to claim every solitary gift I offered. A stranger who wanted to own *me*. I was more than a bit dazed at that revelation.

"So you're still hungry precious?" Jordon asked in a wolf-like voice. "I have something I'm sure will fill you up."

"Mmmmm," I moaned and rolled over with a languid stretch. "May I kiss you, please?"

"Please what?" His smile was seductive as he arched his brow.

"Please, Sir," I whispered, staring at his full, erotic lips.

"No. But I do have something you can fill your mouth with."

He ground his erection against my ass, and I groaned, hungry for every inch.

"On your knees," he ordered as he stood and then wrapped his broad hand into my hair and lifted me from the bed.

I stumbled to the floor as I tried to blink away the fog still clouding my brain.

"I would love to get you so needy, so desperate, that you'd erupt simply by me tugging your soft spiral curls," Jordon whispered as he pulled my hair even tighter. "I'd like to try that sometime, pet."

51

The deep laugh that rumbled from his chest sent a ripple down my spine as I knelt compliantly before him. My pussy clenched and flowed with the image of climaxing for him in the way he described. His voice. His scent. His touch. Everything about him sent my senses reeling. I lusted for this man with an untamed hunger.

I exhaled deeply as the sound of his zipper resonated in my ears. It was torture resisting the urge to glance up and sneak a peek at his cock. I was anxious to see its naked glory. I wondered if it was as huge as it felt pressed against my sore ass. Kicking off his shoes, socks, and trousers, I caught myself as I began to look up. Squeezing my eyes tightly shut, I willed myself to be patient, pleasing, submissive.

"Problem pet?" he asked.

"Yes, Sir," I honestly confessed, still drunk on endorphins.

"Patience running thin, is it?" His chuckle made me laugh softly.

"Oh yes, Sir. Thinner than you could imagine."

"Hmmm. Maybe I should make you kneel there for an hour or two before I allow you to raise those breathtaking emerald eyes of yours. Do you think you could find patience enough for that?"

His finger lightly grazed my jawline as I swiftly shook my head no.

"Aww, surely you have more patience than you claim. You're not that anxious to see the present I have for your luscious, plump mouth, are you?"

His fingers caressed my lips. I opened my mouth, praying he'd slide them inside and allow me to suckle them and show him how ready I was to worship his cock.

"I asked you a question, girl!" His voice thundered as he slapped my face.

Blinking in confusion, my face stung from his assault, and the sublime bliss I'd been floating in vanished like smoke. Yanking me upward by my hair, he angled my face toward the floor, away from his body. Biting back a scream, my brain began to fill with a dark, foreboding fear.

"I'm quite concerned about your failure to answer me in a timely manner. Are we going to have a problem with communication, girl?" His words were slathered in annoyance.

"No, Sir." I gasped and swallowed tightly. My betraying body quivered in arousal as nectar poured from my folds.

"Keep your eyes closed and kneel up," he commanded, stepping in front of me once again. "I'd hate for you to expire from anticipation. I'd much rather keep you very much alive and your beautiful mouth stuffed and busy. I won't have to listen to your bratty snivel at least."

I lifted my throbbing ass from the floor. With my eyes closed, he slid two fingers deep inside my mouth.

"Show me, girl. Let me feel the talents of your mouth. Prove to me you're worthy of my dick."

Red flags were waving in my brain. His sudden change of demeanor once he had me alone was a textbook example of a predator. I shivered and swallowed my fear. He couldn't be a monster. They never would have let him in the club, and Drake certainly wouldn't have given him liberties with me. No. He was testing me. After my horrid first impression, he wanted me to demonstrate my true submissive heart.

Rolling my tongue over his fingers in an erotic fashion, gripping my lips around them, I suckled hungrily upon his digits, wanting to please him and show him exactly what desires I'd kept locked away. Sliding my mouth up and down, my tongue danced in a sensual trail upon his shaft. Tiny whimpers escaped my throat as I projected my willingness to please.

With a quick jerk, he pulled his hand from my mouth and exhaled loudly. "Son of a bitch! Your mouth is sinful, girl."

I nibbled my bottom lip as I wrestled the urge to open my eyes and gaze upon the other appendage I wanted to worship.

He softly chuckled. "Do you want to feast your eyes on my cock, girl?"

"Yes, Sir. Desperately."

"You may not."

I groaned at his rejection.

"Keep your eyes closed and cast toward the floor. Don't move." With a sturdy tug, he released my mane.

"Yes, Sir."

Listening intently, I heard him walk away. The snick of the lock set off a wave of confusion as tingling fear coursed through my veins. Drake's instructions had been clear. The door was to be kept unlocked, yet Jordon was blatantly disregarding his directive. I swallowed tightly, torn between protesting and raising his ire or remaining compliant. I chose to keep my mouth shut. The last thing I wanted to do was disappoint him again.

Grasping my hair once more, he lifted me to my feet and shoved me toward the bed. "Ass in the air, face down," he thundered as he pushed me to the mattress.

Confused and growing more fearful by the minute, I assumed the position but ignored his directive and raised my head. "I thought Drake said to leave the door unlocked. We're supposed to get acquainted, not play, right?"

"What Drake doesn't know won't hurt him."

Red flag. Red fucking flag. I trembled at the sound of a heavy zipper sliding open. "I don't think I'm supposed to..."

"Exactly. Don't think. I didn't order you to think. I ordered you to show me how willing you are to please me. Now shut the fuck up and show me, slut. Use the safe word *'red'* if you must, otherwise, just shut up."

I inhaled a deep breath, gathering my courage to contest his attempt to coerce me into something I knew was not allowed. But before I could confront him, unmitigated pain from some hideous toy brought me upright on the bed.

"Red!" I screamed at the top of my lungs as I tried to crawl from the pain and away from Jordon. Screaming as fire engulfed my ass, shrieked down my legs, and clawed up my spine, I jerked away as he reached for my arm.

"No! No! Don't touch me!" I yelled, scrambling away. Sobbing, I braced my back against the headboard, reeling in the piercing pain.

"Get a grip, bitch! You can take more than that!" His tone was mocking and impatient.

Fear was a potent spoil to the pristine serenity I'd held moments ago.

"Get back down on your knees. I'm not through with you yet." A demented look reflected in his cold and lifeless eyes.

"No! This is over! Get the fuck away from me!" I sobbed, shaking my head, trying to climb from the opposite side of the bed.

"It's over when I say it's over, you ungrateful little whore!"

He rounded the bed and grabbed my arm, brutally yanking me toward him. The soft white sheets felt like knives slicing across my ass as he dragged me from the bed.

He forced my back against the wall, and his teeth clamped down on my nipple ring. With a violent tug, he pulled on my flesh like a caveman chewing meat off a bone. I screamed louder, worried that he would rip the metal jewelry from my nipple. Latching on again, his teeth sank painfully into my breast as he fed on me like a rabid animal.

Panic pumped through my veins. I had to get him off me! A roaring voice inside my head thundered instructions...*Run! Get. The. Fuck. Out. Now!* I struggled with all my might to wrench free.

"Get. Off. Me." I screamed as I slapped and shoved against his rock-hard chest. He towered a good five inches over me and out weighted me by at least a hundred pounds of solid muscle, but I was determined to get free. Somehow.

Popping his mouth from my breast, I looked down to find it red, swollen, and glistening with his saliva as I continued to fight for freedom. Squashing me against the wall with a thunderous force, he knocked the air from my lungs. His slick tongue danced along my neck like a slithering eel while he fastened my thin wrists in his hand, pressing them against the wall high above my head. Using his knees, he roughly spread my thighs, opening me for his pleasure.

"Red! You motherfucker! Red!" I cried, still unsuccessfully gaining my freedom.

"There is no red, bitch! I'm going to fuck you!" he spat in a tone of hatred. "Shut up and submit, whore. That's what you're supposed to do."

This couldn't be happening. This madman was going to rape me. His ocean-blue eyes twinkled in manic delight as my stomach pitched and rolled. Over my dead body! This piece of shit was not going to get inside me. I would never allow him to rape me. He would not destroy me.

"Help! Help! Security! " I screamed at the top of my lungs. "Stop. Now. Stop," I cried in hopes of breaking through his manic craze. His fingers plunged deep inside my wet pussy. "Nooo!" I wailed.

"Oh you like it rough don't you, slut? You're dripping wet for my cock. You might scream for me to stop, but I can feel how much you want it." An evil smirk curled on his lips. "Get on your hands and knees and suck my dick!"

"Never, you son of a bitch!" I wriggled one wrist free and brought it down, pounding my fist against his shoulders and chest. "Get the fuck off me," I screamed.

His fingers gripped my throat. Dragging me across the room, he launched me onto the bed with a feral growl. Breath left my lungs in a loud whoosh, and as I landed, I saw blood painted on the sheets. My blood. The bastard had flayed my ass open. Panic consumed me and a high-pitched scream tore from my throat.

Jordon snagged one of my ankles and yanked me to the foot of the bed. The friction of the sheet brought a new level of agony ripping through me.

Kicking my feet like an Olympic swimmer, I made contact, slamming a hard heel onto his rib cage. Emitting a low "oomph," he jumped onto the bed, straddled my body, and punched my face with his fist.

Pain exploded over my cheek as lights danced behind my eyes. A copper taste filled my mouth as I bucked, trying to toss him from my body. Pinning my arms with his knees, my eyes grew wide in alarm as the thickest, longest cock I'd ever seen was thrust in my face.

My heart thundered in my ears. Without a word, he wrapped his hand around my throat, pinning my head to the bed. I began to gasp, unable to draw air into my lungs.

"Open your fucking mouth, bitch." His face distorted in a hateful grimace.

Bursts of light flickered at the fringes of blackness, obscuring my vision. He was going to strangle me to death. I was going to die at the hands of a madman. Suddenly he released my throat, and I gasped and sucked in tiny gulps of air. I longed for one huge breath, but he was sitting on my chest making it impossible to draw in enough oxygen.

"Stop! Goddamn it. Stop!" I coughed as tears spilled from my eyes. Sliding his finger and thumb to my cheek, he pried open my jaws. Vicious pain burst from where he'd punched me, and I opened my mouth, praying he would lessen the pressure. My heart was lodged in my throat.

"Red. Red." I tried to scream in one last desperate attempt for him to heed my safe word.

"You don't hear so good do you, whore? There is no fucking red. Not now. Not ever. Suck me off, cunt, and do it good," Jordon screamed as he leaned forward, forcing the head of his cock between my lips.

Suddenly the door to the room burst open. Straining my eyes toward the commotion, I saw Drake rush through the door as Jordon's cock jerked from my lips. Blessed relief washed over me.

Heart-stopping astonishment quickly followed. A gasp of surprise froze in my lungs as my heart clenched in my chest. Blinking past Drake, bowed up and ready to kill...standing shoulder to shoulder between James and Tony stood...

Sir Drool.

CHAPTER FIVE

My ghost Dom was *real*.

Bulging milk-chocolate brown muscles and erotic amber eyes lambent in a mixture of desire, panic, and dread stared at me. His rugged jaw clenched, and his hands balled into fists at his sides. Knowing his thick, erotic bottom lip lay tucked beneath the angry, tight line drawn across his mouth, I shivered.

He was real. After all the years, all the dreams, he was real.

The room began to spin. I'd stopped breathing the minute I laid eyes on him. Desperate to draw oxygen into my lungs, I gasped for air. My heart pounded in my chest like a thousand wild horses racing through an open field, and a steady throb beat like a drum upon my clit.

All the nights Fanny-Frustration had brought forth his image, I always wished he was a living, breathing soul. Yet I never allowed myself the luxury of *truly* believing it. But there he was, biceps nearly exploding beneath a black security T-shirt. Flexing. Anticipating relief. Relief he probably wanted to gain by unleashing his boiling rage upon the demented Dom Jordon. His muscles pulsed as if being held back by some invisible force, and his broad sculpted chest rose and fell with each panted breath.

"You're real," I whispered faintly. I was locked in the intensity of his gaze.

"Jordon!" Drake thundered a vicious warning. "Get the fuck off of her!"

"Son of a bitch!" Jordon growled as he shoved me away like a toy he'd grown weary of playing with.

Easing off the bed, I walked toward Sir Drool. I couldn't help myself. The magnetic draw was too overwhelming. Forceful. Demanding. Suddenly everyone in the room melted away. My feet carried me across the room as if I were floating on air until I was standing in front of him. Speechless. I reached up with a trembling hand and caressed his cheek. A tingling current raced up my arm as

58

my fingertips met his delicious brown flesh. His eyes gazed into mine reflecting a combination of lust, sadness, and longing. It was the same heart-wrenching expression he wore in my dream. I felt his body shudder as his chest continued to heave. Did he feel the same electrical current that was still ricocheting through me?

"You're really real," I murmured, gliding my thumb over his lips as my body trembled. "I've been looking for you forever. Where have you been?"

His eyes flashed wide in shock then his brows drew together in confusion. His warm, strong fingers wrapped around my wrist, and the muscles in his arm gathered and bunched as he gently pulled my hand away.

"Get her out of here, Drake!" Dream Man screamed in a scathing tone.

He was screaming...screaming at Drake? Who the hell was this guy? People never raised their voices to Drake.

"I'm staying," Drake thundered back.

"I said get her out of here," Dream Man growled between clenched teeth. His golden eyes narrowed, but he never once took them away. I clearly saw his anger, but there was more, a lot more.

"Fuck! You're bleeding!" Drake spat in a tone of horror.

"Wrap her in a sheet and take her up the back stairs. Go to my office. Drake. I need to get this situation contained. I do not need you here. She needs you. Take her. Now! Go!"

His office? The chocolate-skinned god from my dreams was the owner of Genesis? No. That was impossible. It couldn't be. Nobody knew his identity except the employees, and they never spoke of him. He was like a ghost. A phantom. Just like my dreams. Why would he reveal himself this way? My eyes must have reflected my confusion.

"We'll get everything taken care of. Go with Drake, Emerald." The ferocity in his eyes softened. Lust, sadness, longing, compassion, and a flash of regret reflected as he spoke to me with tenderness.

"Yes, Sir," I whispered in a stupor as Drake encased me in the bloody sheet.

Turning his attention directly toward Jordon, Sir Drool took a protective step forward, blocking me from the monster's view. His voice was low and even but held an intimidating edge. "Don't say a fucking word!" the club owner warned Jordon.

Drake hoisted me into his arms. Pausing for a moment, he turned toward Jordon with a look that would have made me piss my pants.

"You pulled the wool over my eyes, motherfucker. Pray to whatever spawn from hell you worship that I never catch you on the street, you miserable piece of shit. I'll rip your heart out of your chest and let you watch it beating as you die," Drake growled between clenched teeth.

Jordon no longer looked like the Dom God I'd once believed him to be. His eyes glistened with vile hatred. His mouth curled in a combative sneer. The protective, loving Dominant mask he wore was gone. Gone was the sensual erotic smile. Gone was the gentle compassion. Gone was my dream of him being the "one."

Realization that I'd been played by a wolf in sheep's clothing hit me hard. Jordon was a predator, a monster using the lifestyle to attain his victims of prey. Unbeknownst to him, I would never have allowed myself to be a victim again. I would always keep reign of my pride.

"Enough!" Sir Drool thundered. "Drake. Leave!"

I buried my head against Drake's chest as he rushed from the room. I could hear voices from the end of the hall. Snuggling deeper against his chest, I hid my face. With all the yelling and commotion that had come from Drake's room, I shielded myself from any form of pity in the member's eyes.

Drake's body shook with rage and a turbulent heat radiated off him in blistering waves. Without a word, he ran up the stairs and burst through a door. Nodding to a security employee, the man held open a large, intricately scrolled wooden door. After entering the room, the door closed behind us.

Raising my head, I blinked in amazement. We were in an office, but it was unlike any I'd seen. Monitors lined an entire wall. I could see, all too clearly, inside Drake's private room. The image was such high resolution, it was as if I were still standing there with Jordon, James, Tony, and Sir Drool.

My dream Dom appeared to be engaged in an extremely heated, one-sided conversation with Jordon, who was busily putting on his clothes. The owner yanked something from the floor and shook it in Jordon's face. I could see a volcanic rage in the owner's eyes, as well as the ragged control he tried to maintain.

"Come on, baby. Lay down here on your belly." Drake turned me away from the monitors, and my eyes widened in surprise. The entire dungeon lay out before me beyond a bank of tall, heavy glass windows.

"Two-way mirrors," I whispered in surprise as Drake carefully laid me upon a long burgundy leather couch.

"Yes. And I need not remind you that you know nothing of where you are or what you're seeing. Do you understand me?" Drake asked with a tone of warning.

"That man. The owner of the club?"

"Yes. His name is Mika LaBrache. You didn't see him either."

"Yes I did. I've been seeing him for years," I whispered half to myself. "No, I didn't see anything." I quickly amended, nodding in understanding. Drake eased the bloody sheet from beneath my body and draped it over me.

"Seeing him where?"

"Never mind." I shook my head, unwilling to explain my bizarre, clairvoyant visions. "Why did he show himself like that?"

Drake sighed and shrugged. "I can't tell you why he came down, baby. Wearing that T-shirt, the members will just assume he's upstairs security. Only a few of us know who he is, like Sammie and the security staff. Come on, let me see what that motherfucker did to you." Drake carefully lifted the sheet to peek beneath it. "I'll try not to hurt you."

"I know you'll be gentle. I'll be okay."

"I'm so sorry, Julianna. I never thought in a million years...if I'd have even suspected..."

"I'm Emerald here, Moses." I halfway smiled using Drake's real name as he had mine. I looked into his guilt-ridden eyes and raised a hand, placing it against his worried face. "It's not your fault. How were you to know? How was I to know? He'd been thoroughly vetted, right?"

"Yes. And I guarantee we'll be going back through his application with a fine-toothed comb." It was a vow. I could hear it in his voice. "Jesus, Julianna!" Drake's voice quivered as he peeled the sheet from my bottom.

"How bad Moses?" I whispered in a tiny voice filled with fear. Using his real name again, I needed to feel connected with him, not as a submissive but as a trusted friend. "Do I need to go to the hospital?"

"Probably. Shit! I don't know. Fuck! No. We'll need to get you cleaned up, first. There won't be any hospitals. Mika will make a call and a doctor friend will come here if we need him. I'm going to cover you back up, sweetheart. Just lay here and try to relax until Mika comes up."

Drake carefully lowered the sheet back over my burning ass. He sat down on the floor next to the couch and gently traced his finger over my aching cheek. I tensed and sucked in a hissing breath.

"I'm so sorry. He played me. Played *me*! Fucking bastard!" Drake's anger was overshadowed by his expression of absolute remorse. I'd never seen him so out of control before. It was frightening. "Honey, if I'd have thought for one second that he was capable...and after what you went through before, I...Oh God, Julianna. I'm so fucking sorry."

"Moses. Stop. This isn't your fault. I survived that, and I'm going to survive this. Neither one of us are newbies. We know there are monsters out there using our community to fulfill their own distorted view of the lifestyle. Maybe he thinks he acted within reason. Who the hell knows? I'm fine. I'm alive. I've got a boo-boo on my butt. Wanna kiss it? It might make you feel better." I giggled.

"How can you laugh at a time like this?"

"Because you're going to break down into tears any second, and damn it, Moses, I don't think I can take that." I held his warm cheek in my hand, and his chin started to quiver as tears filled his eyes.

"No...no. Please." I pleaded as I wrapped my arms around him and buried my head against his thick neck. His massive body shuddered as we held each other.

"Can you forgive me, Julianna?" His voice cracked as he said the words.

"There's nothing to forgive, Moses." I raised my head and wiped his glistening cheeks. "I love you."

"I love you too, sweetheart."

The door opened, and Mika stepped inside. My breath caught in my throat as I stared, amazed and trying to comprehend that my dream Dom was real. He tossed something heavy onto his desk and exhaled with a loud sigh. Closing his eyes, he stood as still as a statue. Every muscle in his body looked strained like he was trying to center a raging storm. I lay there, drinking in his every nuance. He finally opened his eyes.

"Julianna, are you going to be okay?" he asked with concern and compassion flowing beneath his shimmering amber pools.

"Yes, Sir. I'm going to be just fine." A weak smile curled on my lips. The man was walking, breathing eroticism. Every inch of him oozed Dominance. Control. Sex. But above all else, he was *real*.

A part of me wanted to confess my dreams to him. A much larger part knew I needed to keep that secret to myself. I longed to reach out and touch him just to make sure I wasn't having some shock-induced hallucination. My entire body pulsed with hunger, and I longed to touch him, to feel his rugged, sculpted body against mine.

I was seriously fucked up. I'd just had my ass opened up by a stranger impersonating a Dominant and I was all but drooling and undressing Mika in my mind. Another stranger.

Yeah, I was one fucked-up puppy. And like the train wreck I was, I couldn't look away.

Mouthwatering muscles undulated as he crossed his arms over his sculpted chest. I wondered what size spot I was leaving on his leather couch as my pussy ached and wept. No doubt about it, I was a certifiable head case.

"Somehow I imagine you're going to weather this much better than Moses and I will." He blinked and clenched his jaw as he peeked beneath the sheet.

Mika knelt alongside Drake and looked into my eyes. He tenderly threaded his long, dark fingers through my hair. A shuddering quake of lust rippled down my spine.

A look of realization flashed over his face as if he knew the effect toying with my hair was having on me. "I'm sorry," he apologized and pulled back his hand. "We need to have you looked at. Will you allow a doctor friend of mine to come here to the club and take a look at you? Or would you rather we take you to a hospital?"

"No hospitals." I adamantly shook my head. "I have nothing to fear by outing myself. I mean the worst that could happen is I might lose a few clients. But I don't have any family to protect from my insidious desires." I smiled wryly, trying to lighten the moods of the two brooding Doms. "But please, Sir, if you don't mind, I'd like you to call your friend. I'd rather not have to explain my lifestyle choices to a room full of doctors and nurses who may not understand."

Mika smiled and nodded his head. "Okay. He'll come promptly. Let me make a quick call. Is there anything you need?"

"May I please have some water, Sir?" I asked softly.

"I'll get you some, love." Drake nodded and retrieved a bottle of water from a small refrigerator near Mika's enormous desk. I tried to take the bottle from him, but with a stern shake of his head, he tipped the bottle to my lips.

I took a long pull of the cold, refreshing liquid then smirked. "There's something inherently wrong with this. You know that, don't you?"

"What do you mean?"

"I'm the sub. You, my studly macho man, are the Dom, yet here you are pampering me." I laughed and winked at Drake.

"You're such a smartass. Once your butt is healed, I'm going to take great pleasure in firing it up if you're not careful!"

"Like that's a threat?" I teased.

"Sluts...I swear!" Drake smiled and placed a gentle kiss on my forehead.

Mika ended his call, smiling at our banter. God, his smile was as glorious as a sunrise and as sensual as a sunset. The man positively glowed. With a sudden somber expression, he knelt down next to Drake once again.

"Julianna, if you decide to press charges or sue the club, would you let me know prior to pursing those avenues?"

I frowned, shocked that Mika would even imagine such a thing. "I wouldn't think of it."

"Well, legally you have every right to. I just wanted to be prepared if that was a direction you wanted to go."

"Ah. No Sir, it's not, And no Sir, I won't," I snapped with an indignant huff.

"Julianna?" Drake warned as he raised his brows.

"I'm sorry." I could feel my face flush.

"I'll pass it off as trauma. The shock to your system must have induced your mouth to project that Dominant tone." Mika winked as he broke out in a broad smile.

"Hmm. I think you two have been comparing notes on how...um...never mind." No matter the circumstances, I knew better than to sass either of the two Doms.

"Good girl!" Mika's eyes held a hint of mischief. I watched his smile fade as he looked at me with concern. "When was your last tetanus shot, Julianna?"

"I don't have a clue. It's been a long time, why?"

"I think you're going to need one. I'm going to ask the doctor to also run a test for STDs."

I frowned and my stomach rolled. "But, he didn't...he never...y'all got there before..." I stumbled, embarrassed by the position I was in when they stormed the room.

"I know but the implement he used on you..." Mika shook his head and cursed under his breath.

"What was it? I've never felt anything so horrific and painful in my life."

Mika walked to his desk and returned holding a strange metal flogger-looking instrument in his hand.

"Motherfucker! Where is he? I'm going to kill him!" Drake cursed as he stood and inspected the odd-looking item. "No wonder her ass looks like hamburger."

"Looks like what?" I screeched, nearly jumping off the couch. "Let me see my ass! Get me a mirror."

"Let the doctor fix it up first, Julianna. Trust me. You don't want to see it right now," Drake soothed as he wrapped his broad hand around my shoulder.

"Fine. At least let me see the thing that Jordon used then?" I asked, unsure what to even call the instrument of torture.

I was at a loss for words when I saw the object up close. It was a short leather-wrapped stick with shards of razor blades welded into the ends of numerous long metal falls. The razor blades were rusty and ugly. No wonder Mika wanted me to get a tetanus shot.

"Who uses something like this?" I asked in disbelief.

"A fucking sadist. That cocksucker was only supposed to talk to you," Drake spat. "He only had permission to get to know your limits, your likes, your dislikes. Never once did I even hint that he could take any liberties with you whatsoever. I would never set you up like that, Julianna."

"I know that, Sir."

"Julianna," Mika interrupted in a deep but quiet timbre. "Here and now, you don't need to bother with honorifics. We're friends without the titles. Okay?"

"Yes, Sir." I closed my eyes and shook my head then opened them and nodded. "I'm sorry. Yes, Mika."

"Some subs can't ever get instructions right, have you noticed that?" Drake teased.

"Oh, hush! I'm synonymous for screwing up and you damn well know it," I huffed.

"You've just not met the right one yet girl." Mika's rich erotic voice spread over me like hot melted butter.

"You think?" I asked Mika, raising a brow and curling my lip in a condescending sneer.

"Put my name down on the list to fire up her ass once it's healed, would you Drake?"

"What?" My eyes flew open wide. "You're not serious, are you?"

"Oh, but I am!" Mika smiled mischievously.

I instantly melted at his breathtaking smile, hypnotized by that full, thick bottom lip. If only I could do what I'd always longed to. I'd slip it between my lips, capture it with my teeth, and slowly glide my tongue over every plump inch. *Hold your hormones, girl. That kind of thinking got you into this fucked-up situation in the first place.*

Drake laughed softly and assured Mika he would indeed add his name to the list.

"I need to run down and check on Trevor. I'm sure he's scared half to death and probably pestering the boots off Sammie. Will you be okay for a few minutes, baby?" Drake tucked an errant curl behind my ear.

"I'm good. Please give him a big fat kiss and tell him I'm doing fine. I know he's worried. I would be, too, if I were in his shoes." I smiled and nuzzled my cheek against his warm, thick palm.

Drake leaned over and kissed my forehead then stood and exchanged a quick nod with Mika.

"I'll be right here with her," Mika assured Drake as he reached for the door. "Moses. Don't go looking for Jordon. I'll make sure he's taken care of. Understood?"

Drake mumbled something under his breath, then with a begrudging nod he stepped out of the room.

Mika edged in closer to me, assuming Drake's position on the floor. His eyes were hypnotic pools of splendor as they held mine in a wordless gaze. I finally understood the old adage that the eyes were the windows to the soul. I could see a myriad of emotions flickering through his shimmering amber panes. Longing and fear. Sadness and lust. Concern and sympathy. Involuntarily, I reached out to him.

"Shhh. Lay still. The doctor will be here shortly."

"Why?" I softly asked.

"Why what, honey? Err...Julianna." He cleared his throat and his hand froze, suspended above my face, as if fighting a desire to touch me.

"Why did you come down there?" I asked, wanting to fold my palm over his and nuzzle his dark hand against my face.

"I had to." He lowered his hand and caressed my cheek. "I had to." He repeated in a desperate whisper.

I closed my eyes, savoring the feel of his warm flesh, capturing that one, wonderful sensation and holding it tightly.

"You're so beautiful," he whispered.

I opened my eyes, and his lips were a scant breath from mine. Inhaling, I filled my lungs with his scent. Cinnamon. His warm breath flowed over my skin, and I knew I would forever pluck this one moment from my mind and envelope myself in it the rest of my life. I closed my eyes again, slightly lifting my chin and readying myself for his kiss. I imagined the feel of those full, thick lips upon mine. The heat from his body washed over me like a rolling ocean tide, and I trembled.

"Are you cold, girl?" he asked gruffly.

I opened my eyes to find he'd pulled away, but I caught a fleeting glimpse of panic, or maybe horror. Embarrassed and feeling like a fool, I let loose an internal string of curses.

"No, Sir," I whispered, rejection gripping me in its familiar clutches as tears swam in my eyes.

"I know you're in pain, Julianna. It won't be long. The doctor will be able to give you something to help take the edge off when he gets here." He sighed, wiping away the fat tears that spilled from my eyes.

No point in correcting him. The source of my tears wasn't because of my decimated ass, but rather my decimated heart. No doubt he'd pulled back because he was repulsed at the thought of kissing me. But he *did* think of kissing me, probably out of pity. I closed my eyes and swallowed my threatening sobs.

"Please don't cry, Julianna," he whispered once again. Leaning close, his fingers traced a tender pattern over my cheek.

"I'm sorry."

"Oh, pet. Don't be sorry. I'm sorry. We got to you as soon as we could. I just wish it'd been faster. I had to round up Moses and the security team. I needed them there with me. I was scared to death that if I went in alone, I'd kill him."

"Oh, you wouldn't have killed him. Not for this." I sniffed.

"Oh yes, I would have." The conviction of his voice coupled with the look on his face had me second-guessing my doubts. Pure, bloodthirsty rage burned in his eyes.

"Well, I appreciate all you badasses coming to my rescue." I tried to sound lighthearted and to comfort his intense edge.

"I'll always come to your rescue, girl." He stared back at me with that strange mix of emotions dancing in his eyes, the combination that made my heart thunder in my chest and my clit throb in need.

Oh how I longed to reach out and touch him, caress his face, kiss his mouth. I wanted to make love to his tongue, nibble on that succulent lip, feel his warm, hard body on top of mine. But I'd already gotten myself into enough trouble. Besides, all my ridiculous erotic feelings were probably one-sided. One of these days, I was going to stop setting myself up for these brutal falls.

"Well, hopefully you'll never have to jump on your stallion and save the day." I tried to keep my voice light, but instead it rushed forth like a sex-starved harlot. I should just shut up.

"I'd better not. Ever. Or I'll make sure Drake gives me free reign to your ass." A provocative curl tugged his lips and there was a lewd twinkle in his eyes.

Was this a test? Was he trying to see how much I could take before I rolled from the couch, dropped to my knees, and begged him to use me? I mean seriously. His whole "badass" one moment, "tender, protective" demeanor the next coiled my insides like a fucking rattlesnake.

"Okay, now wait a minute. How is all this *my* fault? Oh, wait. I know. Because I'm the sub and everything's our fault, right?" I asked with a hint of sarcasm.

"No. This is *not* your fault. I'm simply looking for a viable excuse to fire up your ass." His plump, ripe lips drew tight across his mouth and he laughed, the sound a deep, rich, blood-boiling timbre that lit me up like a grand finale on the Fourth of July.

"Like you'd need an excuse to begin with."

"And you'd be opposed to that?"

"Not in this lifetime," I boldly confessed, suddenly worried how it would be received.

It wasn't a smooth, easy glide but an urgent rush as his mouth hovered next to mine. His eyes blazed, hot and alive with desire. His lips stilled torturously close as his hands delved into my hair, holding me motionless. I gasped as a blistering wave of lust careened through my body. Quivering, yearning, I arched toward him, hungry for that first sweet touch of his lips.

CHAPTER SIX

"Fuck!" he growled and released my hair. He launched himself from the floor like he'd been bitten by a snake and began pacing the room.

A light knock at the door saved the awkward moment as Mika jerked then turned and opened it. Drake stood behind a short, balding man with wide, wire-framed glasses. Dressed in khaki trousers and a polo shirt, I was uncertain if the man was the doctor or a golf pro.

Mika introduced the doctor as his friend Martin. "We've had a situation, and unfortunately Julianna here was on the receiving end of a very needless accident."

As Mika explained, in sorts, my peculiar predicament, Drake assumed his position on the floor by my head. His big warm hands massaged my scalp in reassurance and love.

"Hello, Julianna. I'll try to be quick and gentle my dear." The doctor oozed warmth and reassuring comfort. "May I?" he asked.

I nodded and with great care, he pinched the hem of the sheet between his finger and thumb. I hid my face in the crook of my arm. I didn't want Drake or Mika to see any expression of pain or fear on my face. Mika cursed under his breath, and the doctor asked for more light as he cleansed my gnawed flesh. Drake's fingers continued to soothe my scalp, and he murmured soft, loving praises in my ear as I lay motionless on the couch.

It wasn't quite as bad as hamburger, but it wasn't an open welt from a whip either. I needed eleven stitches and a tetanus shot. The doctor drew three vials of blood and gave me his business card, instructing me to call his office first thing Monday morning to make a follow-up appointment. He told me to keep the area clean, covered, and medicated. I thanked him and promised I would call his office for an appointment. Then he left.

Sliding off the couch, I crawled on all fours and sucked in a ragged breath. Both men hovered over me as if I were made of glass. The pain was subsiding but still raw enough to make me pause and gather my resolve before I attempted to stand up.

I raised my head and came face-to-crotch with a glorious erection straining beneath Mika's well-worn jeans. I froze. Not because I was afraid, okay well maybe a tiny part of me wanted to hide behind Drake, but I froze like a statue from the unfathomable realization that I'd aroused Mika. My heart thundered in my chest, and my mouth felt like the Sahara Desert as my eyes fixed at his crotch.

Placing a knuckle beneath my chin, he lifted my face until I was staring into his eyes. Issuing a weak smile, he nodded minutely, but his eyes reflected a disturbing sadness I didn't understand.

"I've got a T-shirt and a pair of athletic shorts in the closet next to the bathroom. If you can tolerate the fabric, Drake and I will take you home. If it's too much, I'll get a clean sheet for you." Mika looked nervous.

"I'll give the clothes a try." I was still reeling from the shock of his arousal.

Standing in Mika's bathroom, I carefully slid my legs through the soft nylon shorts, trying to wrap my head around all that had transpired. In a few short hours, I'd gone from fear to subspace, to orgasm, to fear, to pain. Now I was struggling with absolute confusion. Mika was real. My dreams weren't some subconscious longings but an actual message...maybe? And what was his impressive hard-on all about? Was it me? Had I been the one to provoke such obvious desire? Yes, I'd been naked, but he owned a BDSM dungeon for crying out loud. He'd seen me and every other sub naked on numerous occasions. And if he'd wanted me, why hadn't he come down from his mighty throne and claimed my ass—when it wasn't raw hamburger—years ago?

What kinky episode of *The Twilight Zone* had I stumbled into? My head hurt, my cheekbone stung, and my ass cheeks throbbed. I wanted to go home, slam some of the pain medication the doctor had given me, and go to sleep. The night had been surreal beyond belief.

Exiting the bathroom, I gingerly walked past Mika's desk, narrowing my eyes on the demonic weapon Jordon used on my ass. A photograph on his desk caught my eye, and I blinked in utter shock. It was *her*...Fanny-Frustration, the gossamer angel from my dreams.

I swallowed tightly, averting my eyes back to the toy as I studied the woman's image from my peripheral vision. No wonder I thought I'd been dreaming about myself. Except for the color of our hair, we were identical. She had my green eyes and narrow, oval face. We shared the same ivory complexion, and there was a sprinkling of freckles on the bridge of her nose, like me. Even our lips were shaped the same. It was quite unnerving to see a near mirror image of myself in a photograph of someone else. I couldn't tell by looking at the picture how tall she'd been, or was. Hell, was she still alive? Mika was—maybe she was alive as well. If so, then where was she?

A barrage of unanswered questions raced through my mind. What was her name? Who was she to Mika? His submissive? His wife? I wanted answers to questions I could never ask him. I couldn't just blurt out that the woman had been visiting my dreams for nearly four years, and I wanted some answers. I'd sound like a nut job to both men. And no matter how much Drake loved me, he'd surely cart me away to a padded room.

"Don't worry, Julianna. We're only keeping that as evidence," Drake whispered as he draped a tender arm around my waist. "Come on baby, let's go."

"Thank God." I sighed in relief, pretending I'd been captivated by the insidious toy instead of the beautiful mystery woman's photo.

We followed Mika downstairs and out to the parking lot. I sat next to Drake in his car, and Mika followed behind in mine. My ass burned, and even the smallest dip in the road caused me to clench my teeth and bite back the urge to scream.

"Why does Mika hide in his office?" I asked, trying to take my mind off the growing pain. But who was I kidding? I wanted info on Mika.

"He doesn't want anyone to know he owns Genesis."

"Why not?"

"That's his personal business, pet."

"You don't work for him, yet you know who he is. None of the other members have ever met him, at least none that I know of. Why you?"

"We've been friends longer than Genesis has been in business."

"So tell me about him."

72

"What is it you want to know, girl." Glancing away from the road, he gave me a shrewd look. "You're being awfully nosey."

"No, not really. I just want to know about him. He seems...I don't know."

"Mysterious?"

"No. I think that's how he wants to be perceived, but that's not who he is. He's...sad."

Drake didn't say anything for a long time, but I could tell by his body language and the way he gripped the steering wheel in his meaty hands that I'd hit a nerve.

"We used to frequent clubs, years ago. Me, Trevor, Mika, and his slave, Vanessa."

"Is she the woman in the picture on his desk? The one who looks like me?"

"Very observant, girl." Drake nodded. "Yes, that's her. The four of us were pretty much inseparable. Hell, we *were* inseparable. We vacationed together, damn near lived together. We had some incredible times, that's for sure." A melancholy smile spread across his mouth. It quickly vanished, replaced by a pained expression.

"Vanessa got sick. She had an inoperable brain tumor. Mika's father is wealthy—very wealthy—and has influential friends in very high places. So after Vanessa was diagnosed, Mika took her to every specialist he could find here in the U.S. and abroad. There was nothing anyone could do to cure her. The entire two years she fought the cancer, he never left her side." He exhaled a shaky breath and paused a long time before he continued. "She died on a gorgeous spring morning five years ago. A part of him died with her."

Glancing at me, his jaw clenched. "You repeat any of this to anyone and our friendship ends."

Tears trickled down my cheeks. "I'll never say a word, Moses, I swear on my life."

He nodded and pressed a palm to each of his own eyes. "Good. Yes honey, you do look like her," he stated, and I nodded in agreement. "You act a lot like her, too." He chortled a bit and wiped away another tear.

"But I'm not her. I don't want to be confused with her because I can't be someone's ghost." I sniffed, attempting to talk myself out of the fairy tale fantasies dancing in my head regarding Mika.

"Trust me...he knows you're your own person, Julianna."

"How do you know?"

"We talk. A lot. The night you came to drop off your application to Sammie, he and I were in his office looking out over the dungeon. When you walked in, he stood up, his face went slack, and he started to shake. It was like he'd seen a ghost. He couldn't take his eyes off you. He finally turned to me, and with a pain I hadn't seen in his eyes since Vanessa was lowered into the ground, he asked two questions: How and why?" He swallowed tightly and after a long silence, he finally spoke. "How did you find out about Genesis, love?"

"I drove by one night and saw a woman walking into the building. She was wearing fishnet stockings and fetish shoes under a long coat. It was July. Nobody wears a trench coat in July. So I pulled over and parked across the street. I sat there for over an hour watching men and women enter through the nondescript wooden door. Everyone was wearing coats and jackets, but I spied bits and pieces of fetish wear beneath them. It became crystal clear that even with their flimsy vanilla guise, they were all ducking into Genesis to partake in secret pleasures."

Drake nodded thoughtfully as we turned into my driveway.

"So, nearly every night I sat across the street and watched and waited. I tried to figure out if I was ready to give my submission another try and a way I could get inside the club, to check it out. Then one night a young woman left the building alone. It was Carnation. I rushed across the street and stopped her. I asked how I could be invited to join the party. She nearly jumped out of her skin because I scared the living hell out of her. There wasn't one question she would answer outright. I'm pretty sure she thought I was an undercover cop or something." I laughed softly, remembering how nervous she was.

"I finally lowered my jeans and showed her the tattoo on my hip. I guess she figured anyone who had the international BDSM symbol tattooed into their skin was pretty serious about the lifestyle. After a lot of begging, she finally agreed to meet me the next night. That's when she passed an application to me. The rest is history."

Mika pulled in my driveway alongside us, and I slowly eased from Drake's car, crying out as a knife of pain sliced through my ass. In an instant, Mika was next to me, wrapping me in his arms and lifting me off the ground.

I buried my face in his chest and inhaled deeply. He smelled like rain, fresh and clean, but carried a hint of cinnamon apples, bizarrely reminiscent of my childhood. Dazed by the sudden feeling that in his arms was right where I belonged, tears stung my eyes.

He held me against his warm, solid chest as I sobbed. Emotions, like an angry swarm of bees, buzzed through me. I melted against him, absorbing his power, his warmth, and his gentle tenderness. At the same time, heartbreak for what I could never have made me long to run for the shelter of my house, lock the doors, and hide away from the invisible thread tugging me toward Mika. I wanted to hide from the feelings that had already begun blooming in my heart.

Mika tossed Drake my keys to unlock the front door. Slowly, as if afraid to jostle me, Mika carried me up the stairs and to my room. Drake fluffed my pillows then turned down the cover on my bed as Mika continued to keep me clutched tight and protected in his arms.

Two Dom's taking care of me. I almost laughed. The role reversal was awkward and a bit unnerving, at least to me. Sure Sammie gave me aftercare, but this was far beyond the normal pampering a Dominant gave a sub after a session. Surely a few cuts on the butt weren't enough reason for the two Doms to all but fall over themselves ensuring I was comfortable and had what I needed. I was just a sub. An unclaimed, and for all intents and purposes, an undesired sub. Yet both men were almost bumping into each other to help me.

It was stupid and dangerous for me to feel anything more than gratitude toward Mika. It was stupid and dangerous to allow myself to want and hunger for him. It wasn't only stupid and dangerous, but complete insanity to cling to any thread of hope that my dreams meant something in the real world.

I resembled Vanessa too much. I would be a constant, bitter and painful reminder of what he'd lost. I'd be nothing more than a burden of agonizing memories, never a joy to his heart.

"When was the last time you ate something?" Drake asked as he peeled down the soft nylon shorts.

"Um, lunch with you...well, sort of," I mumbled.

Drake turned and issued a perturbed stare. "You barely ate a bite at lunch. You'll get the lecture about taking better care of yourself later."

I nodded my head with a pensive look.

"I'll make you some tea and toast and then we'll get some pain meds in you. Mika, will you stay with her?" Drake asked.

"Of course. We'll be fine. Come on, let's get you into bed." Mika gave me a little smile.

Drake nodded and left the room.

Mika helped me get into a semi-comfortable position on my side and then carefully sat on the edge of the bed, caressing my shoulder. I wanted to reach up, wrap my arms around his neck, and pull him to my lips. The gnawing need to taste him only reinforced the importance to distance myself. Of course, with his thigh resting against my belly and his warm, long fingers stroking my skin, distancing myself from him was delusional.

"I don't want you to argue. I'm staying the night with you."

So much for detachment. It was so absurd, I almost laughed.

"I promise to be a gentleman, and you can unequivocally trust me. You'll need pain meds in the night, and I don't want you here all alone. If you wake in the wee hours and need something, I'm going to be here for you. At some point Drake will have to go back to the club and pick up Trevor, so it makes sense that I stay with you."

Could I fight him on this? Did I want to? The answer to both those questions was a resounding no.

"Honestly, Sir, you really don't have to stay. I don't want you to feel like you're obligated to me because this happened in your club."

"That has nothing to do with why I insist on staying, girl." He lowered his head and with a severe look of warning, narrowed his eyes.

Then why was he staying? The question was on the tip of my tongue, yet I couldn't find the courage to ask it. I couldn't risk exposing so many raw emotions. Whispering my thanks, I kept my quagmire of cluttered thoughts to myself.

"I can't stop reexamining my actions tonight. I should have demanded to leave the second he locked the door. My gut told me something wasn't right, but I didn't listen. I made excuses. His whole demeanor shifted so suddenly, and I assumed he'd been thoroughly vetted. Drake seemed to have confidence in him. Now I feel like I've just flushed everything I've ever learned about submission down the toilet."

"You haven't, Julianna. Don't talk like that. And yes, Jordon *was* fully vetted before being allowed in. James is going over his application as we speak. James has...hmm, friends." A sly smile curled on his lips. "We'll get to the bottom of it right away because we missed something, something fucking important." Mika's tone was suffused with frustration. "I'm sorry we failed to protect you. Drake's beating himself up unmercifully, and in all honesty I'm trying not to leave bruises on myself as well."

"I know he is. And he shouldn't be. Neither should you." I looked straight into his lusty amber eyes. "I don't want either of you to feel responsible for any of this. Everyone did everything right, except me. I should have known better than to get into a situation like that. After Drake left, I was still floating in subspace and felt so damn foggy it was hard for me to process exactly what was going on. I'd never been in subspace before and didn't know it made you so drunk. Still, that's no excuse. It was stupid of me to ignore the first red flag, I mean, I know all about the predators that gravitate to this lifestyle. How could I have been so damn blind and stupid?"

"Welcome to our world, girl. Drake and I are asking ourselves the same damn thing."

"Well, thankfully you, Drake, and the guys came when you did. I just wish I hadn't been so damn naïve. The person responsible for this mess is Jordon, but guilt isn't always so levelheaded, and I want to will it all away, including my own."

"Jordon is a goddamn player," Mika roared as he launched off the bed and paced the room. "He knows shit about power exchange. The little dickweed was just looking for a kinky piece of ass." His jaw ticked and his full, sensuous bottom lip twitched.

"I wanted him to take me." My confession was fragile in remorse. "I wanted him to claim me. God that sounds so pathetic." Tears slipped from my eyes. "I wanted..."

Mika rounded the bed and knelt, his face just inches from mine. "You wanted the dream, Julianna. There's nothing wrong with that." His words of understanding blanketed me as he wiped my tears with his broad, warm thumb.

"Yes, I did, because I'm a fool. I'll never have the dream. I mean, I want it badly, but I don't think I'm ever going to find it." I sniffed with a disgruntled half-smile that felt more like a kid curling his lip at a plate of stewed spinach.

"You're not a fool for wanting the dream. Hell, we all want the dream. It just takes time to find the right one. Trust me pet, I do know."

"Do you want the dream?" I looked into his sympathetic eyes.

"Every time I step inside Genesis, I can taste it. Yes, girl, I want the dream." Sorrow echoed in his words as he sat down next to me again and began to stroke my arm.

"But yet you don't have..."

"I had the dream once...it died," he subtly confessed.

"I hope the dream doesn't die inside me," I whispered, skirting his confession of loss.

"Don't ever entertain that fear. The dream inside you will never die. Your submission is like air to your lungs. It's who you are, girl." He leaned over and placed a soft kiss upon my forehead. "Lucky is the one worthy enough to claim you."

"I thought I was supposed to be the worthy one. I mean, I've spent all these years learning how to be a good submissive so I am *worthy*." I couldn't help but grin.

"That's exactly why it's called a power exchange, girl."

The erotic baritone timbre rolling from his throat made my heart ache and my eyes blur from tears.

"Oh, pet. Are you hurting?"

"Uh-huh." I lied to disguise the actual reason for the tears trickling onto my pillow. How was I supposed to confess that my heart was breaking over his loss of Vanessa? How could I express my sympathies for life dealing him such a grievous blow? Or confess I'd walk through a field of broken glass for one chance to submit to him.

"Do you want to sit or lay while I feed you?" Drake asked. He stood in the doorway clutching a tray laden with cheese, fruit, and hot steaming tea.

"I'll sit up. I'm going to feed myself, Moses. Thank you, but I'm not an invalid sweetheart...err I mean, Sir." I shook my head and rolled my eyes at the thought of him feeding me.

Both burly men began helping me reposition myself, making

sure I was comfortable. I started to giggle, then softly laugh, and finally burst into uncontrollable belly laughter.

"Don't push your luck, girl," Drake admonished with a scowl on his face.

I somewhat apologized between chuckles. Regaining my composure, I took a sip of the warm tea, and Drake began shoving cheese and fruit into my mouth.

"I can do this myself," I protested.

"Humor me." Drake's eyes narrowed.

"Isn't there a fetish for this?" I rapidly chewed as he continued to pop chunks of cantaloupe into my already full mouth.

"A fetish for what?" Drake asked in confusion.

"Forced feeding."

Mika threw his head back and laughed. I couldn't help but giggle right along with him. Drake shot me a vicious look as I wiped the juice trickling down my chin with the back of my hand.

"All I know is that your ass better heal up damn fast!" Drake growled and then kissed me hard, right on the lips. Pulling back, his eyes were filled with heartbreaking sorrow. "I'm so sorry I wasn't there to protect you."

I set my cup of tea on the tray and picked up his broad hand. Caressing it over my cheek, I placed a tender kiss on his palm.

"Moses. You have been my friend and mentor for years. I've never once questioned your ability to protect me. There is only one constant in my life and that is *you*." Tears began to swell in my eyes as I frowned at his tormented expression. "I will never doubt your love or your friendship, never doubt that all you do for me makes me a better woman, a better human being, and a better submissive. I love you, Moses. Please stop. Please, for me? I've never asked for anything more important to me than this. Don't do this to yourself. It's breaking my heart."

"Goddammit!" Drake groaned, as he scrubbed his palms over his teary eyes and nodded.

"Thank you." I smiled with deep appreciation.

Mika's phone began to buzz. "Yes." He stood and began pacing the bedroom. "Are you shittin' me?"

He was silent for a minute, but I could tell by the way he clenched his jaw he didn't like what he was being told.

"Son of a bitch!" He suddenly stopped pacing and shot a look of rage toward Drake. He shook his head as if in disbelief. "Well, obviously we're going to need to change that now, aren't we? This was premeditated. There's no two ways about it. I'll get in touch with George tomorrow morning. I want this scumbag nailed to the wall."

I watched as a crimson hue climbed over Mika's toffee-colored cheeks.

"Thank you, James," Mika continued. "I appreciate this very much. I won't be back tonight so tell Sammie to put everything in the safe and lock up, would you?"

Mika ended the call and paced a bit more as Drake and I watched him with what I'm sure were matching anxiously curious expressions. He rubbed his hand over his bald head then eased back onto the bed.

"James's connections found something disturbing. Seems Jordon Cartwright isn't the man we approved and welcomed into Genesis. That guy is home in bed sleeping, or rather, he was. The animal that did this to you is Dennis McCollum. Seems old Dennis and Jordon look enough alike to be twins. Dennis stole Jordon's identity, including all his financial and personal information. Jordon, the real Jordon, has been trying to find Dennis for a couple of years. Anyway, that's how Dennis was able to breeze through our vetting process. Bastard set us up from the get-go." Mika placed his elbow on his knee and began massaging his forehead with his fingers and thumb.

"Need a pain pill?" I asked with a tiny smile.

"No. I need a forty-four magnum," Mika growled.

"So that little motherfucker played us all, huh?" Drake groused.

"Listen, if it hadn't been me, he would have eventually found another sub to abuse," I interjected.

"It still shouldn't have been you," Drake hissed.

"And it's not your fault," I hissed right back. "It's nobody's fault, goddammit!"

With his head still resting on his fingertips, Mika turned and looked at me, arching his brows at my outburst.

"Well it's not!" I huffed.

"Yes. I think her ass had better heal quickly." Mika laughed.

"See? And you thought I was overexaggerating!" Drake maintained.

"Overexaggerating about what?" I asked. They'd talked about me?

"Your smart mouth!" they both said in unison.

"Isn't it time for my pain pill?" I snapped with a surly pout.

They both began to laugh, and Drake nodded his head. "I need to get back to the club. Trevor and I will come by in the morning to check on you. Will you be all right through the night or do you want us to drive back and stay over?"

"No need, brother. I'm staying with her," Mika announced, still chucking.

Drake's face went momentarily slack. He opened his mouth to say something, but Mika interrupted him.

"Don't even think it!" Mika warned.

"No. I know. I mean...I'm not." Drake nodded. "Okay, well if you need anything in the night, give me a shout, all right?"

Mika reassured him he would. Drake bent down and kissed my cheek. "I love you, Julianna."

"I love you too, Moses." I smiled. "Thank you for everything."

As both men left the room, I attempted to lean over and retrieve the pain pills from the nightstand, but couldn't quite reach them. Slowly inching toward the side of the bed, I stretched and almost rolled off the mattress.

"Just what the *hell* do you think you're doing?" Mika thundered from the doorway.

CHAPTER SEVEN

"I was getting my pain pills," I answered, issuing a look of challenge.

"Woman, you do *not* want to piss me off." Mika plucked up the bottle, shook out two horse-sized tablets, and placed them in the palm of my hand. I washed down the pills with the rest of my tea and eased back against the pillows.

"What happens if I piss you off?" I asked, trying not to smile.

"Keep pushing and find out." Mika flashed me a feral, evil-laced smile.

Nibbling on my lip, I raised my brows. "That's okay. I think I'm done pushing."

"Novel idea."

I flashed a look of innocence his way, but he wasn't buying it. He merely shook his head and laughed. That gooey timbre reverberated off the walls and penetrated my bones. The muscles on his neck protruded as his rock-hard abdomen flexed. Christ, but the man was potent, gorgeous and bursting with sex appeal. I could stare at him for the next millennium and still not get my fill.

"You certainly know how to keep a Dom on his toes, young lady."

"I'm not all that young, you know."

An awkward silence filled the room. Mika seemed a tad bit nervous. "Are you comfortable in my shirt, or would you like to change into your pajamas?"

I nodded. "I'm okay in the shirt, thank you." Oh, hell was I ever comfortable in his shirt. Too much so. It smelled like him, and it was all I could do to keep from drawing it to my nose and inhaling his erotic cinnamon scent.

"Do you need anything else? A trip to the bathroom? A glass of water? Anything?"

"No, Mika. I'm fine. Thank you." I was somewhat embarrassed that he'd asked if I had to use the bathroom. Silly of me, I know, but it was such a private thing.

"Okay, the house is locked up." A look of anxiety flashed in his eyes before he shook his head and looked at me. "I'm going to take my jeans off and climb into bed with you."

He exhaled deep and began unzipping his jeans. If I'd not been such a chicken-shit, I would have offered to peel them off him with my tongue.

"Please don't be nervous. I'm not going to attempt to do anything sexual with you, but I'm sporting a hell of a hard-on, again." His lips were drawn in a tight line. "You do this to me all the time, girl. But I've already promised that I'll be a perfect gentleman. You have my word on that." His face reflected the solemnness of his vow as he tugged his T-shirt over his head.

But what if I want you to do something sexual, need you to? I silently yearned as I gazed at his massive sculpted chest and stomach. *What if I want to trace every contour of your glorious body with my tongue? You wouldn't stop me, would you?*

"I trust you'll be a perfect gentleman, Mika." Flashing him a confident smile, I looked away just as my eyes reached the waistband of his gray boxer briefs. I tried to focus on the blankets because I knew if I looked at his crotch, I'd be drooling, begging, and pawing at him like a nymphomaniac.

I needed to remain safely encased behind my imaginary walls. Big, thick, honkin' walls. Walls that were hopefully sturdy enough to withstand the myriad of needful, sexually hungry emotions careening through my mind and body. As Mika eased beneath the covers, his torso twisted and he extinguished the bedside lamp.

"Come lay against me, Julianna. You have more stitches on your right butt cheek than the left. Swing your right leg over my hip and maybe you'll be comfortable enough to sleep."

Moving like a turtle, I eased into the position he'd suggested, amazed to discover it actually eased some of the throbbing. But the heat emanating from his crotch and burning my upper thigh was sweet agony. I swallowed a moan of delight and was set more ablaze as he slid his arm beneath my shoulders and eased my head onto his chiseled chest.

"Wake me if you need anything in the night, okay?"

"I will." I nodded when what I really wanted to do was press my lips against his hard chest and grant him a tiny show of appreciation for his tender loving care.

Right. Bullshit!

I wanted to feel his warm skin against my lips and tongue to see if he tasted as sweet as he smelled. My lips twitched as I fought the desire. I wished the pain pills would kick in and make me fall asleep, or at the very least ease the temptation to molest him.

"Mika?"

"Yes?"

"Talk to me. Tell me about yourself," I asked tentatively.

"There's not much to tell," he answered a bit too quickly.

Was he nervous or had I crossed a line?

"You've watched me at the club for God knows how long. You've seen me in every situation imaginable, good and bad. I know you've witnessed a lot of behavior I now wish you hadn't. You know almost everything there is to know about me, but I don't know anything about you."

"Jesus, Julianna. You're unbelievably manipulative, but you already know that, don't you?"

A deviant little chuckle rose from my throat.

"Yeah, just by the sound of that laugh, you're well aware of every button you push."

I could tell he was shaking his head in the darkness of the room.

"Where to start? Well, I'm thirty-one and I know you're twenty-six. I retired from Wall Street and opened Genesis. My father's family emigrated from Haiti to escape the oppressive poverty there and once in the US, my grandparents worked hard and grew prosperous—very prosperous. That was extremely difficult back then with segregation and all. They became US citizens and raised my father with a staunch work ethic, which he still has to this day. It's served him well, and he is highly successful, thankfully, without the prejudice and stigma my grandparents had to endure."

"You're proud of your family. I can hear it in your voice," I sleepily mumbled.

"Very much so. My mother was from Sweden. She had the palest alabaster skin and her eyes were blue as the sky. Her hair was glistening blonde, and it would catch the sunlight in such a way that she literally glowed."

84

I could feel the warmth and love he held for his mother in his voice. "So that explains your beautiful milk-chocolate skin and breathtaking amber eyes." I whispered as my lids drooped, heavily.

He softly cleared his throat and inhaled deeply. He captured my hand and pulled it up to his chest, cupping it tenderly beneath his. My eyes closed as the pain meds began working, and I began to drift off to sleep.

But lying so romantically in his arms, I didn't want to succumb to sleep. I didn't want to miss a single moment curled up against his warm, steely body. I wanted to lie there all night as his deep voice echoed inside his massive chest, resonating in my ear.

Time could have frozen then and there and I would have wished for nothing more the rest of my life. Being suspended for all eternity nuzzled upon his chest was pure heaven. I tried to force my eyes open, but they felt as if someone had sewn them shut.

"I'm glad you found me," I murmured. "Even though you told me you couldn't."

"What?" Mika asked curiously.

"My dreams," I slurred. "You've been haunting me forever."

Mika stopped talking while his rhythmic breathing coaxed me deeper into the murky liquid depths of sleep. I vaguely remember him speaking my name, but I was too far gone to respond.

"Vanessa. Dammit, Vanessa. I know you've sent her to me. I see you in every fucking thing about her. But she's not you. Why are you doing this to me? It's so hard to keep fighting. I've been fighting my desire for her for so fucking long. Why? Why can't I close off these desperate feelings and be content to savor my memories of you? Why are you making it hurt so goddamn bad...still?"

His words were like fringes of lace in a tunnel far away as he whispered a plea to the one he'd lost so long ago. The ache in his voice pierced my heart with a staggering pain. I tried to force myself to listen to him, to hold tight to the edges of darkness, but it swirled me down and sleep claimed me.

~*~

I woke sprawled across a pillow, alone in my bed. Vanessa didn't visit my dreams as I lay nestled in Mika's arms. And while it

85

was nice to have a *real* name for my mysterious dream woman, it unnerved me that she was more than just a dream. She was a ghost. A ghost matchmaker of sorts. Unfortunately, all her emissary tactics were for nothing. I didn't need to be an armchair psychologist to understand that Mika would always look at me as a reflection of her. Sadly, it would be a painful reflection, a knife to the heart for all he once had and lost.

Trying to clear the drug-induced haze glazing my mind, I rolled over. Burning pain enveloped my butt cheeks as I clenched my teeth and hissed in agony.

"Son of a bitch, that hurts! I'd like to find that motherfucker and flay his ass open with that goddamn razor blade flogger," I railed through clenched teeth.

"Such language." Mika tsked from the doorway, his hands fisted around a tray of food.

"Ooops, I didn't know you were um...standing there." I blushed like a child who'd been caught with her hand in the cookie jar.

"No need to apologize. I feel the same way, but I'd like to do a lot more than simply slice the bastard's ass open." Mika's confession was edged in anger as he placed the mountainous tray of food on the foot of the bed. "I'd like to put a bullet through his brain."

"Heavens, Mika. What have you done?" The plates were piled high with scrambled eggs, stacked strips of crispy bacon, and a tower of toast. "I can't possibly eat all this."

"Well, I'd hope not," Mika exclaimed in a shocked tone. "It's for us to share."

"Oh. You scared me." I laughed. "I was beginning to think both you and Drake had forced-feeding fetishes." I winked with a mischievous grin.

Mika laughed and shook his head. "Do you want me to help you sit up or would you rather lie on your belly and let me feed you?"

"Damn it, what is it with you Doms? Do I honestly look that helpless? I can feed myself." Okay so my words held a bit of a curt and indignant tone, but seriously, the thought of him sliding a spoon in and out of my mouth was far too erotic, too intimate.

I didn't want to start my day throbbing and wet. But it was too late. A barrage of sex charged thoughts flashed in my mind. How would I ever find the strength not to swirl my tongue around the

86

utensil while dreaming it was his hot, hard cock? The same cock that twitched so gloriously against my thigh last night.

"You are not going to feed me, Mika."

"Issuing orders now, are you?" He arched one brow and gave me a look of warning. "I think there's a bit of a switch inside you, girl."

"I'm not a switch." I huffed.

"Mmmmm, so you say."

"I'm just strong willed."

"That, my dear, is an understatement of biblical proportions." He laughed with a wicked grin.

I issued a heavy, exasperated sigh.

"Okay, wrap your arms around my neck and hold tight," he instructed as he leaned over and cradled my legs upon his solid, strong forearms. Turning my face against his marble-like chest, I closed my eyes and inhaled deep. Once again, I wished time would freeze. I could spend eternity encased in his powerful arms, cradled against his warm body and breathing in his masculine scent.

Fluffing the pillows behind my back, he eased my bottom onto the bed. Panting as the burn seared, I clenched my eyes shut and rode the wave of pain.

"Do you need some more pain meds?" Mika asked in a tender voice.

"No. Please, no more pain meds. They make me feel foggy and out of control."

"Switch." He smirked.

I raised my chin in challenge and narrowed my eyes. Suddenly his hand was gripping my hair. He gave it a subtle tug. I gasped and shuddered as bolts of erotic splendor zapped my core.

"You need to remember your place, girl, even in circumstances as dire as this." A lurid and all too sensual smile spread upon his inviting lips.

As he released my hair, my eyes were drawn to the straining bulge beneath his jeans.

"Oh yes, pet, make no mistake. You make me want many things." Looking into my eyes with an animalistic hunger, his jaw clenched. "Let's eat."

Yes! Let's eat, indeed. He could unzip those damn jeans and let me feast on him. I licked my lips and imagined how delicious he would taste. I felt my face blaze as powerful, deviant thoughts danced in my brain.

"Food, slut. Let's eat food." Mika chuckled as if he could read my mind.

I groaned low and nodded as he placed the tray upon my lap then sat on the bed next to me.

He took a big bite of eggs and washed it down with a sip of coffee. I watched as his throat worked, wondering if the column of his neck was soft and warm like his hands. Watching me from the corner of his eye, he set down his mug and turned to me.

"Are you always so sexually needy, girl?"

"I think it's the pain meds," I lied, struggling to contain the urge to trace my fingers over his rugged jawline. I closed my eyes and attempted to reign in my zinging hormones. When I opened them up, I realized I was no longer wearing his shirt. I was naked.

"Ummm, where's my shirt?" I asked in confusion.

"Observant much?" He laughed with a twinkle in his eyes. "You're just now realizing you're naked?"

"It's the pain meds. I'm foggy," I protested. "Where is my shirt?"

"Hmmm, you don't remember?"

I shook my head and stared at him, wondering what the hell had happened last night.

"Well, pet, you tore it from your body in a fit of unbridled lust right before you molested me," he said with a straight face.

"I what?" I choked as my eyes flew open wide.

His deep, erotic laughter filled the room as I sat dumbfounded, wracking my brain for any flicker of memory that involved sex. There was nothing, not the slightest inkling. The only thing I could remember was the hazed recollection of his plea to Vanessa.

"You're messing with me, aren't you?" I asked, narrowing my eyes.

"Oh, I am Julianna. It's so much fun." He grinned like an impish schoolboy.

"And you Doms call us subs brats." I huffed in mock disgust. "Seriously, where's my shirt. I know I didn't rip it off in some hot torrid sex session. Trust me, I'd definitely remember *that!*"

His mischievous grin faded to a reassuring smile of compassion.

"You got sick in the night. I think the pain meds were too harsh on your stomach. I was able to get the trash can to you in time, but you did get a bit on you. So I..."

"Oh, God," I wailed in embarrassment. "I'm so sorry. I don't remember any of that."

"Shhh, it's alright." His hand was gentle as he caressed my face. "You're not the first sub I've helped through a night of illness."

"Then you need to start hanging out with some different subs." I sighed, embarrassed that Mika helped as I tossed my cookies. And why didn't I remember any of it? No, that settled it. I wasn't taking any more pain meds.

"I know exactly what I need," he murmured under his breath as he slammed me with a serious and sensual expression. Hunger blazed in his golden eyes. "I need you to eat your breakfast."

Unnerved at the thick, sexual tension filling the room, I nodded. "Yes, Sir."

My body hummed in voracious and insatiable emotions as I began eating with gusto, suddenly overcome with ravenous needs. Ravenous for food. Ravenous for sex. Ravenous to be filled with something unknown. A hollow emptiness deep inside my soul screamed to be complete.

Setting my glass of juice on the tray, I realized Mika was watching me. He wore a somewhat startled expression.

"What?"

"You polished off more than I expected you to. Have you been starving yourself?"

"Oh." I swallowed and blinked at the nearly empty plates on the tray. "I'm sorry. I didn't mean to pig out like that."

"No need to be sorry. I like women who don't eat like a bird."

"Well, you don't get thighs like this from eating celery."

"Your thighs are gorgeous, girl. Don't ever degrade yourself again," he warned with an arch of his brows. "Do you want more? There are some eggs left I can scramble if you're still hungry."

"Oh, no thank you. I'm stuffed." I smiled and patted my slightly distended stomach. "Thank you for breakfast, Mika. It was delicious."

"You're welcome, girl."

"Do you mind helping me get out of bed? I need to use the ladies' room," I asked, feeling my face flush with embarrassment.

"Not one bit in the world."

Before I knew what was happening, Mika lifted me from the bed and walked straight into the bathroom.

"Put me down!" I demanded without thinking.

"I will, Mistress Bossy-Britches, just as soon as I get you to the toilet." He grinned.

A low, menacing growl erupted from the back of my throat, hoping to intimidate him into setting me down. I only accomplished making him laugh.

"Don't drop me in your jovial fit, pal." I warned in sarcasm.

"Yee of little faith." He winked and then his expression turned sober as he looked into my eyes. "I would never let you fall, girl. Never."

A ripple of hope fluttered in my stomach. His decadent mouth was so close. It would be so easy to lean in, and for just one moment, one glorious, magical moment, press my lips against his. I wanted to surround myself with the heat of his body, his full sensual mouth, and his rugged, alluring scent.

I absorbed everything about him. He moved effortlessly, and I could feel the tight muscles of his arms and chest ripple beneath my skin. An internal war raged as I longed to slide my tongue over his bare chest.

"How do you want to do this?" he asked, breaking me from my lust-induced trance.

The immediate visual of me bent over the sink and Mika pounding his ample cock into my pussy sent a swirl of smart-assed responses firing through my brain. *Don't you dare say it,* I warned myself.

"Alone," I mumbled.

Shaking his head, he lowered me to my feet then walked out of the room. The stitches tugged and strained as I carefully eased my backside toward the toilet seat. When I lowered myself onto the hard wooden seat, the pain was so brutal I cried out.

In the blink of an eye, Mika appeared.

"Dammit, Julianna." He clutched my waist and lifted me off the ground.

He held me suspended over the toilet as I clutched his forearms. Tears filled my eyes.

"Do you always have to be so damn stubborn?"

"What the hell do you think you're doing?"

"Holding you here while you urinate."

"Oh no. Oh *hell no!*"

"Will you shut up and piss for God's sake?" His eyes flickered with a golden fire.

"Oh good God in heaven, I can't. It's too embarrassing."

"Girl. For the love of...Piss." He barked in command.

I growled in defiance then did as he ordered and emptied my bladder.

Suspending me with one arm, he reached for the toilet paper with his other hand. Gathering a fistful of paper, he began to reach between my legs.

"Mika. No." I panicked.

"What now?" He huffed in exasperation.

"Don't wipe me."

"Why not?"

Closing my eyes, I exhaled a deep breath. "Because I'll come," I confessed in embarrassment.

It felt as if all the oxygen had left the room.

The silence was deafening.

"Julianna, look at me," he whispered.

I raised my head and was seized by his sympathetic amber eyes as he leaned in and slanted his mouth over mine. I froze for the two seconds it took my brain to process he was kissing me, then I relaxed and melted in his arms.

As his mouth demanded more, I yielded. I poured every ounce of passion I'd ever felt into this one sensual, heart-stopping, life-altering kiss.

A low growl rumbled deep in his chest as his lurid tongue plunged into my mouth, seeming consumed to learn every dip and crevice. I whimpered and clutched my fingers into his shoulders, attempting to mesh him deep inside.

Mika stood and eased me down his sculpted body until my feet met the floor. Framing my face with his warm, strong hands, he slanted his mouth and kissed me again with a demanding, volatile force.

As if impossible, this kiss became more passionate, heightened in intensity. He tasted as sweet as cotton candy, and if this was only a temporary carnival ride, I had every intention of thoroughly enjoying every thrilling second. I hungrily pressed against his body and was ecstatic when his hands slid down my arms, pinning my wrists to my hips.

Forceful.

Commanding.

In total control.

He arched his hips, driving his turgid erection against my center, and began burnishing his hardened shaft against my clit. Needful, muffled moans rose from my throat as I soared to the edge of oblivion. My nails raked across his muscular back and in unabashed hunger, I rocked my hips against his thick, hot erection, all the while feeding on his tongue.

Suddenly Mika tore his lips from mine, retracting his heated cock from my throbbing clit and resting his forehead against mine. We gasped for air, and I groaned in frustration.

"Why did you stop?" I panted.

Before Mika could answer, the doorbell rang.

"I'll be right back." He cupped my hand around the wad of toilet paper and raced from the bathroom.

After mopping up my weeping pussy, I crawled back into bed. My entire body throbbed for more. Seconds later Mika, Trevor, and Drake waltzed into the bedroom. I plastered on a smile hoping I didn't look as horny or as guilty as I felt.

"I'm sorry to barge in on you like this, girl, but Trevor was driving me insane begging to come see you." Drake shook his head with a look of admonishment, but Trevor's smile was so bright he glowed.

"Come here, sweet bro." I grinned, spreading my arms open wide, all the while praying my lips weren't swollen or revealed any sign of the torrid kiss. Stealing a quick glance toward Mika, he seemed perplexed and looked as if he were ready to run from the room.

"I don't want to hurt you, sister." Trevor lightly patted my back.

"I'm not glass. Give me some love!" I demanded, hugging him

tightly.

Trevor gripped me and sighed. "I've been so worried about you. I want to rip that asshole's heart out, if the bastard has one."

"You and me both, sugar."

Trevor turned and looked up at Drake, presenting the saddest puppy dog eyes I'd ever seen as he stuck out his lower lip. "Can I Daddy, please? Please? Please?" he begged like a petulant child.

I knew exactly what he was begging for and followed suit as I mimicked his pitiful expression, pleading to Drake as well.

"Oh for the love of God," Drake thundered. "Kiss her, you little mouth whore." He rolled his eyes in acquiesce.

A squeal of delight peeled from Trevor's throat as he leaned in and pressed his warms lips to mine. His kiss was soft and paled in comparison to Mika's. I ached to have his demanding mouth against mine once more.

"I swear to Christ that boy loves her mouth. I think he's got latent bi tendencies," Drake complained.

Trevor broke the kiss and shook his head. "I do not, Daddy. I just love the way her mouth feels. It's so soft, and that thing she does with her tongue. Lordy, it makes my spine melt."

"Like I said, he's a mouth whore," Drake grumbled as I giggled and wrapped my fingers around Trevor's neck, drawing him back for more.

"Just what is it that she does with her tongue?" Mika's question was low and a bit wistful.

You know exactly what I do with my tongue, Mister, I thought with an inward grin. When Trevor failed to answer, Drake tore him from my mouth by his long blond hair.

"You were asked a question, boy."

"Oh, I'm sorry, Masters!" Trevor chuckled as he licked his puffy, reddened lips.

"She wraps it around my tongue and then sorta slides it up and down in tiny little strokes. It reminds me of the way Daddy..." He stopped as a bashful blush rose on his face when he spied Drake's cautious expression.

"Enough explanation, boy. You may continue kissing," Drake directed. "Just don't get so lost in your imagination that you forget who and *what* you're sucking on, my sweet love."

93

He shook his head and moaned in assurance. I'd never remembered Trevor's mouth feeling quite so delightful before. It felt softer and he tasted sweeter.

Closing my eyes, I imagined Mika's warm, slippery tongue exploring my mouth again. I imagined sucking that succulent bottom lip that constantly commanded my attention. I felt slighted that I didn't have the chance before we were interrupted.

In my mind, I could feel Mika's hard, tight muscles as I ran my hands over Trevor's arms. The voracious hunger was back, burning me alive, screaming to be filled. It was crying to be satiated, demanding the hollow emptiness inside me be quenched.

Rising to my knees, I launched myself against Trevor's chest, plowing him to his back. I whimpered as I raked my throbbing nipples over his cottony soft shirt.

Without warning, I felt a hand grip my hair as my head was jerked back.

"What the fuck do you think you're doing, girl?" Drake's voice thundered.

My body shuddered as I gasped. Trevor looked shocked and more than a bit embarrassed.

"Sister!" he exclaimed in surprise.

"Oh." I covered my face with my hands. I'd all but molested him. I was mortified. Pulling my hands away, I looked down at Trevor, who was wearing a wolfish smile.

"I'm so sorry. I...I...Oh shit." With Drake's thick hand fixed in my hair, I climbed off Trevor, embarrassed that Mika had witnessed my display. I felt shamed and wanted to hide. Hide from them all.

"I'm sorry. I'm sorry." I reached back and placed my hand over Drake's wrist, attempting to dislodge him from my hair. "Please let go."

"What were you thinking?" Drake yanked as he lifted my face upward.

"It's the pain pills, Sir. They've put something in them. Some kind of aphrodisiac," I groused.

"So what are you telling me? That you've been humping on Mika like a bitch in heat because of your pain pills?"

"No, Sir," I snapped in an indignant tone while hoping Mika wouldn't rat me out and confess the little tête-à-tête in the bathroom.

"Well, you had no trouble humping my slave now did you? I'm waiting for a plausible explanation girl."

"I don't have one, Sir." I wished I could slink down and evaporate into the carpet.

"I think sister's just horny, Master," Trevor whispered.

"Is that true?"

"Something like that, Sir."

"Then come, girl," Drake demanded as he wrapped his free hand around my wrist and pushed my own fingers between my legs. "Well? We're waiting. Is there a problem?"

I couldn't do it. I couldn't touch myself. I was still reeling with mortification for how I acted with Trevor. "Please let me go, Moses." My body throbbed in a combination of lust and shame.

"Fuck!" Drake's whole angry demeanor changed in the blink of an eye. He exhaled a heavy, exasperated sigh. "No, I won't let you go, Julianna. You need to come, and so you shall."

"Kneel up on the bed," he instructed as he led me to the foot of my bed.

"Trevor, lay down beneath your sister."

"Master?" Trevor shrieked in alarm.

"You're not going to fuck her, boy!" Drake thundered. "You're going to kiss her while I yank her hair and manipulate that lovely trigger of hers. She can come by her own fingers or not at all. But I'm giving her permission to release the frustration that's governing her actions before she begins fucking the doorknobs. Now if you're both thoroughly satisfied with my explanation, which I didn't owe either of you in the first place, get in your positions both of you. Now." He released my hair with an exasperated sigh.

I couldn't even look at Mika, too terrified by what degree of disgust his eyes would reflect. Drake knew I needed to come and so did I, but I didn't want to masturbate in front of Mika. But with Drake being so hardheaded, I knew I couldn't talk my way out of it. There was no going back.

Feeling debased at what was expected, I tried to swallow my pride as I waited for Trevor to assume his position. Drake directed me by my hair until I was straddling Trevor's hips. I hesitated then descended my mouth to his.

Closing my eyes, visions of Mika once again filled my mind.

95

With my ass thrust upward, the stitches burned beneath my tautly stretched flesh. I whimpered as Trevor's tongue plunged deep inside my mouth. He was being unnaturally forceful, which fed my fantasy like forbidden fruit.

Drake tugged my mane. Dreaming of Mika's tongue, I groaned lowly in Trevor's mouth as I became lost in my fantasy. Sliding my fingers upon my throbbing clit, I rubbed the sensitive knot of nerves. My hips rolled as I fantasized of Mika's broad brown hands clutching my ivory flesh, preparing me, readying me to accept his glorious shaft in my needy pussy.

My body jerked in surprise as warm palms caressed and cupped my breast. It was Mika. It was his hands that were upon me, touching me, helping me climb up and over the edge. I released my lips from Trevor and gasped as Mika plucked and pinched my pebbled nipples. Whimpers, moans, and tiny squeals of delight vibrated in the back of my throat as his magical touch coaxed me higher. His warm breath floated over my ear as he nibbled the column of my neck.

The heat of him surrounded me.

Exploring.

Enticing.

Euphoric.

It was sensual sensory overload. Quaking violently, his broad hands spread my thighs and his fingers plunged through my swollen folds, invading my sweltering cunt. Mika drove into my core with demand, swirling me into a lewd whirlpool of hedonistic splendor. It was a spectacular free fall, and I gave everything over to his masterful control.

Rocking my hips, meeting each deep thrust, my pussy gripped and clutched as my soft, slick tissue sucked upon his embedded fingers. Something warm and slippery slithered across the puckered flesh of my anus followed by his finger that began tracing the ultra-sensitive rim. He persisted upon the fragile tissue and finally penetrated the ring.

It was too much. Too intense. Shards of lightning detonated outward, spreading from the rigid rim of my virgin asshole and tingling through my limbs. I was soaring to the heavens as his finger stretched the delicate opening, flying far beyond my control.

Nothing could have held me back. Nothing could have slowed the spiral as I swirled higher and higher toward oblivion. My whimpering mewls escalated to panting cries, growing louder and more desperate by the second.

"Give it to me, Julianna," Mika's deep, buttery voice whispered in my ear. His fingers curled inside my tunnel, pressing against my hidden bundle of nerves as his other finger steadily seesawed into my ass. "Let me have it, girl. It doesn't belong to you. Christ, your whimpers are like a fucking white-hot spike through my brain. Let go, precious. I want to hear you scream for me. I want to feel your pussy and your ass milk my fingers as you explode. That's it. Fuck my fingers and come for me. Come. Come for me, love. Now!"

His demand catapulted me over the top. Nectar poured from my pussy in a deluge as I closed my eyes and welcomed the crashing thunder.

Drake gave one last hard tug of my hair as my body arched. I tossed my head back and screamed Mika's name as I fragmented into a million shimmering shards of white ecstasy. Convulsing brutally, I clutched Mika's thick fingers, milking them as they plowed in a frantic rhythm inside me, screaming to the heavens as each powerful wave obliterated me.

Before I could even begin to feel the twinges of the fierce tsunami dissipate, Mika jerked his fingers from my body. Lights were still flashing behind my eyes, and my ears buzzed as the powerful release continued to vibrate.

"Trevor, tend to her," Mika snarled. His tone was fused in disgust and anger. "Drake, get me out of her sight. Take me back to the club. Now." Mika stormed from the room, his footsteps echoing in a heavy thunder as he raced down the stairs.

CHAPTER EIGHT

"I'll be back." Drake murmured on a sorrowful sigh.

Was Drake talking to me or Trevor? It didn't matter. The dream was over. Everything I'd longed for and desired just raged down the stairs, out the door, out of my life.

Evidently Vanessa hadn't a clue about my less than stellar track record with Doms, else she'd have known I was *not* the one for Mika. I never would be. She'd have to invade another sub's dreams, one that was worthy of Mika because without one single, solitary doubt, I wasn't the "one."

I fragmented like French lead crystal smashed against a marble pillar. Crawling over Trevor, I curled up into a tight, protective ball. The brilliant white light surrounding me seconds ago dissolved to a black, oily abyss.

Soft sobs turned into mournful wails. Confusion sullied my mind. What had I done? What didn't I do? Clueless, I tried to find an explanation for Mika's sudden onslaught of disgust. My mind could only ascertain the obvious. I was a pathetic excuse for a submissive. Seeing me in action was so disheartening, Mika couldn't stomach my ineptness, couldn't wait to get away from my miserable display. I was beyond hopeless. I was a failure, a complete and total failure, and forever would be.

"Julianna. Oh sweet sis. What can I do for you, honey?" Trevor's words were suffused in sorrow as his tender fingers caressed the side of my face. I shook my head, drew my knees up tighter, and cried. "Oh baby! He'll figure it out. You didn't do anything wrong. Come on, let me love you."

"No," I sobbed. "Leave me alone, Trevor, please. Just let me be for a few minutes."

He exhaled a concerned sigh. "I'll get you some hot tea. That will make you feel better. I'll be right back." With a sympathetic pat to my shoulder, he tucked the covers over me then left the room. Left me alone to wallow in my devastation.

Rocking back and forth, trying to ease the agony blistering my soul, I tried to convince myself that Mika was nothing but a whimsical fantasy. It had never been real. The dreams were simply that, dreams.

Imaginary.

Ghosts.

Smoke.

Smoke that I'd been blowing up my own ass thinking, wishing, I could be more than a disappointment. I'd failed miserably, once again, without knowing exactly how.

I was certain that Mika looked at me as a doppelganger, a far too painful likeness to the ghost of his past, Vanessa. He would never allow himself to align with me because of it.

I was painfully aware that I lacked the grace and beauty worthy of his Dominance. His urgent need to escape painted a ruthless and agonizingly clear picture. He didn't want me. His demand that Trevor tend to my aftercare reinforced his disgust. He couldn't even lower himself to such a menial task.

But it was his acrid, venom-filled demand for Drake to get him out of my sight that decimated me. The echo of his cruel and abhorrent words ripped my soul apart.

Sobs wracked my body as my mind spun like a centrifuge. Dominance. Submission. The quest to find that all-elusive "one" had been nothing but a pipe dream. A fantasy.

And without warning, a light bulb illuminated in my brain and it was all too clear. I knew what I had to do. I had to give up my dreams of submission. If I was to retain any semblance of sanity or self-esteem, I had to let it go. I had to shove it far behind me and forge ahead.

Trevor returned with the tea, his eyes filled with sorrow and pity. Pity! It was the last nail in my submissive coffin. I was a strong-willed woman, a woman fortified with determination. I was also a woman who loathed pity, especially in the eyes of her friends.

No more.

I would take back my control *and* my life.

Drying my eyes, I unfurled my limbs and in my mind began to construct thicker, protective walls, reinforcing the layers of self-preservation. This time I designed them so that no one ever got through to hurt me again.

"Thank you sweetheart." I nodded with a weak smile.

"Are you okay?"

"I'm fine. I'm sorry I broke down. I didn't mean to do that. The onslaught of hormones, I think. I didn't handle that very well now, did I?" The smile I forced felt empty.

"You scared me, Julianna," Trevor confessed in a low, fragile voice. "There's a lot you don't understand about Mika."

"It's not important. If there's anything he wants me to know, he'll tell me." I squeezed his hand.

Trevor nodded then exhaled in a resigned sigh.

"I need to take a shower. Can you help me with the bandages?" I asked.

"Of course. Come on. Let me help you, sis." Trevor's smile was bright. He was happy to be helping me. After all, that's what submissives reveled in.

Helping was how they derived their contentment and they thrived doing things for others. It was something I'd need to learn how *not* to do.

~*~

For the next thirteen days, I stayed away from the club. I concocted a plethora of excuses for my absence when Drake called. And he called daily. Most times I wouldn't even bother to answer the phone, and when I'd relent and pick up, a dubious tone of doubt filled his voice with each pathetic lie I offered up for my absence. Guilt gnawed at me, but there was no going back. I had to buck up and steer my life in a new direction.

I'd followed up with Mika's doctor as promised, and while my backside was mending exceedingly fast, my heart and soul continued to hold the fresh and piercing painful wounds. Wounds that continued to weep and ooze at the loss of my submission.

I'd placed entirely too much hope on Mika in far too little time. Hope inflated by idiotic, obsessive dreams. It wasn't at all surprising that they had stopped. No doubt Vanessa had realized her mistake and was now haunting some other more deserving submissive's dreams. Truth be told, I missed her. But her visits would inevitably have included Mika. I wasn't prepared for that. The memory of him alone was excruciating enough.

It was Friday night, a night I normally spent primping to enjoy with like-minded friends at the club. Yet I sat alone eating a potpie that had the same flavor and consistency of the cardboard container it came in. Restless. Anxious. I sat alone at my kitchen table realizing how much of my life had been centered around the club and its members.

I had no other friends to join for a night out at a vanilla bar or to take in a movie, a dinner. I'd spent the past four years sequestered from anyone or anything outside the realm of BDSM.

Had my choice been a pathetic attempt to fill some void, or was submission at the actual crux of my being? I still didn't know. I *did* miss it, missed the expectation of conforming to a rigid criteria. I missed the feeling of being at peace with my psyche. Even longing for a Dom, I'd felt more centered with people who shared my kink than I did sequestered away like I was now. At least I could achieve my fundamental desires to submit through Drake and my interaction with other Dominants. They kept me under their wings in one way or another, and were a constant reinforcement and reassurance of my submissive status.

This was just stupid. I could do anything I set my mind to. I was a strong, capable woman. Pining over some man a ghost delivered in my dreams was asinine. I needed to get my shit together and start living my life without that infernal club.

Picking at the deceptively delicious-looking crust of my dinner, a knock came from the door. I wasn't expecting anyone, but dread rippled in my belly fearing it might be Drake. Swinging the door open, I was surprised to find Mistress Sammie wearing a long ivory sweater that concealed her fetish wear. A tight, humorless smile stretched over her red, glossy lips.

"Sammie? Errr...come in, please," I stammered. "What's wrong? Is Drake okay?"

"Drake is fine. Maybe you should talk to him when he calls and find out for yourself." Her words were short and clipped. "Get dressed. I've come to haul your ass to the club."

I blinked, speechless.

Sammie snapped her fingers. "Hurry up. I don't have a lot of time. I left James tending the bar, and that's a sure recipe for disaster. The man knows nothing about working my bar."

"Sammie, I'm sorry you came all the way over here, but I'm not going to the club tonight. Please tell Drake that..."

She cut me off, holding her palm toward my face.

"Drake didn't send me to get you, Mika did. Now get your ass upstairs and get dressed."

Mika? My mouth dropped open. "Mika? Why?"

"Go get some clothes on, girl." She smiled, softening her gruff demeanor.

Panic blossomed in the pit of my stomach as a tingling numbness pumped through my bloodstream. "I can't. Please tell him I was busy. I wasn't home. Tell him..."

"I am not about to lie to Mika for you or anyone else," she hissed, cutting me off in mid-sentence. "The man is a saint, and I would never disrespect him in such a way. Now, you march your little ass to your room and put some fucking clothes on. You've got ten minutes to get yourself together, or I'll haul you out that door naked!"

For such a petite woman, she packed a lumberjack punch of authority.

"Why does Mika want to see me? Why didn't he just call?" I asked in defiance.

"You're trying my patience, young lady. You really don't want to do that," Sammie warned as she placed her tiny hand on her slim hip. "Move!"

She took a warning step toward me. I yelped then turned and scurried up the stairs to my room.

Tearing open the door to my closet, I grabbed a black silk gown. Digging out a pair of heels, I had stripped and dressed in a matter of seconds. Rushing to the bathroom, I looked in the mirror. My face was flushed, and I trembled at the absolute panic reflected in my eyes.

"What the fuck are you doing, Julianna?" I whispered at my image. My heart thundered in my ears. "Calm down. Don't be an idiot. It has to be something to do with Jordon, err...Dennis. Pull yourself together. He doesn't want to see *you*. Not the submissive *you*. Maybe Genesis is pressing charges because of the attack and he wants you to sign something."

Scolding myself for the seeds of hope taking root in my heart, I tried to calm the anxiety crawling beneath my skin. Quickly dabbing on some makeup, I turned and scurried down the stairs. Sammie was waiting for me on the porch, holding the front door wide open.

"Get in the truck," Sammie ordered without looking back.

"I can drive myself."

Spinning on her spike-heeled boots, she shot me an angry glare. "I was told to drive you. Now get in the truck," she growled.

I climbed in and slammed the passenger door. I was pissed. Pissed that I was being treated with indifference by Sammie. Pissed at being carted off in the night and expected to appear just because I was summoned. Pissed that Mika didn't have the balls to call me himself and discuss whatever this was about. Setting my lips in a tight rebellious line, I huffed in annoyance. The man had nerve. What ego. What gall.

"So tell me, Sammie. Just who is Mika? Is he the Lord Alpha Dom of the planet? Is he the great and powerful Oz? I mean, honestly. He yells at Drake, orders him around like he's some kind of minion, and now he's sent you to pick me up, to run his errand like I'm his dry cleaning or something. Who the hell is this guy? Better yet, why do you Dominants so readily submit to him?"

Sammie gripped the steering wheel so tight her knuckles turned white. Her nostrils flared and her jaw ticked. "I'm going to dismiss your insolent tone this once, but if you know what's good for you, you'll shut your piehole and drop the sarcastic tone now. Every lifestyler in this community owes a huge debt of thanks to Mika for providing us Genesis. He's the one taking all the risks to ensure we kinky folks have a safe place to realize our dreams. You think it's easy to keep a club like that open? You think it's easy to keep the holier-than-thou religious fanatics, the cops, or the press from swooping down like a swarm of locusts and shutting it all down? Where do you think we would go if we didn't have Genesis? Nowhere. There's not another club like it within a two hundred mile radius. And if you were any kind of submissive worth your salt, you'd realize that without having it spelled out to you, girl!"

"Yeah, well, I'm not a submissive anymore. So I guess you spelling it out was necessary," I snapped right back.

Sammie slammed her foot on the brake, pulled to the curb, and shoved the truck into park. She whipped her head and looked at me with eyes wider than I imagined possible.

"What the hell are you talking about? What do you mean you're not a submissive? If you're not a submissive, I'm a fucking nun." She sighed heavily and frowned. "Why, for one New York minute, do you think you're *not* a sub?"

"It's been four years, Sammie. The only Dominant I've had a chance to spend time with turned out to be a sadistic wannabe that flayed me open before he tried to rape me. I'm so fucking undesirable, I couldn't turn a Dom's head if it were on a spring!"

"You don't know shit! Not turn a Dom's head?" She choked out a strangled laugh. "Honey, there's an ass load of Dom's who wouldn't think twice about tossing their subs aside if they thought they could have you."

"Bullshit!" I spat, rolling my eyes.

"It's not bullshit. And don't talk to me like that or I'll beat your ass so hard you won't sit for a month."

"Oh yeah, they're all lining up every night holding up numbers. I have to push my way through the hordes of Dominants wringing their hands just waiting for me to bow down and submit to them. Sorry, Sammie, but you're on crack."

"God, what I'd give for a ball gag right now," Sammie growled, flashing me a furious look. "Just because they're not pawing all over you doesn't mean they don't want you. You have no idea how many times Drake's been approached by Dominants interested in you. And he's not turning them away because of your lack of submission. It's because he knows none of them have the backbone to keep you in line. None of them are strong enough to handle you. Like it or not *princess*, you're a wee bit hardheaded."

I growled, and she tossed me a condescending grimace.

"Shut it," Sammie growled right back at me. "The only reason Jordon, the weaselly little fuckknuckle, was even allowed to spend time with you was because you ran out on Drake when he told you to wait for him at the bar. He realized he was holding on to you too tightly. He wasn't allowing you to grow. So he eased up and let that fucktard...well, Drake's still kicking his own ass for what happened."

A wave of guilt swamped me behind an even bigger wave of

anger. "He's been doing what? Keeping Doms away from me? What the fuck? He thinks none of them could handle me? Just how the hell would he know? He never let any of them try!"

"Oh, get over yourself." Sammie rolled her eyes.

"No. That just proves my point now, doesn't it? Obviously, I'm too high maintenance for any Dom to *handle* me! And after four years, there never will be. So why even bother? Why keep searching for someone and something that's never going to come? Why waste my time? And if Drake's so goddamn protective of me, why didn't *he* come drag me to the club himself?"

"Christ. You want a Dom handed to you on a fucking silver platter, is that it? As for Drake, I'd hazard it's because you've been lying to him for about two fucking weeks. And he's so pissed by the way you're treating him, he doesn't trust himself not to beat your ass bloody!"

I closed my eyes and hung my head as guilt gnawed through me. I was so wrapped up in my own self-pity I'd repeatedly lied to Drake just to save face. I'd lied to my best friend assuming he wouldn't understand how devastated I'd been at Mika's parting words.

"You're going to have to make some serious heartfelt apologies to him. You've hurt his feelings. I mean deeply hurt his feelings. And that pisses *me* off, Miss Thing. I thought you two were friends. A friend doesn't shit on someone the way you did. He's been the best thing that ever happened to you and you damn well know it."

Sammie's lecture made me feel two inches tall. She was on a roll, and I knew better than to interrupt her now.

"I know all about your past. I know all about the hell you went through with that wannabe Dom when you first started exploring the lifestyle. And let me tell you something, Drake loves you as much as he loves Trevor. That's not something you throw away. He most definitely doesn't deserve you kicking him to the curb just because you're in the throes of a pissy little temper tantrum."

Feeling broken every way imaginable, I wanted to open the door and fling myself from the truck. Anger. Guilt. Embarrassment. Every ugly, worthless emotion I'd been trying to wash away over the past two weeks came flooding back with a vengeance.

"Just take me back home, Sammie. I can't do this anymore. I'm sick to death of constantly fucking up my life and everyone else's, too. I'll find a way to apologize to Drake. And I'll find a way to deal with all these other shitty emotions swirling inside me. You're right. Drake has never been anything but golden to me, and all I've managed to do is hurt the one person who means the world to me."

"I'm not taking you home, Julianna. I'm not giving you an easy out. But I *will* give you some advice. Haul your ass off the pity pot and start putting into practice all the training and knowledge you've learned, everything Drake has painstakingly taught you. You owe him that much. At least you should." She pulled the truck from the curb, and we rode the rest of the way to the club in silence.

Sammie parked in the back lot, behind the building.

"We'll go in this way."

I followed her to a small metal door. She punched in a code and the lock disengaged. Without a single word, I followed her inside.

"Go up those stairs. Tony will be waiting for you." Then she turned and walked away.

"Great," I mumbled under my breath as I climbed the stairs, the same stairs Drake had carried me up the last time I was at Genesis. The night my world crumbled.

I encountered another door, this one locked, so I hesitantly knocked and waited.

The door swung open. "Hey, Emerald. How are you feeling?" Tony asked with concern in his eyes.

"Wonderful, thank you," I lied. "Is Mika in?"

"Yes." He nodded toward an ornately carved door. "I need to go check on some things downstairs."

Of course you do. I stood staring at the intricately scrolled door. Glancing up, I spied a small camera mounted above the frame. Cocking my head, I glared at the lens. I placed one hand on my hip, and balled my other hand into a fist as I pounded on the door and waited. And waited. And waited. Impatient, I nibbled my bottom lip and looked back up into the camera's lens.

"Well, I'm here. Just like you commanded, oh great and powerful Oz. Open the damn door!" Still nothing.

I knocked again, this time harder than before. Still nothing.

"Open up!" I cried, annoyed at the stupid pointless game Mika was playing.

"Fuck this!" I spun on my heel, turning the knob on the door I

106

had arrived through. I found *it* was locked.

"Seriously?" I whipped back around to look at the camera. "You've got to be fucking kidding me."

I was at Mika's mercy.

"Really? You brought me *all* the way down here to make me stand outside your door." I folded my arms across my chest in rebellion. "Fine! I'll stand here until you grow some balls and open the goddamn door. And since I'm not a submissive anymore, I'll just stand here and wait your ass out!"

My feet ached in my uncomfortable heels as I waited for what seemed like hours. I issued a low, feral growl and sat down. Staring at the scrolled design on the massive door, I wondered when or if Mika would decide to open it.

For a man so anxious to talk that he'd sent Sammie to fetch me, he sure wasn't fired up to start a conversation. I waited hour after pointless hour. Finally fed up with the whole game, I laid down on the plush, soft carpet where I eventually drifted off to sleep.

She was back. Vanessa hadn't haunted my dreams since I'd met Mika. As she floated before me, I wanted to wish her away, to take back control over my dreams.

"You can't wish me away any more than you can wish away what you truly are. He can't wish you away or what he is, either. Open your heart. Embrace your desires. He needs you more than you realize, more than he can comprehend. I've done all I can for now. You'll have to do the rest. If you want it bad enough, you'll figure it out."

"Come on girl. It's time to go." Sammie shook me from the confusing dream.

"What?" I felt disoriented. "What time is it?"

"Three thirty. The club's closed. I need to take you home now."

"But...Mika. He didn't open the door."

Sammie issued a slight shrug then helped me to my feet. Disbelief flooded my veins. He'd kept me waiting all damn night and never opened the stupid door. Glaring at the camera, I wanted to spit on its lens.

"I hope you enjoyed yourself. I had a dandy time. We'll have to do this again real soon. Maybe in another fucking lifetime. Buh-bye." Sarcasm rolled off my tongue, thick and bitter.

"Now!" Sammie ordered.

I could tell she'd run out of patience with me. Well join the damn club, lady. My patience had long run out as well.

The drive home was quiet. I was stewing in a boiling pot of anger. Why had Mika yanked me out into the night only to leave me sitting outside his mighty throne? What was the purpose of it? What was he trying to prove? Did he get his jollies manipulating me? I was at a complete loss.

As Sammie pulled into the driveway, she put the truck in park and turned to me. "I'll pick you up tomorrow night at six thirty. Be ready."

"Don't bother. I'm not going back there. I'm *never* going back." I scrambled out of the truck, slamming the door and stomping toward my house.

Sammie ignored my words. "Be ready tomorrow at six thirty or I'll drag you out by your hair. Don't piss me off. You won't like it."

CHAPTER NINE

Yeah, well if I'm not home, you can't pick me up, now can you?
I slammed the front door to my house and let loose my rage with a
bloodcurdling scream. Racing up the stairs to my room, I tore off my
clothes and shoes then threw myself onto the bed as fury bubbled in
my veins. Burying my face in the pillow, I cried myself to sleep.

Sunlight poured in through the curtains. I looked at the clock
and groaned. Nine thirty. Great. Reminding myself how far behind I
was with work, I took a quick shower then began digging through
the mountains of paperwork.

Glancing at the clock, I blinked, so focused on work I'd lost
track of time. It was five forty-five, and my stomach issued an empty
growl.

"Sorry Sammie, but there's no way in hell I'm going to subject
myself to another night of humiliation and boredom for a man who
gets his rocks off watching me sleep." I grabbed my purse and
stormed out the house.

Pulling into the parking lot of Maurizio's, I looked at the clock.
It was six o'clock. A pang of guilt rent through my veins as I closed
my eyes. Screaming in frustration at my own weakness, I threw the
car in reverse and drove back home, cursing the entire way.

Standing near the front door, dressed once again in a long gown
and uncomfortable high heels, I peeked through the curtain as
Sammie pulled into the driveway. Slamming the front door behind
me, I walked solemnly to her truck.

"Let's go," I growled in disgust.

"What did you learn last night?"

"Umm, let's see...his carpet is very soft and plush."

The pasted-on smile I flashed obviously didn't impress Sammie
as all she did was stomp the gas pedal and flip me off.

"It'd be nice if he'd at least leave a pillow and blanket, maybe
even a bedtime story. Does he seriously think a solitary slumber
party is a flipping picnic for me?"

"Is that all you learned? That the carpet was soft and you think he's enjoying this?"

"What else am I supposed to learn, Sammie? I was all alone, just me, myself, and I. The three of us aren't really that interesting conversationalists, you know. If the great and powerful Oz would open the fucking door, then maybe I'd have a chance to learn whatever the fuck it is I'm supposed to. Maybe I should just click my heels three times and say, 'there's no place like home.' Would he open the goddamn door then? Or maybe I need a broomstick. Yeah, that's what I need, the Wicked Witch of the West's broomstick. Then I can shove it up his ass!"

"Oh, girl. You have no idea how badly I want to slap you. Keep it up and you'll be sitting outside his door for months!"

"No, I won't. Because after tonight, I refuse to participate in his little game. He can kiss my ass. Tonight is it. After that, I'm done. Either he opens the fucking door and talks to me like a man or it's over."

Without a word, she nodded as her lips pressed together in a firm, unhappy line.

Repeating the same steps as the night before, I stood alone outside Mika's door. I brought my hand up to knock then lowered my arm. Looking up at the camera, I simply waited. Once again, I was ignored.

Incensed that I'd allowed myself to repeat the same humiliating nightmare of the previous night, I began pounding on the door. Fuck knocking civilly. I'd lost all patience with civility. He'd open the damn thing up even if I had to knock it down.

Possessed with a rage I never knew existed inside me and screaming at the top of my lungs, I pounded on the door. Rage and humiliation consumed me. The only cognizant thought in my brain was that I was being played by the Alpha Dom inside. No doubt the man was laughing his ass off seeing what he'd reduced me to. And no doubt, he was loving every fucking minute of it.

"Open the door you motherfucking bastard!" I pounded and kicked like a woman possessed.

Moments later, the door behind me opened. Drake stepped into the foyer with James right behind him.

"Drake," I sobbed. "Make him open the goddamn door."

The look in Drake's eyes was cold and lifeless. It was as if he were looking through me and not at me.

"Drake?" I screamed as tears streamed down my cheeks.

"Hands behind your back," Drake commanded in a calm and far too detached voice.

"No," I cried as I stepped away from him. "I don't want to play his goddamn game!"

"Julianna," he warned as he took a step toward me. "Put your hands behind your back, *now!*"

"Why, Drake? I'm not a submissive anymore. I'm nothing. I'm just a fucked-up, confused woman. Why am I even here? Why are you doing this to me? Why is *he* doing this to me? Please, just let me go home. I swear I won't come back. I swear I'll just go away. Nobody will ever see me again." Tears streamed down my face.

"Hands. Behind. Your. Back." His deep voice reverberated in the small alcove.

"Why are you doing this to me?" I sobbed as James stepped behind me and with a firm tug pulled my wrists behind my back. "Drake! Please! Just let me go home."

Drake also moved behind me and a pair of cold metal cuffs snapped around my wrists.

"He isn't the God you all think he is. You know that, right? You don't have to do this shi—" My hateful tone was stilled when a big red ball gag was shoved into my mouth and the leather straps fastened behind my head. My eyes flew open wide in fear as I turned and issued a pleading look at Drake. For one brief second, I saw a flicker of regret in his eyes. Just as quickly, it vanished as he heaved a heavy sigh.

"You need to start remembering what's inside you, Emerald," he whispered into my ear then turned and left the vestibule. James stood with his arms crossed over his massive chest, watching me with a slack, unreadable expression.

I wanted to sob even more, but I knew if I lost control, my nose would run. With my hands restrained behind my back, I wouldn't be able to wipe the mucus from my face. Flopping to my side, I curled into a tight ball on the floor. It was then that I spied a pillow and blanket lying in the corner. There was a book propped up on top of the pile. It was a copy of *The Wizard of Oz*.

A muffled growl tore from behind the ball gag as I unleashed a string of obscenities in my mind. Obstinately ignoring the comfort provided me, I remained in the awkward semi-inverted fetal ball on the floor.

A furtive glance at James confirmed my suspicions. He wasn't there to help me, he was there as a safety precaution. He was watching over me, ensuring the cuffs didn't cut off my blood flow or that I didn't choke on the ball gag. Casting him the most pathetic look I could muster, James arched his brows.

"Dream on. You don't honestly think I'll fall for that pathetic look, do you? You know me better than that, girl." James chuckled with a sharp tone of annoyance.

Great. James just had to choose that moment to be in Dom mode. He couldn't be in his submissive role and grant mercy on a fellow sub. No. Of course not. Huffing a loud exasperated snort from my nose, I closed my eyes and waited for him to remove the cuffs and gag. I wondered how long I'd have to remain nearly hog-tied and unable to speak. Within a few minutes, I drifted off to sleep, and this time Vanessa's ghost did not pay me a visit.

In the wee hours of the morning, Sammie woke me once again. I was surprised to find the gag and cuffs had been removed, and James was nowhere in sight. Of course Mika's door still remained closed nice and tight, just as I'd expected. *The rat bastard.*

The drive back home was quiet and unnerving. Sammie obviously wasn't happy about having to haul Mika's excess baggage around every night.

"And what did you learn tonight?" Sammie asked as she yawned, breaking the awkward silence.

"I don't know," I mumbled. "What am I supposed to be learning, Sammie?" Feeling dejected and confused, I rolled my stiff shoulders and rubbed my aching jaw.

"That's what you're there to figure out. It's something only you can determine. I can tell you one thing. The answer is unique for everyone. There's no right or wrong lesson."

"But you know the crux of what I'm supposed to learn from all this...hell, I don't even know what to call it. Abuse?" I felt confused and defeated. "Torture? Fucking cruelty?"

"Yes, I know the end results the lesson provides. But honey, it's not something I can fix or figure out for you. I don't hold the answer. It's something you have to work out on your own. Nobody can do this for you. If we could, trust me, Drake would be the first to give you the road map. I've never seen him so torn up. He loves you. He loves you with all his heart."

"I know. And I feel so guilty for lying to him. But worse, I feel guilty for failing him."

"Stop feeling guilty. Do *something* to fix it."

"But I don't know how."

"Sure you do. You've just got to figure it out."

"And what the hell does Mika have to do with all this? What does he want from me? I can't do this anymore, Sammie. I can't go through another night of waiting outside his door, wondering what the hell he expects me to do."

"It's all tied together. It's all pieces of the same puzzle, sugar." She smiled softly as we pulled into the driveway. "You're fighting this tooth and nail, baby. The more you fight it, the more it will elude you. Listen to me—stop fighting it."

"Thank you, Sammie. I don't know why, but I feel better. I'm not so pissed off now."

"Get some sleep. You'll be picked up again tomorrow night at six thirty."

"But it's Sunday. The club's not open. Besides, I'm not going back."

"You *are* going back, so stop arguing the point. The club will be open just for you." She smiled softly. "Remember, quit fighting what's in your heart. Now go on inside and get some sleep."

I eased from the truck feeling numb, almost dazed. Climbing the stairs to my room, I crawled into bed. As soon as my eyes closed, Vanessa appeared in her brilliant gossamer light. A fearful worry etched her beautiful face. Frantic. Impatient. Even more demanding than ever before, she forced me down a long corridor of opaque glass walls, then ushered me down a dark foreboding hallway containing thousands of closed doors. She pushed me forward, insisting I *"find the key."* I searched my pockets but had no keys, and each knob I attempted to open was securely locked.

My frustration to find a key was growing urgent, and Vanessa's eyes were filled with an almost hysterical fear. I frantically tried to open every door, but not a single one would budge. Finally, the very last knob I wrapped my fingers around opened.

Yanking back the door, I found a solid brick wall glowing in a strange golden light before me. The bricks seemed to undulate, almost breathe in a stunning pulsating light. It reminded me of a throbbing heartbeat of sorts.

"What's behind it?" I asked.

"You have to see."

"But how do I get in?"

"You have to go through it."

"I can't. It's brick."

"Then knock it down, silly." A smile filled with relief spread across her lips, then she kissed my cheek and vanished in a silvery flash.

Nervously placing my hands on the wall, I expected it to be solid and sturdy, but was amazed to discover it bowed beneath my fingers. Pushing harder, two bricks popped out, landing on the other side. The light emanating through the opening was spectacular. Bright. Soothing. Alluring. I had to see more. Methodically, I began pushing upon the bricks, giggling in childish glee as they fell away. Beyond the opening, the shimmering golden light beckoned me, calling to some hidden force clawing inside my soul. I didn't know why, but I knew there was something of importance on the other side. A gift, a treasure of infinite value, awaited me if I could just get through the damn wall.

Like a demon possessed, I threw myself against the bricks, clawing, slapping, and punching, determined to break through. And when I finally did, I stood frozen in shock at what lay before me.

Kneeling on the ground, wrists crossed behind my back and engulfed by the warm pulsating light, was me. My skin glowed as prisms danced over my skin. I looked beautiful.

Serene.

Content.

At peace.

From the other side of the room, Mika appeared. A broad smile adorned his sensual lips as he looked at me staring at my own image in astonishment. He turned his attention to the other me, the one kneeling in the center of the room. His erotic amber eyes instantly filled with pride, with love.

"Stunning, isn't she?" he asked, looking back at me and capturing my attention with his hypnotic gaze. Extending his hand in offering, he waited.

When I placed my fingers in his wide palm, the golden light exploded in a blinding white flash. I could feel his power and control sluice through my veins like liquid silver as I was coalesced in a tranquil serenity I'd never felt before.

"I'm so glad you've found your way, pet. I knew you could do it. I'm so very proud of you. Are you ready to join her? She's been waiting for you for a very long time."

As tears streamed down my face, I nodded. "Yes".

Opening my eyes, I thought I was still dreaming. Bright light filtered into my room as I sat upright in bed. The dream! It was the answer. *Stop fighting it. You've been fighting it tooth and nail.* Sammie's words echoed in my head, and Drake's floated right behind. *Remember who you are, girl.*

All the training, the knowledge imparted over the years, held a deeper meaning than ever before. I'd been given the ultimate test and had learned the ultimate lesson. Of course it was different for everyone, just like Sammie said. The meaning for this glorious lifestyle was as unique as the individual living it.

I knew what I had to do. It was so simple, yet I had been pushing it away, fighting it tooth and nail. I'd been trying to purge it, force it from inside me, when it had been there all along just waiting for me to open my mind and...my heart.

I'd been so insistent on trying to mold my submission to what I thought it should be, and when it wouldn't conform to my own preconceived notion, I'd tried to exorcise it from my being. But the harder I tried to banish it, the more miserable I became.

I *was* a submissive.

It was in my blood, my heart, and my soul. Trying to deny the fundamental core of my being was like trying to amputate the very arteries sustaining my life. I couldn't change who I was any more than I could pluck a cloud from the sky. It was in every fiber of my being.

At six thirty that night, I was dressed and waiting. A calmness I'd never experienced had settled over me. The knock at the door no longer filled me with trepidation. Instead, it was a sound of comfort. Sammie had once again come for me, and this time, I was ready.

Lowering my head as I knelt upon the floor, I called for her to come in.

"Julianna?" Drake asked in a startled tone.

Snapping my head up, amazed to hear the sound of his voice, I issued a look of penance. "Daddy Drake, Sir?" Feeling a monstrous wave of guilt crash over me, I wanted to wrap my arms around his neck, kiss his warm cheek, and beg his forgiveness. But I willed myself to remain in my submissive posture.

"Are you ready girl?" he asked brusquely.

"Yes, Sir. I am."

"Rise. Let's go."

A shiver rippled down my spine at the sound of his familiar, commanding tone. When I stood, he wrapped his arms around me and pulled me close.

"You've figured out the lesson, haven't you girl? You've finally recognized who you are."

"Yes, Sir. Without a doubt." I nodded with conviction. He damn near squeezed the stuffing out of me as he hugged me tighter and then kissed the top of my head.

"Thank, God," he murmured under his breath.

Seated next to Drake in his car, I could feel his intermittent gaze upon me.

"What are you feeling, girl?"

"Extremely sorry for the way I've treated you over the past few weeks."

"We'll discuss that later, pet. What else are you feeling?"

"Centered. Calm. Complete." A slight smile curled on my lips.

"You make me proud."

"Daddy, I'm so sorry that I lied to you. You deserved more respect. I should have never treated you the way I did. I'm so damn sorry."

"I accept your apology, Emerald. I know the past few weeks have been extremely difficult. I know that I own a part of the

116

responsibility for what you've been through. There will be no repercussions for your actions. I should have been a better protector for you. I'm just happy, no, I'm thrilled, that you have completed the circle and that you are whole."

"I feel whole, Daddy. I feel small and..." I sighed trying to find the right words. "I can't describe it, Sir."

"You don't need to. I understand. I can finally see it reflecting in your eyes." He smiled, beaming with pride.

We pulled into the nearly vacant parking lot. Drake punched in the code to the back door.

"You know where to go, and I think this time, you know what to do."

"Yes, Sir. I do." I nodded and kissed his cheek. "I love you, Moses."

Looking deep into my eyes, he smiled. "I love you too, Julianna."

I walked up the stairs and with a gentle knock, I waited. James's warm smile greeted me and then like before, he left me alone. Glancing up at the camera, this time filled with hope, I inhaled a deep breath and then lowered my head. I gracefully kneeled on the floor before the scrolled door, the same door I'd screamed at, pounded at, and cried at the past two nights. As I cast my eyes to the floor, I crossed my wrists behind my back.

Closing my eyes, I waited, praying the beautiful Dominant behind the door could sense what was in my heart. I hoped he would find me worthy to open the door and allow me to give my power to him, to give it to him freely, without the tiniest reservation.

Before anxiety had a chance to decimate me, my heart leapt to my throat as I heard the door open. I didn't move, didn't raise my head, didn't utter a sound. I remained as still as a statue. Hope took flight and soared.

"Thank you for coming back, girl." Mika's deep buttery voice was sweet music to my ears. I hadn't realized how much I'd missed his erotic timbre. "Rise and enter."

Keeping my eyes cast downward, I rose to my feet and followed him into the massive office. I watched with my peripheral vision as he sat down in a leather winged back chair. I once again gracefully knelt, only this time I yielded before his feet and not at his door.

"Look at me, Julianna."

I raised my eyes and feasted upon him. My heart thundered in my chest and rang in my ears as I tried not to whimper. Looking at him, I wanted him so badly I ached.

Mika was as incredibly gorgeous as before, but something was different. He looked fatigued. While his eyes were still mesmerizingly erotic, there was an untold shadow lurking within, like a man heavy with worries.

"I've been waiting to apologize to you, girl. The last time you saw me, I was...I was not myself. I took something that did not belong to me. I took you." He paused for a moment as if gathering his thoughts. "I need to tell you something, but I'm not quite sure how to explain it all, so I'll start at the beginning. My parents lived this lifestyle to the fullest. I was raised in the beauty of a Master/slave household. My mother submitted with a grace and beauty I've come to appreciate now more than ever. I was taught that everything she did, every scrape she kissed, every meal she prepared, every chore, every word of praise or chiding scold, was a gift, a precious gift she bestowed upon me and my father. We were to cherish and treasure that gift. She was the light of our lives, my father's and mine. She was our angel, a blessing that taught me unconditional love and how to respect all aspects of life. Cancer took her from us ten years ago. It felt like a part of me had died. And sadly, part of my father did die."

Mika paused, and I could feel the depth of his pain reflected in his voice as he relived the death of his mother. I wanted to reach out to him, to comfort him, but I held my posture and my tongue.

"Dad raised me with the principle that the slave we claim will be bound to our hearts and souls for all eternity. It's a bond stronger than marriage. There is only one in the lifetime of a Master."

My breath froze in my lungs as the meaning of his words crashed down on me like a ton of bricks. He could only have one sub his entire life? How damn unfair was that? Who the hell came up with that outlandish rule? I finally figured myself out, was ready to give him every ounce of my submission, and he couldn't take it? Was this some kind of sick joke?

"I realize it's quite an archaic concept compared to what transpires in the BDSM community these days. Dominants claim and release submissives like they change their clothes. I've never understood that practice, but I don't judge others for the way they find fulfillment. I can only live my life based on my own beliefs."

His ideology of the lifestyle was archaic indeed. I palpably felt every drop of hope I'd carried into the room sliding between my fingers. I wasn't hurt. I wasn't angry. I was sad. Sad that he would spend the rest of his life bound to a ghost, to the memory of what he once had, knowing it could never be reclaimed.

"Would you do me a favor, Julianna?" he asked with those fierce amber eyes gazing down at me.

My heart pounded in my ears the way it always did under his scrutiny. I nodded eagerly.

"Would you please get me a cranberry juice from the fridge? Get something for yourself, if you'd like."

I nodded again, unsure if I should speak, then rose and retrieved the juice. I removed the cap and discarded it before kneeling before him once again. I lowered my head and extended my hands, offering the bottle to him.

"Very nice." His words of praise filled my heart as I raised my head. An approving smile spread upon his handsome, rugged face. His knuckle caressed the back of my hand as he accepted the drink. A shiver raced down my spine as a soft tremble rippled through my core. Placing my hands behind my back, I crossed my wrists.

"Nine years ago I met a slave. She was...was...my 'one.'" His confession was almost a whisper. Taking a long drink of juice, he cleared his throat. "Five years ago cancer took her as it did my mother. After she passed, I was lost, empty, void inside. Those first months I spent a lot of time with my father. He helped me work through my anger and depression of losing her. He's a phenomenal man. I love and respect him a great deal."

I smiled at his carefree confession.

"Shortly after Vanessa passed, I opened Genesis. I needed to feel connected to her in some way. Watching Doms and subs find fulfillment, well it helped. Helped me heal. I can't explain it any other way."

I wondered why he was sharing so much of his private life with me. His personal enlightenment made it difficult for me to tamp down my hopeful feelings. Was he revealing all these details to squelch my dreams, or was there a big fat "but" on the end of it all? Would he decide to throw caution to the wind and claim me? God, I couldn't hope for that. It would be like a storybook, a happily ever after. And I wasn't convinced endings like those even existed. As he continued to speak, I tried desperately to quiet the fantasy and focus on his words.

"I know it sounds insane, but each night before I go to sleep, I talk to Vanessa. For years, I begged her to help take the pain and emptiness away. I naïvely thought she would heal my heart, but I can't help but believe she's answered my prayers in a way I never expected. And in a way she knows I can never accept."

I knew what was coming, and dread filled my veins. The need was so strong to slap my hands over my ears like a terrible two-year-old to prevent his words from penetrating my brain. Or scream for him to hush and not say another word. I knew what was coming, and try as I might to block the inevitable, I knew that would be like trying to stop a freight train with a feather. I closed my eyes and lowered my head, shrouding the pain that would soon be screaming in my heart from his view.

"I vividly remember the day you walked into the club. I'd never been so shocked, so shaken to the core, in my life." Suddenly his fingers were beneath my chin, tilting my face upward. "Open your eyes, Julianna. I know you don't want to hear this. And I'm truly sorry to have to say these things to you. I can read you like a book, girl, but I need you to look at me. Let me see your eyes as I confess my guilt."

CHAPTER TEN

Swallowing tightly, desperately reaching for a fragile thread of inner strength to carry me through, I inhaled a fortifying breath and opened my eyes.

He smiled soberly. "Thank you, girl."

I steeled myself for the walls of hope to crash down with the words I knew were forming on his tongue.

A frown settled on his mouth. "You resemble Vanessa to an almost frightening degree. The first time you walked through the doors of Genesis, I thought I'd seen a ghost. Her ghost. But it wasn't her. I knew that. Still, it didn't keep me from wanting to wrap you in my arms, breathe in your scent, and claim you. But I knew better. I knew you weren't her. I knew she hadn't returned from the dead to ease the emptiness in my heart. I've watched you, watched you for days, months, years. I've reveled in your growth as you blossomed from behind your timid walls of apprehension and grew into a graceful, elegant submissive. I've sat in my office watching every session you've had with Sammie and wishing to hell and everything holy it were my hands on you as you shattered. Hell, I've watched everything about you, from your demure smile when you're unsure of a Dom, to how you toss your head back laughing in gusto and unadulterated joy. I've felt a sense of pride as I watched your smoldering embers of submission grow into a blazing and all too enticing flame. See, as your submission has grown, so has my temptation for you. I've felt the pull of you for what seems like a lifetime. You tempt me, girl, more than anyone I've ever known. I want you so badly it's like a hot blade searing inside my soul."

I could feel the heat from his body, smell the fringes of his arousal in the air. I couldn't stop myself from hoping he'd toss aside his beliefs and claim me as he confessed of wanting to do.

"You *are* a submissive. You doubted that even before Dennis abused you. And what I did to you only caused that misconception to multiply. I'm so sorry for being the reason you questioned your submission, Julianna. I can't begin to convey my remorse for what I've done to you. I failed you in the worst way, and like Drake, I'm wracked with guilt over failing you."

I lightly shook my head no. I didn't want to hear that either man was still shouldering the blame for the horrid events with Dennis.

"Moses and I are more than friends. We're like brothers. He and Trevor spent many years with Vanessa and I. When Moses told me about the lunch you two shared, when the longing inside you to find your 'one' had gotten to the point of you doubting your desirability to Dominants, I was livid." He leaned forward and wrapped his warm palm beneath my chin. "Nothing could be further from the truth, sweet girl. You're a coveted submissive not only in my eyes, but in the eyes of almost every member here. Moses felt he'd done you a disservice. He'd virtually kept every Dominant that voiced an interest in you away. His own guilt was what precipitated him to allow Dennis to spend time alone with you. Guilt for withholding prospective Dominants now pales in comparison to the guilt he carries for allowing that bastard to abuse you the way he did."

Tears dripped from my cheeks. My heart ached as I listened to Mika reveal the depth of Moses's guilt. I wanted so badly to fix him, to take his guilt away, but I didn't know how. I softly sniffed and exhaled a quivering breath.

"I know how much you love him. He's far more than just your protector. He is a brother, a father figure. Let him back in your heart, girl. He deserves it."

"He never left my heart." I sobbed, unable to hold back my raw emotions. "I will do anything to repair the damage I've done. I swear."

"I have no doubt, pet." He inhaled a long, deep breath as if steeling himself for something. "As I said before, Vanessa and I spent almost all our time with Moses and Trevor. We took vacations together, played with our respective slaves in the same dungeons. We were more than friends, we were family. The four of us had a very special and unique relationship, which brings us to the morning in your bedroom...or rather my actions that day. As I watched Trevor kissing your mouth and gazed upon your naked, voluptuous body, I was overcome with a feeling of déjà vu. It was as if I were back to a time when my heart no longer ached, a time when I was complete. I lost my grip on reality, sweet one. I couldn't fight the longing and the tormented hunger for you anymore. The demand to feel you beneath my hands—just to touch you, feel your hot flesh beneath my fingers—was too much. I lost control. I lost my ability to resist my overpowering need for you. When I plunged my fingers deep inside your pussy, I knew I could never walk away. I had to claim and own you. You are simply too perfect."

I blinked in surprise, hope and relief winding together like silken scarves binding my heart.

"Make no mistake, girl. It was you I wanted, not the ghost or carbon copy of Vanessa, which you're not. You never will be. Trust me when I say both my heart and head know the difference. You're an almost perfect submissive, Julianna. An almost perfect fit to what I've ached for all these years. That morning in your room as you climaxed, as your delicious hot tunnels convulsed around my fingers, I was imprisoned by a combination of heaven and hell. Then the guilt slammed through me. I knew I had failed. Failed myself, and most regrettably, failed you. I took what was not mine, what could never be mine. I took your gift. Up until that morning, I'd not touched another submissive since Vanessa died. She was my 'one.' So my apology to you is from my heart, my soul. I'm no better than Dennis for the betrayal I've committed."

I sucked in a gasp of disbelief at his comparison. I started to speak, but Mika shook his head and moved his hand from my chin, placing a broad finger against my lips. His eyes reflected a gut-wrenching sadness. I bit back the sobs burning my throat as tears stung my eyes. He was nothing like Dennis. How could he compare himself to that despicable animal?

"I'll forever need to fight this unappeasable hunger inside to claim you. But that's my burden, not yours. I will find a way to cope with what I can't have."

Gazing at him in disbelief, I was unable to wrap my head around the harsh restrictions he placed on his Dominance. I knew I had no right to judge his principles or try to sway them no matter how desperately I longed to. But it was beyond my understanding how he could deny his need to dominate. He paused as his words continued to penetrate my brain and torment my soul.

"Moses and I have talked. He will no longer shield you from the

Dominants who wish to pursue you. However, none will be allowed private liberties with you at first. Either Moses or I will be present during any sessions, public or private."

What? That couldn't be. Mika was going to cast aside the anonymity he guarded so vehemently and mentor me? And why in the hell would he subject himself to watching another Dominant use me if it would only cause him heartache? Surely he'd not put himself through such hell for the likes of me, would he?

"Kneel up, girl," he whispered in that erotic velvet voice that always made my heart thunder and my pussy weep.

I rose to my knees. He leaned forward, and I stared into his sensuous eyes.

"Who are these tears for?" Using the broad pads of his thumbs, he wiped my cheeks.

"For you, Sir," I whispered on a quivering breath. His gentle touch was like a white-hot fire surging electricity through my body.

"Why? Why do you shed tears for me?" His brows pulled together in concern.

"Because you've vowed to never touch another submissive and are burying your Dominant needs. My heart breaks knowing you can only live out your desires through memories. That's too much for anyone to suffer, to endure. I'm sorry. I know I'm speaking out of turn, and I don't mean any disrespect to your beliefs, Sir, it's just I can't imagine, can't fathom living with such emptiness, longing, and pain inside. It has to be unbearable."

"Yes." He nodded as a bittersweet smile tugged the corners of his mouth. "But you're forgetting one important aspect, girl. I *did* achieve a Master's fulfillment. I was honored with the gift of a lifetime and the memory of it is a treasure, one I will cherish till I die."

He was ripe with gratitude for the short time Vanessa shared his life, and I knew the memories of her filled every corner of his heart...still. A feeling akin to jealousy seeped into my soul. She shouldn't still have claim over him. She was dead and gone. He was the one left here to suffer without recourse. He should have the opportunity to find, with someone else, what he had with her. How could sharing something so primal for such a short period of time sustain someone for the rest of their life?

"Moses and I will do our best to help you find your 'one.' All I can say is that he'll need to be one hell of a Dominant for your precious submission. Don't be too anxious, little one. This might take some time."

A warm smile stretched over his succulent bottom lip as his broad finger caressed my jaw. I longed to taste his decadent mouth one last time, to feel the warmth of his body against mine. Even though the door of hope had been slammed shut, I yearned for one last good-bye.

He stood from the chair and extended his hand. "Let's get you home, girl."

"Sir? May I say something?"

"Of course."

"I'd like to apologize for my behavior over the past two days. Well, for longer than that, actually. I didn't mean the things I said outside your door."

"Oh, I think you did." He smiled wide and fought back a laugh. "But I forgive you. Don't worry. It's all fine, and you're going to be fine, too. Moses and I will make sure of it. You're damn lucky you know. How many subs have two Doms as protectors?" he teased and winked mischievously.

"Hmm..." I smiled. "I'm not sure if that's a good thing or a bad thing."

"Depends on your behavior, I would say. Could be twice the reward or twice the punishment." He raised his brows as a twinkle of delight danced in his eyes. "Come. Let me take you home."

I followed Mika down the stairway that two days ago felt like a pathway to a beleaguered prison cell. It no longer held the oppressive dread it once did. Stepping out into the dimly lit parking lot, he gently placed his palm against my lower back. A shiver rippled through me as he led me to a shiny black Escalade parked alone in the darkness.

"I am more than a bit curious, Julianna. What happened between yesterday and today that produced such a dramatic change in you?"

"A dream."

"A dream? Tell me about it." He stopped and tilted his head with a curious look.

"Actually Sir, it's been a lot of dreams...years of them in fact that culminated to one prophetic dream. Your Van—"

"Emerald!"

I stopped in mid-sentence as a voice dripping with hate screamed my name. I whipped my head toward the source as fear coursed from my stomach to my throat and a rush of adrenaline slammed me.

Standing at the edge of the building, eyes filled with pure, unadulterated hate, stood Dennis. A lone streetlight scantily illuminated the parking lot, and I saw the shimmer of a gun in his hand. My heart knocked in my chest as my stomach swirled in a violent knot.

"No," I murmured, unable to draw my eyes away from Dennis's advancing form.

"You've fucking ruined my life, you whore!" Screaming in a demented tone, he stalked toward Mika and me. "My wife left me. My children think I'm a monster! It's all your fault you fucking cunt!"

His gun was pointed at me. I wondered if I should dive for cover or remain frozen in place. Both options held the potential for catastrophic outcomes. Even in the dimly lit surroundings, I could see a look of demonic hatred reflecting in his eyes. It was more frightening than the weapon in his hand. His lip curled in an almost inhuman snarl as my heart continued to jackhammer in my chest, reverberating in my ears. I fleetingly wondered if I could explode from fear. Unable to look away from the deranged man, I sensed movement. Mika was reaching for something behind his back.

"You're going to pay for this you fucking bitch!"

Time slipped into some lethargic, sluggish dimension. Everything began to move in slow motion, as if some higher power flipped a switch, commanding time and space to unravel a millisecond at a time. Dennis's manic screaming continued as his wide strides were eating up the distance between us. The barrel of his gun remained pointed straight at my face.

Mika's strong arm wrapped around my waist almost instinctively as he slung me to the ground behind him. He'd placed himself between me and the crazed lunatic still approaching. Gravel pierced the thin fabric of my gown and stung as it dug into my knees. Raising my eyes, I watched Mika's posture alter. Crouched low to the ground, he assumed what resembled a fighting stance. The muscles in his shoulders and arms bunched as he extended something in front of his body. He was holding a dull black handgun that was leveled and steady aimed at Dennis. Undaunted, the maniac continued to advance, the frightening gleam in his eyes clearly visible.

"Mika!" I choked out softly.

"Stay down!" he roared. His voice was loud, flat and unwavering.

"Get away from her motherfucker! You can't protect her this time!" Dennis screamed.

"Not happening! Put your gun down," Mika warned.

"Fuck you!"

Simultaneously two shots split the night. Blood curdling screams filled the air. My screams. Mika's body lifted from the ground and slammed back against the Escalade. Then, like a ragdoll, he slid to the ground. Dennis fell backward with a sickening thud. Blood poured from Mika's chest as I scrambled across the gravel, kneeling next to him.

Frantically digging through his pockets, I retrieved his cell phone, casting a quick glance over my shoulder to assure myself that Dennis was indeed dead on the ground. I punched in nine-one-one as I violently trembled.

"My friend's been shot. I think he's dying. Please send an ambulance. The parking lot of Genesis. Seven forty-three Myers Street. Oh, God. Please. Please hurry." I screamed as I threw the phone to the ground and cradled Mika in my arms. Blood poured from the gaping wound in his chest, and I firmly pressed my hand over the streaming red river.

"Mika! Mika! Please don't die. Please don't leave me." Blinking through the tears streaming down my face, I saw his eyes were open, glassy and unfocused as he groaned.

"Mika! Stay with me. Please stay with me."

"Vanessa," he softly whispered. His glazed eyes widened as if in surprise.

"No!" I sobbed "Please Mika, no."

He was seeing Vanessa. It could only mean she had come to take him away.

"No!" I screamed in a panic. "You can't have him. You promised, goddammit. You can't have him. He's mine."

I was yelling at the ghost of my dreams, fighting an invisible phantom for his life, his love. Deep inside I knew his heart didn't belong to me. He wasn't mine and never would be. Every fiber of his being belonged to her. She was the one who would forever hold his heart and soul. The only one he would ever love. Ever dominate. Ever cherish, in this life or the next.

A mournful wail echoed through the night as I sobbed, knowing what I had to do, yet unsure I could find the strength to do it.

"I'm sorry, Mika. I'm so sorry it can't be me. But oh God, how I wanted you to want me." Screaming through my sobs, I looked down at his lifeless face.

"Go to her, Mika. Go to Vanessa. She's your 'one.' Your only one. She's the one you've been waiting for. Soar with her to the heavens and be free from all the pain you carry in your heart."

There was nothing on this earthly plain of value that I could offer him. Only Vanessa could grant his freedom, freedom from the chains encasing his heart. I was powerless to stop the inevitable no matter how desperately I wanted to try.

"Go with her, Mika. Find your peace." Blood oozed between my fingers as I attempted to keep him tethered to this life even as I coaxed to set him free. "Oh, God. I can't do this. What am I going to do without you now, Mika?"

Screeching sirens blared as numerous police cars careened into the parking lot. Keeping my hand pressed firm against his chest, I prayed against the cold uncertainty filling my soul that I could somehow save him. It was a selfish notion I had no right to own, yet I couldn't stop myself from trying.

I heard voices. Shouts. But the words weren't connecting with my brain. Strong arms lifted me from the ground as two men in crisp white shirts converged over Mika's lifeless body.

"Shhh...This way ma'am. Let the paramedics do their job." A man's low, soft voice finally permeated my frightened haze as I was led away from Mika. I looked up and was met by brown eyes filled with warmth and concern staring back at me.

"Is he dead?" I cried, filled with fear.

"I don't know." He shook his head. "Let them work on him and

128

get him to the hospital. They'll do all they can, but we need to stay out of their way. What's your name? Is he a friend of yours? What's his name?"

The officer's questions were measured, and when I didn't respond, he would simply ask something different. "Do you know the other man over there?"

He pointed toward Dennis's dead body. I knew Dennis was dead. I saw the bullet pierce his forehead as he fell back.

Finally, the officer's questions filtered through the numbness, and I nodded. "I'm Julianna Garrett. Yes. He's my friend. His name is Mika LaBrache."

"Do you know the other man?"

"No," I lied.

"Did they have an argument? Was there a fight or something?"

Unsure what to say or how much information I should reveal, I shivered uncontrollably. "I need Moses."

"Who is Moses?"

"A friend," I whispered, choking back a sob.

"Here." The officer slid a cell phone into my hand. "Can you call him or do you need me to?"

"I can." I sniffed, watching the paramedics work in frantic but adept choreography over Mika's body. Clear ropes of tubing had been embedded into both his thick, corded arms. They were talking loudly to one another with a frightening tone of urgency in their voices.

The officer stepped away as I called Moses. Somehow between my blubbering sobs I was able to tell him that Mika had been shot.

"Don't say a word. Don't say anything to the cops. Nothing. I'm on my way. If Master George gets there before I do, let him handle things. Just, please Julianna, don't say anything. Do you understand?" His tone was stern and adamant.

"George? Why would he be coming here?" I asked in confusion.

"He's a judge, and Mika's legal adviser," Moses confided. "Just don't answer the cop's questions, honey. I'm on my way."

"Hurry." I begged and ended the call. The officer reappeared, and I handed him back the phone.

"Did the other man and your friend Mika have a fight?" the officer pressed.

129

"I can't think right now. Give me a minute," I stalled, wishing Moses would appear like a genie from a bottle. "Can you please ask someone if he's alive?"

I was unable to look away from Mika's unresponsive body. The paramedics lifted him onto a gurney as the officer nodded and stepped away. Nervously scanning the parking lot, I wrung my bloodied hands, whispering for Moses to hurry.

The officer returned. "Yes...he's alive, but he's very unstable. They're transporting him to St. Agnes. I need you to stay here with me to answer some questions. I need to get a statement from you, ma'am. Were you a witness to the shootings?"

"I need to go with him," I cried as I rushed toward the gurney rolling toward the ambulance. The officer caught my shoulder with a firm grip, holding me back.

"We'll get you to the hospital in a cruiser just as soon as we can," he explained in a calm voice.

I numbly watched the ambulance scream down the street as more headlights flashed across the parking lot.

"Julianna!" Master George yelled over the commotion, pushing his way past the officers. He gripped me in a tight hold, oblivious of the blood covering my flimsy silk gown. "Is he...?"

"He's still alive, but he's unconscious. They said he's very unstable. They're taking him to St. Agnes." Thankful to have George's familiar presence sheltering me, I exhaled a deep sigh.

"What have you told the police?" he whispered in my ear, removing his jacket and wrapping it around my trembling, blood-stained body.

Resting my head against his neck, needing to feel the warmth and reassurance of a friend, I whispered in his ear. "Just mine and Mika's names. I lied when the officer asked if I knew Dennis. He asked me more questions, but I didn't answer any of them."

"Good girl," he praised. "Come. Sit down with me on the steps. I need you to tell me exactly what happened."

I began retelling the horrific details to George as more uniformed officers and men in suits descended upon the scene. A tall, middle-aged man wearing a dark suit walked up as we huddled on the stairs.

"Your Honor." The man in the suit extended his hand.

"Patrick. Good to see you, my man." A grim smile formed on George's lips as he shook the suited man's hand. "This is my friend, Julianna Garrett. Julianna, this is Detective Patrick Daniels."

Flashing a nervous glance at George, I slightly nodded to the detective.

"Julianna witnessed the shooting. I'm sure you'll find it's a clear case of self-defense, but of course you'll make that determination."

"Ms. Garrett." The detective smiled a somber greeting. "We need to get a statement from you, but I'd like to do that at the hospital. It will be safer." The detective turned back to George wearing a grave expression. "I think you should take her there now. It won't be long before the media shows up. I'm surprised they're not already swarming."

"I understand. We'll meet you at St. Agnes."

George wrapped his arm around my shoulder and pulled me from the stairs just as Moses came rushing through the crowd with Trevor at his side. Horror reflected in their wide eyes as they looked at my blood-soaked gown.

"Are you hurt?" Drake gasped, running a burly hand over my stomach. I shook my head no and broke down. Mournful sobs shook my body as I clung to him.

"Moses. We need to get her out of here, now," George informed Drake in a low whisper as he started leading us toward the edge of the parking lot. "Take her to St. Agnes. I'll be there shortly with a friend of mine, Detective Daniels. But right now he wants her out of here, before the media shows up."

Without a word, Moses scooped me into his arms and ran past the milling police officers straight to his car. He slid me into the front seat. Trevor jumped in the back and had his seatbelt engaged before Moses opened the driver's door.

"We're going to stop by your house before we head to St. Agnes. I want you to get cleaned up, but do it fast, do you understand?" Glancing from the road, he looked at me. "Are you sure you're not hurt?"

"No. It's Mika's blood. There was so much blood." I sobbed as I told the details of the shooting to Drake and Trevor. "I'm scared to death he's going to die."

Moses careened onto the main road, heading north towards my

house.

I inhaled a deep breath, trying to decide if I should tell Drake the rest. Of course I needed to tell him. Mika was like a brother. "He called out to Vanessa. I think she was there. I think she came for him."

"Aw, fuck!" Moses cursed on a mournful groan. Unhooking his cell phone from its holder, he passed it to Trevor in the backseat. "Call Emile, baby."

CHAPTER ELEVEN

Trevor's face was etched with fear as he dialed the phone then handed it back to Moses.

"Emile. I don't have a lot of details to give you right now, but Mika has been shot. He was shot in the chest outside the club a few minutes ago. They've taken him to St. Agnes, and I'm on my way there now. I will arrange to have Trevor pick you up from the airport. I'll call you when I get to the hospital and give you an update on his condition." There was a short pause. "I will and hang in there. I'll call you shortly."

"Was that his father?"

Moses nodded, sliding his phone back in its pouch. "I need you to really hurry when we get to your house."

"I know. I'm just going to wash my hands and change clothes. I don't even want to go home. I want to go straight to the hospital, but I understand I can't go waltzing in like this."

"Good girl," he whispered as we pulled into the drive.

I ran inside my house and straight to my room. Within three minutes, I had washed up, changed, and was back in the car and buckled up.

As Moses raced down the streets, a blanket of fear hung heavy in the air.

"Moses, what am I supposed to say to the detective?"

"Probably not much. I'm sure George has taken care of most everything. Just follow his lead, okay?" He gripped my hand with a brief reassuring squeeze and I silently nodded. The remainder of the ride to the hospital was eerily silent.

All three of us rushed into the emergency room, frantic for information about Mika. When a tight-faced nurse informed us she could only give patient information to family, I thought Moses was going to wrap his beefy hand around her throat and strangle her. Luckily for her, his cell phone began to ring, and he answered it with a frustrated growl.

"Emile. We just got here. They won't tell us a goddamn thing because we're not family." He paused. "Yes. One moment."

Moses thrust the phone to the closed-mouthed nurse. "It's Emile LaBrache, Mika's father."

The nurse took the phone with an air of annoyance. At first she appeared distracted and uninterested, but suddenly her face went slack as she blinked and swallowed tightly. A dark crimson hue burst over her cheeks.

"He was brought in twenty-two minutes ago. He expired in route, but the paramedics revived him. After being triaged, he was immediately taken into surgery. He is in critical condition."

The nurse paused. He'd expired in route? Oh, God.

"No, sir. I don't know how much longer he'll be in surgery. I can get that information for you though. Would you like to hold?" She nervously licked her lips and nodded. "Yes, sir. I understand. I will relay your wishes to the staff in surgery as well as ICU. Yes sir, everyone. Thank you."

She quickly passed the phone back to Moses as if it were a snake.

"Emile." Mosses nodded as he listened to whatever Mika's father was saying. "Trevor will be at the gate waiting for you."

Trevor clasped his hand in mine, holding it in a death-grip, then nodded his head. I could see the depth of worry on his face. There was no doubt mine held the same intensity as I silently willed Mika to hang on.

After another brief pause, Moses's lips set in a grim line. "I will. I have been. I'll see you in a few hours. I'll leave messages on your cell with updates." He ended the conversation as the nurse hurried from behind the white-topped desk.

"If you'll follow me, I'll take you to the surgery waiting room. I'll go back to the OR and tell them to keep you apprised of his condition." Her eyes danced in a nervous jerk between the three of us. I had no idea what Emile had said to the woman, but whatever he'd told her, it had made a major impact.

Everything seemed to fly at the speed of light. Racing down the long, astringent-scented corridors, we wound our way deeper into the belly of the hospital. The nurse ushered us into a large empty room were couches and chairs were arranged in an inviting atmosphere, but it did little to soothe our anxious nerves. The nurse disappeared after assuring us she would return with more information.

Trevor pulled me to the couch and held me tight as Moses paced the speckled tile floor. Moments later, George and Detective Daniels walked through the doorway. I trembled as I looked up at the two men.

"How is he?" George asked, greeting Moses first.

"He's in surgery. We don't know anything yet. A nurse should be back with more info, soon. We're just waiting."

George nodded in solemn understanding then turned to me. "Julianna, I've relayed the events of this evening to Patrick. He needs to ask you a few more questions. He's also informed me there has been a rash of carjackings in the area recently. It was unfortunate that Mr. McCollum chose Mika to perpetrate his carjacking crime against." George's eyes held mine with an underlying intensity, and his words were slow and steady, as if willing me to absorb the crux of an alibi.

"It's a bit ironic. Just a few weeks ago, I received an anonymous tip that Dennis McCollum had stolen another man's identity. The D.A. had recently initiated an investigation and charges had been filed. He was arrested a few days ago but posted bail only hours before the attempted carjacking. We think he may have been trying to flee the city." The detective's eyes were locked on mine, and I felt as if he were performing a visual lie detector test.

"I see." I nodded, trying to focus on the cleverly constructed lie and not the scrutiny of the detective's gaze.

George had indeed taken care of the situation. The story was a plausible one that protected Mika, Genesis, and me. I wondered if George was not only safeguarding us but himself as well. I looked at the detective who issued a grim smile.

"I only have a couple of questions for you, Ms. Garrett."

The moment I'd been dreading had arrived. I watched as the detective and George each pulled up chairs and sat across from Trevor and me. Moses hovered behind the men, his body visibly humming with worry as he watched me.

"Did you notice anyone else with Mr. McCollum when he approached you and Mika?"

"No, sir."

"Did he say anything to either of you?"

I nervously looked at George. "I..."

"I'm sure he probably said 'give me your keys' or something to that effect?" George volunteered.

I nodded, praying I wouldn't be hauled away to rot in jail for giving false information. Nervous, I licked my lips, then cast my eyes to the floor. I wanted to slip into my submissive repose and escape the fear consuming me. Where was the calming center from my dream? I needed to find it and cling to it in order to get through these fearsome questions. It felt as if I were walking an imaginary tightrope stretched as tautly as my nerves. I knew one wrong word and I'd plummet into a terrifying and wholly uncertain abyss. Already having lied to one law enforcement official, I worried if a condemning amount of guilt was reflected on my face.

"Did you know Dennis McCollum?"

"No, sir." I shook my head. It wasn't a lie, not really. I'd never been formally introduced to him as Dennis McCollum. I knew the bastard as Jordon. Escaping the truth by semantics was still an escape, and one I could live with.

"Who fired the first shot?"

"It was...both shots were fired simultaneously. Mr. McCollum had his gun drawn and pointed at us. Mika pulled a gun from behind his back and both shots rang out. I saw the bullet hit Mr. McCollum in the head as he fell backward, and I crawled to Mika's body. There was so much blood..." My voice cracked as a tear slid down my cheek. Inhaling a deep, quivering breath, I continued. "Blood was pouring out of Mika's chest. I found his cell phone and called nine-one-one, then tried to slow the bleeding until help arrived."

"Thank you, Ms. Garrett. I don't have any further questions. It looks like an unfortunate case of self-defense. If you remember anything else you feel is important to the case, please give me a call." He handed me a business card as he stood.

"Thank you." I nodded, wiping the tears from my face.

"I'm sorry this happened to your friend. I hope he pulls through."

"Thank you, Patrick." George nodded, shaking the detective's hand.

"The press has been handled."

"You're one in a million." George patted Patrick's back and walked him to the doorway.

Within moments of the detective's departure, the nurse reappeared.

"He's still in surgery and is still listed in critical condition. They've removed the bullet and are repairing the damage it caused. It's probably going to be a few more hours. As soon as the surgery is over, they will move him upstairs to the intensive care unit. The surgeon, Dr. Williams, will come out and talk to you as soon as he can. I'll arrange an escort to take you to the ICU waiting room and make sure you are introduced to the team that will be taking care of Mr. LaBrache. Is there anything you need while you're waiting here?"

"No thank you." Moses shook his head and reached for his phone.

The nurse issued a weak smile and then quickly left the room.

Moses spoke into his phone, leaving a message for Emile. He handed his car keys to Trevor and rattled off Emile's flight information. Trevor kissed my cheek then walked out the door with George, who'd instructed Moses to phone him when Mika was out of surgery.

Moses finally stopped pacing and joined me on the long, somewhat lumpy couch.

"Are you doing okay?" he asked, drawing me into his arms and snuggling me against his broad chest. "I've been so wrapped up in my own worry I've not been taking very good care of you."

"Don't add me to your list, Moses. Please. I'm doing okay. I'm just scared, like you."

"I know you are, baby. I'm sure it was frightening beyond words."

I nodded as I hugged his barrel chest. "Where is Emile flying in from?"

"Washington, DC. He should land in about an hour. He sounded like he's keeping it together, barely. He and Mika are tight. This is going to be extremely hard on him. Mika's all he's got left."

"I know." I nodded, praying that Mika made it through surgery. Engulfed in Moses's strong arms and warm body, I began to relax and closed my eyes. I was so grateful he was there. He was my rock. He always had been, and I melted against his massive frame.

A deep thrumming vibration drew me from a dark, dreamless sleep. It took me a minute to realize the rumbling was Moses's voice vibrating against my ear. There was another voice, much deeper, nearly the same timbre as Mika's but laced with an enchanting accent. French. It had to be Emile. Suddenly, I felt intimidated and nervous about meeting the man. Remaining motionless, I kept my eyes closed. I wasn't trying to eavesdrop on his and Drake's conversation, but I didn't want to intrude either, so I played possum.

"Mika told me how similar they are in appearance, but my God I never dreamed in a million years the resemblance would be so uncanny. No wonder the boy has been beside himself for all these years."

"I know. For the first few months, I had to stop myself from blurting out, 'Remember when we...or wasn't it funny that time we went to...' The déjà vu was unsettling to say the least. But it didn't take long before I came to know the woman inside. She's a spitfire. Strong willed. Hardheaded. She'll make a Master earn her gifts when she finds the one strong enough to handle her. And when she does, she'll no doubt earn those gifts right back."

"How much longer do you think it will be?" The man's deep voice was thick with worry. Still feeling the need to stay hidden, unsure of my place, I continued to feign slumber.

"I don't know. It's been over two hours. Hopefully the doctor will come out and talk to us soon."

"Can I get you anything, Emile, Sir?" Trevor asked.

"No son. I'm fine. I had bourbon on the plane to help calm my nerves. I'll switch to coffee once I know my Mika has made it through surgery."

He sounded like a Master. His velvet voice was rich and commanding. The subtle accent lacing his words sent a shiver down my spine. The desire to remain invisible overshadowed the desire to peek at him from beneath my lashes. I knew it was only a matter of time before I would be face to face with the man, but I wasn't ready, not yet. From his words, I knew Mika had spoken about me, but I didn't know what details he'd shared with his father.

All too soon, my hopeful reprieve to stay hidden ended.

"Julianna. Come on baby, wake up. The doctor's here." Moses shook me then pulled me from his chest and helped me sit up.

Rubbing my eyes, I looked up and saw a stunningly handsome dark-skinned man. His eyes were deep brown, but the erotic lips and defined facial features were identical to Mika's. A shy, embarrassed smile curled on my lips as the man stared into my eyes, a look of disbelief etched upon his face.

"Emile, Julianna. Julianna, Emile." Moses made a hasty introduction as a weary-looking doctor walked in.

"I'm Doctor Williams."

"Emile LaBrache. I'm Mika's father."

"Pleased to meet you." The doctor nodded, taking a seat facing us. "Mika is out of surgery and so far doing well. If he continues to remain stable, we will upgrade his condition in the morning. He sustained a lot of internal injuries that we've repaired. The gunshot badly bruised one lung, so we've put him on a ventilator. He'll be on the vent and unable to talk for a few days. He did suffer a cardiac arrest en route to the hospital, but was revived in the ambulance."

Tears swam in my eyes as my heart thundered in my chest. Having already heard that he'd died didn't make the chasm opening beneath my feet any less terrifying. The pain reflected in Emile's eyes was gut wrenching, and I swallowed the lump in my throat as I continued to listen.

"There is always the possibility of brain damage when the heart stops, but the paramedics revived him quickly, and we're hopeful there'll be no long-term effects. We'll be moving him up to ICU shortly. He'll be hooked up to a lot of machines. I want to prepare you for that. It's a bit overwhelming when you first see him. He won't be conscious for the rest of the night and probably the better part of tomorrow. We'll be keeping him sedated to let him rest and allow his internal injuries a bit of time to heal. We'll monitor him closely for the next forty-eight hours." The doctor was quiet for a few moments as if waiting for all the information he'd just explained to sink in. "Do you have questions?"

"How long will he be in ICU?" Emile asked.

"For the next forty-eight hours at least. When he's strong enough, we'll move him to a lower level of intensive care, then eventually to either a private or semiprivate room."

"When can I see my son?"

"As soon as we get him moved up to ICU and the team gets him set up. We'll let you know when you can go in and see him."

"When will we know about any brain damage?" Emile asked with a grim expression.

"We should know relatively quickly. We've already done some neurological tests and it all looks good, but we'll know for sure once he's conscious. Like I said, I doubt he's suffered any brain damage, but I wanted to let you know there is that chance."

"Thank you, doctor." Emile solemnly nodded, extending his hand.

"If you think of any other questions, I'll be here all night checking in on him. Just have one of the nurses grab me, and I'll come talk to you. Someone will be out shortly to take you up to the other waiting room."

"Thank you, again." Emile smiled then exploded a heavy exhale.

After the doctor left, Emile rose and walked toward me. The urge to slide to my knees and assume a proper submissive posture was almost overwhelming. I lowered my head, casting my eyes downward as my heart thundered in my chest.

"Such a beauty," Emile softly whispered. "Julianna, my dear, there is no need to honor me with your gifts. I simply wanted to greet you properly."

He extended his hand and I timidly placed my fingers into his palm as he gently coaxed me from the couch and to my feet. Wrapping me in his long arms, he held me tight.

"Thank you," he whispered against my ear. "Calling for help so quickly saved my son's life. I am forever in your debt, sweet girl."

"You're welcome, Sir." A wave of guilt slammed me. There was no way I could confess I'd told Mika to die and leave this earth to be with Vanessa. Even if Emile understood the meaning behind my action, it would make me appear to be a cold, heartless bitch, uncaring whether Mika lived or died. I nodded as an awkward silence filled the room.

"Would anyone like a cup of coffee?" I asked, filling the silence I thought might swallow me whole.

"Yes, please." Moses nodded.

"I'll get it for you, Daddy," Trevor volunteered as he shot from the couch. "Emile?"

"No, sweet boy. I'm fine for now, but thank you."

I sat back down on the edge of the couch, leaving a spot for Trevor to sit next to Moses. I'd monopolized enough of his warm, sheltering body. He needed his lover's comfort now.

It wasn't long before a nurse motioned for us, and we followed her to a much larger waiting room. A handful of people were sprawled out sleeping in decidedly awkward positions. A few talked quietly on cell phones. Others read books, and some stared off vacantly into space. A soft-spoken nurse introduced herself and assured us she would return after Mika was settled. We found seats in a tight corner of the room where once again we prepared to wait.

I was barely able to control my anxious restlessness. I *needed* to see Mika, to gaze upon him with my own eyes and confirm he was still on this earth, still breathing my same air.

So many questions filled my mind. Why had Mika come back to life in the ambulance? Vanessa had undoubtedly appeared to him in the parking lot. Why hadn't he gone with her? What was keeping him here? Was it because he didn't want to leave his father with yet another loss to endure? Perhaps it wasn't his time yet. Perhaps he was destined for something more in the grand scheme of things. Maybe something awaited him later in life, some task he'd not yet completed. Too many unanswered questions fluttered through my aching brain, yet I couldn't shut them off.

Trevor leaned against Moses's shoulder and in an instant was wrapped within his strong, burly arms. Moments later, both men had drifted off to sleep. I was relieved that Moses had finally relaxed, but it left Emile and me to fill the uncomfortable silence enveloping our little group.

"Mika talks of you often."

"He does? I didn't know that, Sir."

"Yes, I know." A soft chuckle escaped his throat, smooth and deep, just like Mika's.

"Evidently I'm the only one that didn't know about that." A smile of embarrassment curled on my lips, and I shook my head at the irony of it.

"Unfortunately, I'm afraid there's a lot you don't know which isn't fair to you. My son is an extremely private person. I think he gets that from me."

"We had a long discussion earlier tonight, Sir. Well, rather Mika talked and I listened." I swallowed the anxiety clogging my throat. "I understand why he guards his privacy, and I know the reason he's closed himself off, especially toward me."

"Ahh. So he has told you about Vanessa." Emile nodded in understanding. "Do you also know the internal war he battles in regard to you?"

"I know that I remind him of her."

"You're far beyond a reminder, dear girl." He smiled and gave me a knowing wink. "You're like a constant open wound to his heart."

Guilt and sadness washed over me. Emile confirmed the depth of pain my presence, even unwittingly, had been to Mika. It was a heart-crushing revelation.

"Maybe it would be best if I caught a cab home and terminated my contract with the club."

"Nonsense!" Emile practically roared. "Have you never yearned for something so desperately that you ached from it?"

A humorless chuckle bubbled from the back of my throat. "Every day of my life," I confessed, thinking about the lack of a Master and my burning desires for Mika. "But it's pointless. What I want, I can never have. There comes a time when longing becomes so painful you have little choice but to raise a white flag and simply concede."

"Perhaps. I've been doing a lot of thinking, soul searching so to speak. A few weeks ago, I received a call from Mika. He was beside himself over a situation that occurred involving you, my dear." I knew exactly what *situation* Emile was referring to. "Since then, I've given a lot of thought to the lifestyle principles that I was taught. I have to honestly say that I too am having second thoughts in regard to their validity."

"Second thoughts? I don't understand, Sir."

"When I was a young man, I had a wonderful mentor. Through him, I came to terms with what I thought were dark demons in my soul. They weren't demons but rather misunderstandings about my need to dominate. He instilled the belief that Dominants were

destined to have only one submissive their entire lifetime. I'm
beginning to wonder if his own insecurity that his sub might leave
him cultivated his stringent guidelines. Who knows? It's all moot.
The man's been long dead for years." His lip curled in a half-smile
as he tossed his hand in the air. "Yet on the other hand, as I watch
the lifestyle evolve, I find it hard to refute his beliefs. The carefree
claiming and releasing of subs, as if there are no bonds to the soul,
reaffirms to me that his teachings were probably correct. But when a
treasure is taken, not by another man but by the Almighty Himself, is
the one left alone on this earth meant to remain that way?" He
pursed his lips, pondering his own words.

Listening to Emile, I weighed his words. He made sense in a
strange and unfamiliar way. I knew of subs who wore so many
different Dom's collars it was a wonder they could keep their Master
of the moment straight. And I knew of a couple of Doms who would
toss aside their sub the minute a new girl joined the club. In no time
at all they'd slapped a collar of ownership around the new sub's neck
as if it were a game of chess. It was like they were collecting pawns
for some purpose. I never could understand people like that.

"I know the constant yearning to dominate has never waned in
all my years alone. I know Mika feels that same clawing need, but
exponentially stronger since you came into his life. I'm truly
surprised he had not succumbed to you before that day."

Before I could respond, the soft-spoken nurse approached.

"Mr. LaBrache, you may go back now."

I glanced over at Moses. He and Trevor were still sound asleep.

"We'll go in first and then wake them when we get back. Come.
Let's go see my son and your..." Emile didn't finish his sentence but
instead flashed a knowing smile.

My heart was lodged in my throat. Emile extended his elbow. I
wrapped my arm through his, and we followed the nurse through a
wide double door.

Sliding glass doors lined the hall, behind which were beeping
machines tethered to patients. It was hauntingly reminiscent of the
opaque glass doors from my last dream. I could feel an invisible
thread tug my soul, coaxing me to the end of the hall. An icy
premonition of déjà vu raced down my spine. Fighting the urge to
run, I focused on keeping in synchronized step with Emile.

Even with the doctor's warning, seeing Mika with so many tubes and leads connecting him to the numerous machines was shocking.

"Mika. Oh, Mika," Emile whispered as he rounded the bed and caressed his fingers over Mika's bald head. "My sweet boy."

Tears streamed down my face as I tried to choke back my sobs.

Emile's voice cracked as he bent and placed a tender kiss on Mika's forehead. "I've met your girl. She's beyond perfect, so you must get well...for her. For me. For Moses and Trevor. There are boundless joys ahead of you son. You must fight and heal yourself. She is definitely worth the battle, my boy. Not because she is a memory of another, but because she is Julianna. She is yours. Now get well and complete that missing part of your soul."

Emile was negating every ideal that held Mika prisoner to his past, tearing down the walls that had confined him to a life alone and unfulfilled.

The symmetry of the long, frustrating nights Mika forced me to wait outside his door, wielding his power, forcing me to decimate my own walls, filled my mind. He'd challenged me to peel back the layers of self-protection I'd desperately clung to. He'd opened my eyes, my heart, and my soul to the submissive serenity within me. And now Emile was eradicating Mika's barriers, peeling back his layers of self-protection so that his son might find happiness and serenity.

Standing on the opposite side of the bed, I gingerly cradled his limp hand. Leaning down, I caressed it with my tear-streaked cheek, peppering his russet flesh with tender kisses.

"I'm here Mika. I'll always be here if you want me." I wondered if my confession was out of line. I was nervous about allowing hope back into my heart, especially after everything Mika had told me.

All too soon, we made our way back to the waiting room. I woke Moses and Trevor so they could spend a few minutes with Mika. I declined their offer to drive me home, opting to stay at the hospital with Emile. After hours of talking, exhaustion took its toll, and I laid my head upon Emile's lap and slept.

CHAPTER TWELVE

Early the next morning, the waiting room began to fill with employees and members of the club. Drake and Trevor clung to one another, offering support in a poignant testament of love and commitment. Sammie smothered me with tenderness and soothing reassurance.

A stark realization struck me as I looked around the room. We were a group of multifaceted people with one common denominator: we were a family full of unconditional love and acceptance. Not one person asked me what had happened, they simply doled out compassionate hugs and offers of everything from meals to shoulders to cry on.

The local television reported the attempted carjacking. While some of us knew it was more sinister than what was reported, not a soul acknowledged Dennis's previous actions or involvement with the club. Our tight-knit community was also a closed-mouth community. We were protecting our own, protecting our family.

"Did you find your answer?" Sammie asked, brushing her long, glossy red fingernails through my hair.

Without responding, I looked into her sparkling aqua eyes and smiled. Clasping her other hand in mine, I drew it to my lips and placed a tender kiss on both the palm and back. A soft sigh of satisfaction swirled from my lips.

"Oh you did, girl. You most certainly did." After flashing a broad smile, her soft lips caressed the top of my head as she squeezed me against her ample breasts. "I'm so proud of you. I knew you could do it. Sometimes we get lost along the way, but those of us who find our destiny in the power exchange always wander back to the path that leads us home. For some it's an easy transition. For others, not so much. I'm proud and happy you're back."

"Me too."

"It wasn't too terrible a journey now was it?"

"Let's just say it's one I'd rather not repeat."

145

"You and me both, girl." She chuckled lowly. "You have no idea how badly I wanted to whip your ass bloody. You can try a Dominant's patience to the nth degree, no doubt about it."

I rolled my eyes and smirked. "I'm not that bratty."

"You were." She arched her brows in emphasis.

Master George entered the room and bestowed a warm, grandfatherly smile. He walked toward where Sammie and I huddled close on the couch and extended his hand. I glanced at Drake, who issued a subtle nod, and then I took George's hand and rose from the couch. He led me to an unoccupied corner of the waiting room, and with my back against the wall, he leaned in and wrapped me in a warm hug.

"Thank you for allowing me to cover the bases last night. Keeping the details from the uniformed officers on the scene kept this whole unfortunate incident from being entirely more complicated than it needed to be." His voice was low as he spoke. Anyone watching us would only observe a semiprivate moment of compassion between two people. "Please don't think less of me that I skirted the facts to protect people I dearly love."

I tilted my head, as if placing a kiss on his cheek and whispered in his ear. "Never, Sir. I am forever in your debt."

Pulling back, I saw a broad smile form over his lips, stretching the weathered lines on his face.

"No, sweet girl. All this is water under the bridge. It's best if we allow it to flow out to sea and stay lost forever." Stepping back, he placed his hands on my shoulders and winked. "I need a moment with Drake and Emile, but I want you to call me if you or Emile need anything. Understood?"

I nodded in assurance.

"Drake has my number, and I expect you to use it."

"Yes, Sir. Thank you for everything. I can't begin to tell you how relieved I was to see you last night. I was so scared. So..."

"I know, dear." He gave my shoulder a reassuring squeeze. "It's been a horrific scare to all of us. But Mika will recover from this. He's a strong young man. He comes from good stock."

He motioned for Drake and Emile to join us, then George presented Emile with an envelope. It was a directive that Mika had drawn up when he first opened Genesis that Drake oversee the day-to-day operations in the event of his death or incapacitation.

Drake accepted the responsibility solemnly and soon he, Trevor, and Sammie left to ready the club for the evening's guests. I knew most of the members would be at the club, not only to offer their support, but to try to glean more details about the shooting. Of course none would be given. Drake would make sure the news account was the exact version retold at the club. Besides, no one who knew Dennis McCollum's alter ego would spill the beans.

Feeling a bit vulnerable with Drake, Trevor, and Sammie gone, I curled my legs beneath me on the couch next to Emile while he made a litany of phone calls. Waiting was always so damn hard.

The soft-spoken nurse finally appeared and whispered something into Emile's ear. His eyes sparkled, and he nodded his head.

"Come, dear. He's awake." Emile beamed with joy.

Butterflies dipped and sailed in my stomach. Suddenly struck with a brutal case of anxiety, I had no idea what to say to Mika. After everything that happened, would he even want to see me? After all, it was my fault he'd been shot.

"Shouldn't you go see him alone?"

"Nonsense, child. We go together." Emile extended his hand, and we made our way down the glass-lined hall.

As he stood next to Mika's bed, Emile gently called his name. Mika's eyes flashed open in a combination of fear, relief, and love.

"It's okay, son. Everything is going to be fine. You gave us one hell of a scare, though." Emile smiled and once again kissed Mika's forehead. "Are you in pain?"

Mika slowly shook his head no.

"Good. I know you can't talk and it's probably frustrating, but there'll be time for that later. Right now, I just want you to work, son. Work hard on making yourself well." Emile squeezed his hand and nodded emphatically. Mika nodded gently and closed his eyes.

Surrendering to the ache, I slowly slid my hand into Mika's. Gently caressing my thumb over the back of his hand, he opened his eyes and turned his head toward me. A low groan rumbled in his chest.

"She is a treasure," Emile praised. Mika nodded, his eyes searching mine as if he were longing for an answer to some elusive question.

"I'm so sorry. All this happened because of me," I choked, sobbing on my guilt. "I never imagined he'd come after me like that. I'm so sorry, Mika."

Blinking through my tears, I felt Mika's hand tighten around mine.

His eyes suddenly reflected sadness as he shook his head no. Releasing my hand, his finger traced a strange gesture in the air in a somewhat lethargic, caveman type of communication. Emile and I were at a loss. He tried again and again, but we had no idea what he was trying to convey. Mika was becoming exhausted and agitated at our inability to decipher his pantomime. Emile bent and lovingly caressed his scalp, quietly reassuring Mika that there would be plenty of time to talk once he was healed.

~*~

The next three days were an exhausting blur. Emile and I spent our allotted fifteen minutes every hour at Mika's bedside. Each time I apologized to him, and each time he shook his head and his eyes filled with sorrow.

Something was very different about the way he looked at me. Each time I sat by his bed, he would draw my hand to his cheek and nuzzle it softly. Emile constantly praised the rate at which he was healing and encouraged him to keep fighting.

I couldn't stop touching him. It was as if I needed the constant reassurance that he was alive. Even when we would venture back in the wee hours of the morning, I would slide my hand beneath his and hold it. Feeling the comfort of his steady pulse in my hand gave me a silent security that he was still here with me if only for a little while.

The steady stream of friends from the club lending their support never waned. Trevor brought clean clothes for Emile and me along with a survival kit of snacks and goodies daily.

On one of our many walks through the hospital, Emile purchased a notepad and pen from the gift shop. Mika was still trying to communicate with his undecipherable pantomime and each time we walked into his room, he would snatch up the notepad and scrawl the same message.

Everything has changed. I need to tell you both. Too much to write down. Get this damn thing out of my throat!

On the fourth day, the ventilator was finally removed. Emile and I stood at his bedside, anxious to hear what Mika had been so obsessed to reveal.

"What is it you need to tell us, son?"

Mika swallowed with a pained expression then inhaled a deep breath. Reaching out, he held both Emile's hand and mine in his.

"First of all, what I'm going to say will sound unbelievable." His voice was still deep but horribly scratchy, not the buttery-soft timbre I was accustomed to, and his eyes held such a powerful urgency, it gave me chills. "But trust me, it's true. I know it is. It wasn't a dream. I know with every cell in my body it was *real*."

"Okay." I nodded solemnly, wondering what could possibly evoke so much passion in his words and eyes.

"I think I died and was brought back to life." He wrinkled one brow as if looking for confirmation of his suspicion.

Emile sadly nodded, confirming Mika's suspicion.

"Vanessa came to me. She told me that she sent you to me, Julianna." Mika smiled broadly.

A chill raced down my spine. If he only knew of Vanessa's nightly visits, he'd realize that the story he was revealing wasn't so unbelievable. I, too, had a story that would surely rock him to the core. But not today. It could wait for another time.

"You knew she came for me that night. Did you see her, too?" He looked at me expectantly as if I could corroborate his experience by confessing to have seen her ghost as well.

"No. I heard you call her name. I knew she was there to take you away with her."

"I heard you talking to me. I heard every word you said. You told me to go to her, to be happy with her."

A wave of guilt nearly took out my knees. I could feel Mika's stare, feel his eyes burning though me.

"Were you anxious for me to leave this mortal world, Julianna? To leave you?" A sly smile formed on his gorgeous lips.

"No." I blinked in mortification as my stomach pitched. "No. Of course not. That's not what I wanted. I knew why she was there. And I know how much you love her. You're so miserable without her.

149

I...I wanted you to finally be happy." I lowered my head, ashamed that he thought I didn't want him to live.

"So you gave me the ultimate gift you could give, complete self-sacrificing love." The warmth, understanding, and praise in his voice had me softly sobbing at his side. "You were willing to give me up simply for my own happiness, is that right?"

I nodded as tears spilled from my eyes. A bleak sob tore from my throat.

"Shhh, Julianna. Please don't cry. I am in awe of you. I keep wondering what I've ever done to deserve someone as precious as you."

He raised his hand and caressed my face, wiping away my tears as they streaked down my cheeks. I held my breath, waiting for him to continue speaking.

"Vanessa told me that she'd answered my prayers, that she sent you to me to take away the emptiness and pain. She said I was too damn stubborn to see the gift in front of my face. She was quite pissed at me for it, too." He grinned. "She told me the rules I'd been raised with were wrong, that the potential to love more than one is inside all of us. She said that we shortchange ourselves when we limit sharing that love with just one."

He looked at Emile with sad eyes. "I'm sorry, Dad, but I believe her. The love I felt in whatever place I was in was indescribable. I was engulfed with such a powerful feeling of unconditional love, I can't even begin to explain. My skin glowed with a golden light so bright, so warm and accepting. No human words can give it justice."

A sudden serious frown formed on Mika's lips as he looked at his father's smiling face. His brows drew together in concern, and his eyes held Emile's as he licked his lips and took a small sip of water. He was already growing tired from expending so much energy talking.

"Mom was there," he finally announced, watching his father's expression warily.

Emile threw his head back and laughed. He smiled broadly, looking again at Mika. "How did she look?" he asked as tears glistened in his eyes.

Mika's chin quivered and he struggled with his own emotions. He swallowed tightly and nodded. "Like an angel."

"That doesn't surprise me. She always did." Emile choked, pride in his voice.

"She said you were also wrong about only claiming one. She said that it was the second time in your life you were wrong and that it was a bigger mistake than the car. I don't know what she meant by that." Mika shook his head in confusion.

Once again Emile laughed, but it sounded like a strangled cry of pain. Tears spilled from his eyes. "Ahh, yes, the car." He swallowed audibly and palmed away his tears. "I bought a used car when you were just a baby. It was a rickety old piece of crap, but I was proud of it because I'd saved like a miser and paid cash for it. I brought it home and smugly announced it was our new car. Your mother cried she was laughing so hard."

I wiped the tears from my eyes and smiled at his memory.

His lips curled in a broad smile as his eyes twinkled with tears at the memory. "She brazenly told me that I'd been hoodwinked and that it was a piece of junk. She said we'd be lucky if it ran to the end of the block. I was incensed. She'd never scoffed at anything I'd done before, so I punished her. I punished her for all the wrong reasons. I claimed she'd undermined my authority and that she didn't have faith in my decisions. Just as she'd predicted, I had decidedly been screwed. That damn car broke down three times within the first week. It was then that I had to make amends to her. I had to apologize not only for punishing her unjustly, but for wasting hard earned money on such a worthless piece of shit."

We were all three grinning broadly, then Mika nodded and once again took on a somber expression. "She said you need to open your eyes and stop being so hardheaded. She wants you to look at what's in front of you and to stop being such a stubborn fool. She wants you to get on with your life, Dad."

Emile's eyes hardened and his jaw ticked, rebelling in the notion that he should move on.

Mika held up his hands in defense. "Her words, Dad, not mine."

After taking another sip of water, he lowered his head and closed his eyes. "Mom said she sent someone to you, but just like me, you're too stubborn to see her. I know you don't want to hear this, but she wants you to stop mourning her."

A tear slid down Mika's cheek as he swallowed a muted sob.

"She wants you to start living again, to find happiness with the gift she's sent you." He finally opened his eyes and saw the tears sliding down Emile's cheeks. "Do you know who she's talking about?"

Emile sadly nodded his head yes.

"She loves you dad. She loves us all. She wants you to be happy. She wants me to be happy. Both she and Vanessa just want us to live the rest of our days here fulfilled. They both want us to embrace our futures and not hold onto the past."

Emile nodded, wiping his tears away, then cradled Mika's face in his hand and gazed upon him with a love so absolute it made me smile. "Then we will do as they ask. We owe them that much at least."

Mika then looked back at me. "Come closer, Julianna," he whispered.

I leaned over the bed, and he spread his palm over my cheek. His liquid amber eyes penetrated deep into mine. "I love you. I've loved you for a long, long time. I've been a fool, a stubborn, hardheaded fool. I don't expect you to love me. But I pray you'll give me a chance to show you, to prove to you who I am and what's in my heart. We have a lot to learn about each other, but there is no doubt in my soul that I want you as mine. You are my one, my second one. I want to share my life with you." His eyes sparkled as he pulled me to his lips.

I returned his passionate kiss as every emotion I'd tried to deny detonated, erupting through me like blistering lightning as it surged through my body nearly taking me to my knees. His lips were full and warm and his erotic flavor exploded over my taste buds. I savored his potent demand. Coaxing the seam of my lips wider, he masterfully opened my mouth and claimed what was his. What would always be his—me.

Oblivious to Emile's presence, I whimpered, needing more. More of his tongue. More of his lips. More of his love. And he gave it to me. Passionately. Erotically, without the slightest reservation. And I took it all. Greedily. Hungrily. I slipped that provocative full bottom lip into my mouth, tugged it gently with my teeth, and slid my tongue over its sweet, plump flesh.

The soft-voiced nurse came rushing into the room, skidding to a halt. Raising my head, I looked into her panic-laced eyes. An almost instantaneous look of relief washed over her face as her shoulders sagged. The tension in her body deflated like a balloon.

"Mr. LaBrache, you nearly took ten years off my life. The alarm on your heart monitor just went berserk. But I now see it wasn't a pending heart attack that caused the sudden spike." A mischievous twinkle flashed in her blue eyes.

Emile began to laugh as my face burned hotly.

"I'm going to have to ask you to curtail your...um...amorous activities until you get home," she admonished with a sly grin, then turned and left the room.

"I guess we'll have to wait." Mika's sensual eyes danced with delight. His broad, beautiful smile filled my heart with fiery anticipation as my clit ached in desire. I gave him a shy nod then planted a tender but brief kiss to his lips.

"We'll be back in an hour," Emile announced. "But I'll guard the girl much closer next time we come. You don't want your heart monitor broadcasting your desires."

"That's probably a good idea. This little vixen has a habit of stealing my control." His deep sensual chuckle turned my legs to Jell-O, and a torrid rush of honey spilled from between my folds.

My entire body shuddered as I sucked in a quivering breath.

Reaching up, he wrapped his hand around my wrist, and he pulled me toward him. He nuzzled his mouth against my ear, his warm breath wafting over the column of my neck. "I can smell your arousal, pet. It's so fucking intoxicating." His teeth nipped at the creamy flesh of my throat and he released my wrist.

"Oh you'd better hurry up and get well...um, Sir," I moaned with a hungry plea.

"I intend to." The promise in his eyes left little doubt he would soon be up and running around in a matter of days. As he lowered his gaze, I followed his eyes and bit back a pitiful whimper. It took every ounce of willpower I had to turn and walk away instead of launching my mouth over the massive arousal tenting the thin hospital sheet.

Emile was still laughing as we left the room. My body was on fire. I wanted to rush back to Mika's room, rip off my clothes, straddle him, and feed every sinful inch of his glorious hard cock deep inside me. Inhaling a slow breath, I attempted to calm the ricocheting flames singeing me from the inside out.

Emile wrapped his arm around my waist, still chuckling even as we walked back into the waiting room. Raising his head, his body froze like a marble statue. He stared in disbelief at an extremely tall, willowy older woman with thick, shimmering blonde hair. A combination of heartbreak, shock, and embarrassment reflected in her huge, sparkling azure eyes.

She wore a dark pencil skirt and an ivory silk blouse that barely contained her brimming breasts. A blazer was draped over her arm. She looked exotic and earthly erotic atop her high-heeled shoes. Her shoulders slightly sagged as she observed me ensconced in Emile's arm. Her sense of rejection and remorse was heartbreaking palpable.

"Sarah." Emile's startled reaction caused the woman to jump. "What on earth are you doing here? Is there something wrong with the company?" He rushed toward the trembling woman as she blinked back glistening tears.

"No, sir." She shook her head and swallowed tightly. "I'm sorry. I should never have come and intruded into your personal life."

"Nonsense." Emile blinked as if he finally understood the swirling emotions roiling within the stunningly beautiful woman. "Sarah, this is Julianna Garrett. She's Mika's girlfriend."

Removing his arm from around my waist, a warm smile tugged his lips as if trying to ease the pain reflecting in Sarah's eyes.

"Julianna, this is Sarah Mills. She is my personal assistant."

"It's an honor to meet you," I said with a broad smile, hoping to alleviate the misconception that I was with Emile in a more personal capacity.

"Oh." Her body language softened at once. A broad smile of relief stretched over her full, ripe lips. "It's an honor to meet you too, Julianna. I'm so sorry to hear of Mika's accident. How is he?"

"He's doing much better," Emile interjected. His brows furrowed as he looked into Sarah's eyes. "Why exactly are you here, dear?"

"I...I'm sorry Mr. LaBrache. I shouldn't have come. I realize this now. I have no business intruding into your personal life. I'm sorry, sir, but I couldn't take another minute sitting at my desk worrying about you and Mika and wondering if I could help out in some way for you here." Her words nervously poured out like a waterfall.

I wanted to laugh. I wanted to cry. I wanted to shout to the heavens. This woman...Sarah, Emile's assistant, was the one Mika's mother had sent to him. The woman practically oozed submission from every pore.

Desperate to bite back my giggle, I studied Emile's expression. The fight between a lifetime of steadfast rules and Mika's enlightening revelation was waging a full-scale war in the poor man's brain.

"I shouldn't have taken it upon myself to simply fly out here, but as I said, I've been beside myself, sir. Really, I should just leave. I'm sorry." Nervously smoothing her palms over the blazer resting on her arm, she cast her eyes to the floor then back at Emile. The poor woman was a hot mess. "I need to go back home and take care of things for you from the office."

By the looks of it, Sarah was backpedaling like crazy, desperate to grapple not only her embarrassment but fear of Emile's rejection.

I giggled. I couldn't help myself. Emile looked absolutely shell shocked. His mouth was slightly agape as he stood in stunned silence. But there was a twinkle in his eyes, a glimmering light I'd not seen since he'd arrived.

I had to do something. I couldn't just stand there watching these two dance around one another getting nowhere. While Emile might think I was topping from the bottom, I didn't care. There was no way I was going to let Sarah prance back out of the hospital, and possibly out of his life, not after Mika's disclosure.

I took her hand and issued a warm smile. "I'm sure Emile doesn't want you to leave, Sarah." I led her to the same couch Emile and I had claimed over the past three days. "I know he's deeply touched that you came all this way out of concern for him and Mika."

A quick glance over my shoulder told me that Emile followed behind us looking dazed and confused.

Sarah slightly turned, looking back at him. "I just wanted to be here in case you needed anything," she whispered in a soft confession.

As if his body and mind finally meshed, Emile took her arm

155

from mine and placed his hands on her thin shoulders.

"I'm glad you're here, Sarah. And no, absolutely not. You will *not* turn around and fly back home. There's nothing that can't be handled here." He looked into her eyes with such a powerful gaze that it sent a ripple of excitement down my own spine. "Indeed, there is something I need you to do."

"What is it, sir?" she asked in a near breathless whisper.

"Have dinner with me." His broad smile couldn't hide the lustful, animalistic desires dancing in his eyes.

"I'd like that very much, sir." A deep crimson blush rose upon her cheeks as she smiled. Her breath was low and shallow, almost panting, and the sexual tension between the two was as thick as a London fog. I somehow managed to keep the ecstatic laughter bubbling inside me buried as I watched the fireworks ignite between them.

CHAPTER THIRTEEN

"Oh my God, Mika, you should have seen them." I was all but dancing in my excitement next to his bed as I told of Sarah and Emile and the near sexual combustion in the waiting room. "She's such a sub. Everything that came out of her mouth was submissive. And oh, she is so beautiful. She's tall and thin. She looks regal with long, thick waves of blonde hair and, oh my God, she's got the most expressive blue eyes. Her lips are like plump, ripe fruit. She's a goddess."

"You've just described my mother." He beamed with pride.

"Oh, and your poor father." I couldn't help but giggle in excitement. "He hadn't a clue what to do. Thank goodness he quickly explained that I was your, well, that I wasn't *his* lover." I amended my words, unsure if I should assign myself the label of "girlfriend" quite as freely as Emile had.

Mika's smile reflected his absolute gratitude, and he cast his eyes toward the ceiling, issuing a heartfelt thanks to his mother.

"Where are they now?"

"Oh! That's the best part. He went with her to make sure she got," using my fingers to illustrate quotation marks, "'checked in' to her hotel safe and sound. I bet they're busting up the furniture as we speak."

"Lucky bastard!"

"You'll have your turn soon, Sir," I blurted out without thought.

"No pet. You've got that backwards. You'll have *your* turn soon. But I like the way you think." He flashed an evil smile that sent a ripple of anticipation through my entire bloodstream and growled low and menacing. A pained expression quickly etched his face.

"Does your throat hurt?" I reached for a cup of ice chips.

"A bit." He nodded, opening his mouth as I spoon-fed him the soothing ice. Within seconds, an erotic gleam returned and danced in his eyes. "I need to feel you, pet. Climb on the bed and rest your head on my stomach."

I blinked. "What about your heart monitor? It will nark you out again."

"Not if I control myself."

"And just *how* do you plan on doing that?"

He scrunched up one side of his mouth, contemplating. "I'm not sure yet."

I laughed.

"Come here," he instructed, patting his stomach.

"Mika? We can't..."

"I just need to feel you. I'll keep my heart rate in control. I'm a Dom. I can keep all kinds of wild things in control, including you." He grinned mischievously.

"But you're all hooked up...there's no way."

"Julianna? Do I need to shut the door and make you wait outside it again?"

"Oh, that's not *even* funny." I groaned as I took great care weaving my body beneath the various tubes attached to his arms. Gently resting my head on his stomach, I tilted my chin and looked into his decadent amber eyes.

He chuckled as his warm hand caressed my face.

"About that..." I lowered my eyes in embarrassment then looked back up at him.

"Yes?" he asked, arching his brows.

"I'm sorry I was such a...a bitch."

"You weren't a bitch. You were angry. And you've already apologized to me."

"Yeah, I was angry and then some. I certainly wasn't a poster child for submission."

"No, that you weren't." He laughed. "But I knew why you were angry and part of it was my fault. I probably shouldn't tell you this, but that night with the ball gag and cuffs? I was laughing my ass off inside my office. You were having a full-on temper tantrum, pounding on my door, demanding...*demanding* that I open it."

"So, let me get this straight. You were laughing as I nearly lost my mind?"

"I *tried* to make you comfortable, precious. I set out a blanket and a pillow, and even a bedtime story. But you were a bit too obstinate to use them." He smirked.

"Well, that's because I was cuffed and gagged, Mister. That was about the same time I realized you'd heard every horrid word I'd said." I cringed at the rage I'd unleashed opposite his door. "I'm sorry for all the hateful things I said."

"I only requested the ball gag once. I thought I was being extremely lenient since you called me...what was it again? Oh yes...a fucking bastard, wasn't it, love?"

I groaned in shame for my insolent behavior as Mika laughed.

"I showed great restraint otherwise, especially when you kept calling me 'the great and powerful Oz.'" He grinned and winked as I once again groaned. "Yes, I heard every word you said from the time Sammie and Moses picked you up until you went back inside your house."

"You what? How?" I blinked, more than a little dumbfounded.

"I had James plant little receivers on their clothing. You thought you'd lost your submission. I knew better. But I was a bit panicked when I thought I'd lost you on the second day. When you left your house and drove to Maurizio's."

"How did you know about that? Did you plant a GPS in my bra?"

"No, smartass. I followed you. After the first night, I suspected that stubborn streak of yours would win out and you would run. I was right," he announced with a slight smirk. "I was fully prepared to have Sammie haul you out of the restaurant if need be. Thankfully, you ended up going back home. I'm damn glad you did."

"So you heard everything I said to Sammie and Moses?"

"Yes, I did. I listened for the simple fact that you are far too special to me to allow you to run away from your destiny."

"But you didn't want me," I mumbled.

"What?" he choked in shock. "What in the hell are you talking about? I've always wanted you. Where did you get such an outlandish idea from?"

"That morning at my house. After you...made me come. You ran out and you told Moses to get you out of my sight. I thought I repulsed you."

"Oh, Julianna. No. Hell, no." The pain and sorrow reflected in his eyes stabbed my heart. "It wasn't you. I was angry with myself, repulsed by my own actions for what I'd taken from you."

He cupped my chin with his palm and slanted my head back as he gazed deep into my eyes.

"It was never you, beautiful, never. I was angry with myself. I'd taken your gift. And at the time, I felt I'd violated my vow to Vanessa, that I'd shamed her by my weakness for you. I know differently now, but then I felt as if I'd failed myself as a Master to her, and failed you by using you."

"All this time I thought it was because I repulsed you," I whispered as the rejection I'd harbored since that horrific morning began to melt away.

"You could never repulse me, love. I can still feel your tunnel contracting on my fingers, feel the heat of your burning, slick nectar pouring out and coating my palm. I still smell your sweet fragrance." He heaved a disgruntled sigh. "All this time you thought I didn't want you? Dammit, Julianna. I've wanted you since I first laid eyes on you. The longer I've watched you, the harder it's been to deny myself. That morning at your house, I caved, and caved hard."

"I've never been touched that way before," I confessed in a shy voice.

"What do you mean?"

"I've never felt so controlled. I've never been spoken to like I was a real submissive, commanded and enticed."

"Never?"

I could tell by the tone of his voice he was surprised. I shook my head no.

"Well get used to it, girl." His smile was full of promise. "You never told me about the dream that opened your heart."

"Oh, the dream." I nodded. "It seems like a lifetime ago."

"Aww, princess." He traced the pad of his thick finger over my lips. I couldn't help myself. The need to taste him was overpowering. I suckled his finger into my mouth, wishing it was his cock, that glorious hard cock throbbing against the back of my head.

"Careful, girl. I can't promise I'll control my heart rate with you doing that."

I giggled and popped his finger from my lips.

"I'll stop. We don't want you getting another lecture now, do we?"

"No. It undermines my authority in front of *my* girl."

My girl. God, I'd waited so long for a Dominant to call me that. Swallowing the massive lump in my throat, I blinked the tears stinging my eyes. Lifting my head, I was met with Mika's dazzling smile, and my heart melted. His sinful bottom lip looked even thicker stretched across his mouth. I wanted to suckle his lips, wanted to kiss him passionately again. I wanted so much, maybe too much. A tiny voice inside my head pushed away my doubt, demanding that I take it one day at a time and enjoy them to the fullest.

Cupping his hand around my cheek and caressing me tenderly, he gazed into my eyes. "Tell me about your dream, love. I'm curious to know what caused such a profound change in you."

"Ah, yes. The dream." I sighed in a low hum. "Actually it wasn't just one dream. I need to tell you something about a lot of dreams."

"You can tell me anything. In fact, from now on you *will* tell me everything."

I nodded in understanding and inhaled a deep breath then began to confess my nightly visits from Vanessa, ending the encounters with the last dream of the golden brick wall. "And there you were, standing before me like the great and powerful Oz...Ooops." A mischievous chuckled rolled off my lips.

"You're such a brat," Mika replied with a dry smirk and a sexy flicker in his eyes. "Please continue with the dream and not your um...sassy interpretation."

"Yes, Sir." I grinned and winked.

"Anyway, when I awoke, the symbolism of the dream made me realize with absolute clarity that I was a submissive. The core of my being wasn't something I could cast off. I had to embrace it. And no matter what path I ended up walking, the journey would be exactly as it was meant to be for me. I had to stop fighting what I thought I wanted for my walls to come down. I knew it was the only way I would find whatever peace and serenity was destined for me. You made me see that. Thank you."

"I *am* proud of you, pet." His eyes reflected the same intense love as in my dream. I smiled through the tears that slid unchecked down my cheeks. "I knew you'd found your way back the moment you knelt outside my door. I nearly exploded with pride."

Neither of us spoke for a long time as he trailed his fingers through my curls. Tiny quivers tingled through my core, and it clenched and ached to be filled.

"I don't expect to hear you say it, not for a while anyway, but I love you."

My heart clutched in my chest. "I think I want to love you too, Mika," I whispered my confession. "I need some time, though. I could easily fall in love with the idea of you that's in my head, but I need time to learn more about you, the person you are in my heart."

"Yes, you do. But there's something you need to know. I'm a very patient man. However long it takes, whatever you need from me, just ask. My heart is yours, pet. Just don't make me wait a lifetime. I feel like I've already waited that and more for you."

~*~

A few days later, Mika was moved to a private room. The doctors were impressed at how fast he was healing and regaining his strength. Emile and Sarah stayed to make sure he continued to progress without any setbacks.

However, I think Emile had other reasons for their lengthy stay. Moses had given him a key to Genesis, and during the day, he taught Sarah some of the finer pleasures of the lifestyle in private. Of course she'd been full of questions, and the four of us spent many hours in Mika's private room candidly discussing her newfound submission. It was just as I'd suspected. She was a natural born sub and once she discovered her "place," she literally blossomed from the inside out. Emile was equally lambent, wearing a constant smile of Dominant pride. It was heartwarming to see such a change in him. Sarah had brought him back to life.

While Mika recuperated at the hospital, Drake and Trevor moved my clothes and toiletries into Mika's house, convinced that I should be the one to help him finish recovering at home. I was more than willing to volunteer for that job. In fact, wild horses couldn't have kept me from it.

It wasn't long before Mika was released from the hospital and sent home. Emile hovered over him almost twenty-four-seven as a loving father would. Passing by Mika's room one morning, I caught my name in conversation as Emile gave him a sponge bath. Okay, so curiosity got the best of me and I paused to listen.

"You know, Dad, Julianna can do this for me. You don't have to."

"I know, son, but if I allowed her to touch your bits...you've not healed well enough for the exertion of wild jungle sex, not quite yet." A hint of amusement laced his words.

"Shit. Don't lead my mind down that path, Dad. Just thinking about everything I want to do to her, all the ways I want to claim her and knowing I can't, it's driving me out of my mind. She comes in the room and her scent carries on the wind. She leaves, and I sit here like a fucking pussy, inhaling the ghosts she's left behind. Christ, I've lost my damn mind over her."

Emile's deep laughter echoed from the room. I smiled, not at Mika's torment, but with the knowledge that we were both on a razor's edge of sexual need. It was all I could do at night not to slide my fingers over my tingling nub and bring myself off in a mind-numbing climax. I didn't, though. I wanted to save the swelling explosion for his pleasure. He needed to see and feel the level of desire he fostered in me. And if I allowed myself to focus too keenly on the continuous ache, I'd never keep my fingers away. God help the poor man once I unleashed all that was trapped inside. I might kill him after all.

Scurrying back to the kitchen, I took in my surroundings, anything to take away the focus of my aching clit. Mika's home was massive, as regal as the man himself. At first I was intimidated by the sheer size of the mansion, but slowly I grew accustomed to the elegant, spacious rooms, the dark masculine décor, and the private dungeon, especially the private dungeon. Catching myself standing at its doorway, more often than not my mind seemed to fill with all the immoral, decadent things Mika might subject me to within the wicked walls. Of course it was self-induced masochistic torture and only ratcheted my level of frustration higher, but I simply couldn't stop myself.

As the days progressed, he needed less and less help from me. I was unsure what his expectations of me were. Would he want me to continue living with him once he'd fully healed? I didn't know, and I was too scared to ask. Thankfully, I didn't have much time to dwell on my insecurities as the house was usually filled with visitors. And I was happy pampering Mika and his guests. I'd not even given much thought to my clients who I'd passed off to a very capable number crunching CPA friend of mine. In all honesty, I was grateful for the reprieve of dealing with the IRS. Most of my time was spent cooking, cleaning, and tending to domestic chores for him. It was strange, but I found doing tasks for him rewarding. Taking care of Mika filled me with joy. It was funny, though, because I'd always dreaded doing the same chores for myself.

We'd spent a lazy morning tangled in bed. Mika's fingers tortured me unmercifully, taking me to the edge of oblivion over and again. Each time I was ready to surrender, he would stop and softly talk me down from the ledge. Frustration coiled like an angry snake, hissing and slithering through my veins.

Mika's engorged shaft bore witness that the doctor's orders were taking their toll on him, too. He'd been instructed to do nothing but rest until his follow-up appointment. With the sexual tension humming through the air, I knew I needed to do something to take the edge off, something non-sexual to undo the thundering knot beneath my clit.

"I'll get your shower ready whenever you'd like me to."

"Now would be fine, pet. Thank you." There was a strange twinkle in his eyes as he smiled at me. "I think I'd like it if you joined me this morning."

Tilting my head, I shook it, narrowing my eyes. "When the doctor says you've healed, remember?" Heading toward the spacious master bath, I tried to calm my zinging horny hormones. Turning on the shower, I felt Mika's hot body heat behind me. A ripple of excitement sliced my spine as his warm breath caressed the back of my neck.

"I am healed enough, girl. Take off your nightshirt and join me." His soft, full lips trailed over the column of my throat.

It wasn't a request. It was an order. My knees turned to putty. His commanding words pebbled my nipples as a brutal ache clutched deep in my womb. Trembling, my blood pumped with exhilarated anticipation. My fingers fumbled at the button of my nightshirt, and I

164

could feel the heat of his eyes as he watched me with a voracious intensity.

"Are you nervous, girl?" A sly smile spread over his mouth.

I swallowed tightly and nodded.

"Why?"

"I don't know what you're going to do to me."

He nodded thoughtfully as a fire leapt in his eyes. "Why, take a shower with you, of course. You certainly don't need to be nervous about that, do you?"

"No, Sir." Unsure if that was all he intended, I felt vulnerable and edgy.

"Get in, my sweet. I'll join you in a minute."

And with that, he left the bathroom. I stepped into the shower and rolled my shoulders as the numerous showerheads massaged my body. When the shower door opened and Mika stepped in, I couldn't stop staring. Drinking in his sculpted body, I wanted to weep at his pure, unadulterated masculine beauty. Even the clear adhesive bandage over the wicked puckered wound couldn't diminish the absolute splendor of his physical form.

Delineated muscles rippled over every inch of his light ebony skin. Legs and arms bulged with thick, corded muscles, and I was dying to slide my tongue over every inch of his sweet milk-chocolate flesh. His heavy cock, thick and long, was framed with tight, black curls that glistened beneath droplets of water. I had a desperate urge to drop to my knees and worship it with my mouth until the end of time.

My soft whimpers echoed off the tiled walls. Swiping my tongue languidly across my bottom lip, I sucked in the plump flesh, nibbling it between my teeth. Impatient for his command, I gazed at him through thick lashes in a silent plea for that first taste of his cock.

A predatory gleam flashed through his hypnotic eyes. Taking a step closer, he raised his hands and cupped my breasts. I arched as electricity sizzled through my veins and raced to my needy clit. His broad thumb traced over each turgid peak as I gasped.

"You're so fucking beautiful, Julianna," he growled in a hoarse, desperate tone. "I need to feel you, taste you."

"Yes," I murmured, melting against his hot, hard body.

165

Tilting my head back, he pressed an erotic kiss upon my lips. I opened for him, greedy and hungry, as I accepted his slippery warm tongue. Dizzy with the force of his virile kiss, I groaned as I devoured his mouth. I ardently tugged his bottom lip between my teeth, flicking my tongue over the sweet full flesh as I throbbed for more.

His taste alone unleashed a voracious, brazen vixen hiding inside. I couldn't have contained her if I'd tried. Silently screaming for more, I consumed all he'd allow with a carnivorous hunger. And he allowed, oh God, how he allowed.

Separating my mouth from his, I lowered my head in desperation and sipped the beads of water from his chest. I drank my way down until I'd settled upon my knees. Brushing my lips against the broad crest of his glorious shaft, my mouth watered. Looking up, I knew he could see the urgent demand blazing in my eyes.

"Take what you want my love," Mika permitted as his strong fingers massaged my scalp.

My heart soared as I buried my nose beneath his shaft. Deeply inhaling his masculine scent, I rubbed my mouth against his heavy, warm sac and snaked my tongue over each of the fuzzy orbs. I licked the water from his dark wiry curls then eased them into my mouth. Massaging the base of his cock with my nose, we groaned in unison as I rolled my tongue between his tightly drawn balls.

"Fuck, Julianna. You're killing me!" His fingers gripped my saturated curls. A muffled cry bubbled in the back of my throat as my body quivered in uncontrollable tremors.

Releasing him from my mouth, slurping my saliva from his balls, I opened wide and edged my lips over his broad, glistening crest. I wedged each pulsating inch of his cock into my mouth. My pussy wept in euphoria. His sweet, tangy essence exploded over my taste buds.

Savoring the taste of my "one," I indelibly inked his unique flavor into my soul. This was the essence I would crave day and night for all eternity. A tear of happiness melded with the water sprinkling my face as I realized this was the shaft that would claim me, own me, complete me.

Floating my tongue over the thick veins, I made love to every engorged inch as my hands cupped and massaged his sac. Slick, hot nectar poured from my tunnel and slid down my thighs while my clit throbbed and my nipples ached. With lurid swirls, I danced my tongue over his cock. I sucked until the broad crest caressed the back of my throat then swallowed, coaxing, enticing. I was anxious for him to fill my mouth and shower my throat with his milky-sweet treasure.

"Your mouth is sinful, fucking heaven." His fingers clutched my hair as he fucked my mouth in a steady, urgent rhythm. "I'm going to scald your throat, pet. Take it, love. Drink my come."

An ardent whimper vibrated in my throat as I swallowed the crest of his cock once again. His column swelled and a loud, primitive growl filled the room as his hot, thick treasure jettisoned down my throat. Stream after stream of his salty, slick seed ensconced my tongue as I gulped every savory spurt. His cries of uninhibited pleasure filled my ears as I laved my tongue around his jerking shaft. It was the most rapturous music I'd ever heard. Listening to his panting breaths, I licked and sucked every drop from his still erect shaft.

"Turn around and close your eyes, sweet girl." A slow smile of pleasure curled on my lips as I lifted to my feet. Turning, I waited, anticipating how the heat of his cock would singe the entrance of my pussy. Instead, his long, strong fingers began to massage shampoo through my wet ringlet curls. His deep, erotic voice blanketed me with praise, calming the urgent sexual need that hummed through my veins.

"I don't want to confuse you," he murmured as he turned me to face him and began rinsing the soap from my hair. "I will claim you today as a man. Today we are lovers. Equals. I don't want you holding back anything you feel. I will give you no commands to follow. Don't keep any desires or needs locked inside you, love. Let them go. Show me, tell me what you want. I ache to explore you, to please the woman inside the submissive. No holding back or allowing your submissive side to take over. I want you to take your fill. Don't get me wrong, I desire your submission. God, I crave it. But our first time together we're simply two people exploring and fulfilling desires. You'll want to give, it's who you are, but I want you to take as well. Take what you want, what you need. Do you understand?"

Realizing he'd just given me carte blanche to all the carnal desires I held inside, an evil giggle escaped my throat as I nodded.

"Oh, Lord. That was a wicked little laugh. Should I be scared, love?" His brows arched as he smiled wide.

"Only if you're afraid of enjoyment." I winked mischievously.

"Hrmmm, you're pretty sure of yourself, are you?"

"Oh yes, I am. Indeed I am." Raising my hands, I wrapped my palms around his face then softly rubbed my thumb over his wide, velvet bottom lip. "I love your lips. They're so...erotic."

My eyes fixed on the plumpness, aching for another taste.

"Take me to bed, Mika. Make love to me, please." I slanted my lips over his. Holding nothing back, I kissed him with a fiery passion. My fingers and palms skimmed in urgency over his hard rippling shoulders, corded arms, and tight firm ass cheeks. Memorizing each contour and bulge, I couldn't absorb him fast enough to quench the blistering need blazing inside me. Whimpers of my hungry demand echoed off the marble walls, drowning out the resonant droning of the water.

His hands were as frantic as mine. Thick fingers tugged my nipple rings, massaged my breasts, and plucked each aching peak. Tearing his mouth from mine, his tongue lashed each pebbled, cranberry-colored nipple. Gripping my nipple rings between his teeth, he gave a solid tug on each silver sphere. Arching my back, I cried out in delight.

The heavy, musky scent of arousal infused the steamy mist. Uninhibited and desperate, I reached between my legs, stroking my needful clit as I rolled my hips against his.

"Do you want to explode for me here, love, or on the bed with my tongue driving deep in your wicked cunt?" Growling, he plunged two fingers inside my empty, fluttering pussy.

I cried out a garbled answer and launched my head back as my muscles clamped around his embedded fingers. My hips pumped a furious beat against his hands.

"Look at me, baby. Look into my eyes. I need to watch you shatter."

Forcing my heavy lids open, I was met with sparkling approval reflecting in his eyes and a feral smile curling on his lips. My body buzzed as a familiar tingle spread down my legs and up my spine.

Fire burned and pooled deep in my womb. Hovering on the brink of orgasm, I waited for his command, his permission to plummet over the edge. I begged him with my eyes to grant the free fall into orgasmic bliss. Panic melded with demand when I realized he had no intention of verbally sanctioning my release.

"Please, Mika, please," I gasped, begging for his instruction. "Help me."

"What do you need, precious?" Taunting fingers full of command danced and scissored inside my clutching tunnel.

"Permission," I wailed as tears stung my eyes.

"Oh, darling girl. You've not allowed yourself to come without a directive? Can you not slip over the edge without permission, my love?"

Frantically in need, I shook my head no as a pitiful whimper filled the air. "Please. Give me your permission."

"And if I don't? If I withhold one word, you'll be stranded right where you are? Caught between ecstasy and misery?"

"Please no. Please don't torture me," I begged, panic stricken.

Then without warning, he slid his fingers from my core.

CHAPTER FOURTEEN

My eyes flashed wide. "No. No. No." I moaned, thrusting my hips into the air as he turned off the shower and gathered a soft, fluffy towel. Unable to speak in the throes of frenzied deprivation, my mind raced in fear.

He couldn't leave me on the cusp like this. It was inhuman. What happened to taking what I want and need? I needed a fucking orgasm. Surely he wasn't going to leave me like this, was he? I wanted to scream and claw at him, to pound on his steely chest and demand he put me out of my misery. Yet all I could do was undulate and whimper.

"Shhh," he whispered as he wrapped the towel around me. "We're going to the bedroom. I'll help you, pet, but you'll achieve your release without my permission."

"I can't," I cried, on the verge of hysteria. Tears slid down my cheeks.

"Yes you can, gorgeous. You just haven't done it in a long time. There's a line inside you between woman and submissive. Today you're going to find it for me. I want you to realize how much power you possess before I accept it, take it from you. Show me the degree of entitlement you're going to hand over to me when I claim you as mine."

"Mika, I can't. I swear, I can't do it. You have to say the words. You have to tell me to come. You...you can't leave me like this. Please. Help me."

"Trust me, precious. Just trust me," he soothed as he led me out of the bathroom and to the bed. "Relax. Let me take care of you. On your back, sweetheart. Spread your legs wide for me."

Mika climbed between my splayed legs, pulling the towel away. His warm breath caressed my thighs. A violent shudder rippled through my body as I looked down, watching his full brown lips sprinkle tender kisses over my alabaster flesh. My skin was alive. Every nerve ending burned with intense sensitivity. The softness of his lips combined with the scratchy stubble of his face caused my hips to arch in demand.

His eyes were fixed on my sex. "Your glistening cream is pouring out like a waterfall. Do you always get this wet or is this something special for me?"

"You, because of you," I mewled as his wet, pink tongue took a slow glide over his bottom lip.

"Then I think I'll need to lick it up, if it's all for me." A lurid smile curled on his mouth as he gave me a playful wink.

Arching as his mouth devoured my swollen, aching center, our cries of mutual delight melded together in a primitive call of carnal magic. Within seconds, I had soared back to the precipice of orgasm beneath his masterful tongue. His fingers plunged inside me, stretching me, filling me. I soared so high I could almost touch the stars flashing behind my eyes. My low guttural moans grew to desperate, frantic screams as I writhed and thrashed beneath his assault.

"Please. Please," I panted, begging in a delirious fog.

"You know what to do, Julianna," he growled.

"Help me."

"Show me, love. You can do this."

"I can't."

"Yes, you can. I know you can."

"Please. Oh, God. Please, Mika. Please just say it." I screamed.

"It's all up to you, love."

I started to cry as I looked down into his passion-filled eyes. I was failing him.

Frustration overwhelmed me, and I dug my heels into the mattress and crawled away from his skilled tongue and decadent fingers. Wrapping my arms around my knees, I clutched my thighs together. Hiding my head beneath my arms, I sobbed in misery.

His strong, warm arms were around me in seconds.

"Shhh, baby. Don't cry. You can do this. I know you can. I wouldn't take you to the edge and just leave you there. Come back to me."

"I can't. I can't do it myself."

Cradling my face in his hands, he forced me to look at him. "Give it one more try. Let me take you to the edge, and if you can't go over without me, I'll give you the command. I promise. Shhhh, don't cry. This isn't supposed to be hurtful. I want this to be beautiful. I want you to feel the love I have in my heart for you, baby. Release your will, my sweet, and give yourself permission."

"I'm sorry Mika." I sniffed. "I'm not trying to fail you. It's just that I haven't released without permission for years. I've forgotten how."

"You've never failed me, love, and I doubt you ever will. Be patient. Let me reteach you, baby." Mika wiped the tears from my eyes, and with my essence coating his lips, pressed his mouth to mine.

Unfurling myself, clinging to his hard body, I melted against his broad chest. Wrapping my arms around his neck, I devoured his lips and tongue while his hard, thick shaft prodded against my tingling cleft. I was desperate to feel him driving deep into my aching core.

As if sensing my fervid level of need, urgency consumed him. His broad hands careened over my breasts and gripped my supple flesh while his thumbs and fingers pinched and tormented my taut nipples.

Sliding down my body, he spread my thighs wide and abraded my distended clit. Shudders of pleasure raced through my body as I rocked against his fingers. He stopped for a brief moment and sheathed his cock in latex then centered his enormous, delicious brim between my slippery folds.

"Oh God, Mika!" I cried as he eased the thick-crested tip inside my fluttering core. He stretched the sensitive skin as a delicious burn spread through me, filling me one glorious, agonizing inch at a time.

"Let me in, baby. You're so fucking tight. Relax around me. I'll be gentle," he coaxed, stilling to allow my narrow opening to accommodate his ample width.

Capturing my breast in his mouth, he sucked, nipped, and laved his tongue over my turgid nipple, tugging on the silver ring. Wrapping his hand in my riotous curls, he didn't yank or pull, but instead teased with a scarce, tormenting tug. It was enough. My walls relaxed and ceded, allowing more of his engorged shaft to squeeze through.

I moaned as my quivering muscles sucked his column deeper inside, stretching and dilating my fragile tissue with his cock. I cried out at the sublime painful pleasure.

"Fuck! You're so goddamn tight. So fucking hot. I want to stay buried inside you for days."

His hands gripped my hips, hoisting my ass from the bed, repositioning to drive deeper inside my clutching center. I wrapped my legs around his narrow waist, crossing my ankles behind his back as he inched his shaft in and out of my fluttering tunnel. With each thrust, his thick column burnished my clit as arcs of delight pulsated through every nerve ending in my body.

"I've dreamed of being inside you forever, but never in my wildest dreams did you feel this fucking good. I'm never letting you go. You can love me or hate me, but you're mine. Do you hear me? Mine. You've got such a hungry little cunt. Hot. Sinful. I can feel your muscles sucking my cock. It's just begging to be showered with my come, isn't it baby?"

His words were like fingers pulling me under a whirlpool of swirling, boiling lava. My limbs grew numb as the swell deep in my belly grew. As the fire rushed over me, a ribbon of sparks unfurled, then gathered, converging to consume me.

"Son of a bitch! I can feel your pussy fluttering around my dick. Open your eyes for me baby, let me drown in the reflection as you shatter."

Mika's growl yanked me back from the crumbling edge just long enough to lift my heavy lids. Shimmering amber pools reflecting demand and desire stared back at me as I watched the sweat trickle down his neck onto his rippling chest. He powerfully launched his shaft inside me. The crest of his cock hammered against the entrance of my womb. It was blissful heaven.

"I love you, Julianna," he whispered as I flew over the edge, fracturing into a million shards of bursting light. Screaming out his name, my pussy convulsed in violent spasms around his driving cock. I thrusted manically against him while savage seizures wracked my core, his gaze never leaving mine.

Hammering like a piston, he drove into my clutching center. The sounds of slapping flesh filled the room. His eyes narrowed as a loud, animalistic growl rose from his chest. His shaft swelled larger inside me, and as he exploded with a savage thrust, he cried out my name.

Lowering my hips to the bed, Mika draped his sweat-soaked body over mine. Burying his face in my neck, he held me as we both panted, desperate to fill our lungs with oxygen.

I licked and kissed his slick, salty shoulder, mewling like a sated kitten as his shaft remained twitching inside me.

Slowly our breathing began to settle. He raised up on his elbows, and I slung my arms over his wide shoulders. I smiled as he leaned in and playfully tugged my bottom lip between his teeth.

"I love you, Mika."

His cock jerked inside my pussy as a huge smile spread over his sensuous mouth. "I can die a happy man now."

"No," I scolded as my eyes grew wide. "You've already tried that once. I'm greedy and needy, and I want you here with me forever."

"You've confessed your love to me, pet. You're never going to get rid of me now. And as I see it, I'm one lucky bastard."

"No. I'm the lucky one."

"You are the one, there's absolutely no doubt about that." He grinned.

We spent the rest of the day and clear into the wee hours of the next morning exploring one another. Mika induced so many orgasms I lost count. His mouth, fingers, and cock coaxed me with thunderous and intense demand. I couldn't help but oblige and shatter for him.

He filled my belly with his tart, sweet seed more than once, and I nearly came apart when he showered his hot, sticky treasure over my breasts and face. Seemingly fascinated with my tight puckered anus, his fingers and tongue unraveled me time and again. The sensation was so overwhelming that I nearly crawled out of my skin.

When I confessed that I'd never had anal sex, a mischievous sparkle flickered in his eyes.

"So when I claim you as mine, you'll not only be giving me your power but your anal virginity, too?"

The broad smile on his face was much too feral. I nodded, more than a bit fearful as to how my tiny opening could accommodate his massive cock. "Don't worry baby. I'll be gentle and won't hurt you."

After our third shower and yet another powerful orgasm beneath the thundering showerheads, Mika carried me to bed. Covering me with a soft, clean sheet, he climbed in next to me. Lying side by side, he wrapped his arms around me. With his hot cock nestled against the crack of my ass, he pulled me against his chest.

Boneless and exhausted, my body hummed. The man was beyond astonishing, and if everything I'd experienced was just a dream, I prayed never to wake.

But I did awaken with his warm, strong arms banded around me. I smiled as I listened to the rhythmic sound of his light snoring. Peeking up at his rugged, handsome face, that damn bottom lip was the first thing that captured my attention. Never was anything more erotic to me, except for his eyes, and of course every epic sensation his masterful body bestowed me. But it was his lip that had me enthralled. Even though he was sleeping, I couldn't resist a little swipe.

Holding back a giggle, I eased over his body and leaned in. With a light swipe, I licked my tongue over his full lip. He woke with a start and growled as I sucked it into my mouth. Suddenly I was gasping and quivering as his fingers cinched my hair, pulling me from his lips.

"Did you have permission to wake me, girl?" he asked in a deep, bellicose tone.

I swallowed in fear and shook my head no.

"No, you didn't. Did you think I would allow you free reign indefinitely?" He almost smiled as his brows arched, and he looked into my wide, startled eyes.

Again, I shook my head no.

"Good. I'm glad you won't be disappointed because the freedoms I so generously granted yesterday have come to a crashing halt."

He looked threatening and dangerous with anger etched on his face, but then a slight curl formed on the corner of his mouth as he forced my lips to his. The big ol' bear was just roaring. He wasn't pissed, just asserting that knee-knocking, panty-melting Dominance over me. His generous carte blanche had just been rescinded. *Thank God!*

He claimed my mouth with a totally different kiss from the day before. This one was forceful, demanding, possessive. As liquid rushed from my sore folds, my heart pounded in my ears. A part of me longed for one more day to enjoy him without restriction while another part longed to be under his firm thumb. The thought of being immersed in submission made me almost giddy, and I tried to imagine what the day would bring.

"We will play in the dungeon today, pet." A wicked smile played on his lips as he gave a firm tug on my hair. I whimpered my acknowledgement. "You have no idea how much I've been looking forward to it. It's almost as much as I looked forward to making love to you."

Tossing back the sheets with one hand, his other wrapped in my hair, he guided my head down to his turgid erection. The veins on his column throbbed and a clear pearl of come adorned the dark, bulbous crest. I licked my lips and flashed a pleading look into his eyes.

"Hungry, pet?"

"Oh, yes Sir."

"You may." He nodded and allowed my head to descend upon his beautiful engorged shaft. I moaned as my lips slid over the broad crown and my taste buds exploded with his now familiar tart, salty taste. Engulfing his velvet-steel shaft, I rolled his tightly drawn sac between my fingers, massaging the rippled skin separating each sphere.

He sucked in a long hiss that filled me with pride. Satisfaction at bringing him such pleasure sent my heart soaring. Voracious and needy, I launched my mouth up and down his shaft and swirled my tongue along the sensitive ridge as he growled low and deep.

"Are you trying to force my scalding seed down your throat, pet?" he hissed between clenched teeth.

"Uh-huh," I moaned, still devouring his shaft in a gluttonous hunger.

A muffled cry tore from my throat as he fisted my curls. Instantaneously another torrid rush of cream flowed over my swollen folds. My nipples throbbed with the synchronized rhythm of my pulsating clit.

"You enjoy topping from the bottom, don't you pet?"

With my mouth stuffed full of his cock, I shook my head no.

"Touch yourself. Rub your clit. Rub it hard!" Growling his demand, he yanked my hair.

Whimpering as a wave of raw lust crested through me, I slid my hand to my cleft. Skimming my nimble fingers over the distended bud, I groaned and rose to my knees. His thick, hard cock slid further down my throat as another ragged groan vibrated over his embedded shaft.

Yanking on my hair, he pulled me from his cock with an audible pop. "Enough!" he barked, wrapping a burly arm around my waist as he flipped me onto my back. "Keep fingering yourself, my sweet. I want to watch."

Without instruction, I spread my legs wide for his viewing pleasure. Arching my hips upward, my fingers busily burnished my clit. A lurid, predatory gleam illuminated his eyes as he inspected my sex. I bated my swollen nub back and forth, taking myself higher and higher.

"Don't come, girl," he warned. "You don't have permission. You don't have the freedoms you had yesterday."

Swallowing a groan, I watched him lean in between my splayed thighs. I could feel his warm breath rasping over my skin. The intensity of his gaze drove me to the ragged fringes of release, and when he reached out and caressed my slickened labia, I jerked and cried out in delight.

"Who do you belong to?" he whispered as he swiped a finger along my outer lips.

A strangled moan ripped from my throat. "You!" I gasped.

"You what?"

"You, Sir!"

"You what, girl?"

"You, Mika."

"Let's try this again, my sweet." Taunting me with his words, he teased me with his fingers, sliding two deep inside my dripping tunnel. "What are you?"

"Ahh, I am a submissive," I panted, squeezing my walls tight around his imbedded finger.

"What are you?" he asked, arching his brows high and driving another finger into my quivering chasm. He stretched my sore channel, strumming his digits, spiraling me higher by the second.

"I am your submissive, Sir," I mewled as I milked his fingers.

"No." Shaking his head, he dragged his hand from my quaking

channel.

"No? Yes, I am," I cried in confusion as I thrust my hips toward his hand.

He leaned over my needy body and whispered in my ear. "You're my slave, precious."

As soon as the words were out of his mouth, I froze in terror. My fingers stilled against my throbbing pearl as my heart hammered in my chest. The term "slave" made my brain revolt in absolute panic.

"No. No. No," I gasped in panic-laced whispers and shook my head. Mika's brows furrowed as he rocked back on his knees. Confusion mixed with concern reflected in his eyes.

"Stop." He gently pulled my hand from my mound and threaded his fingers in mine. "Sit up, pet."

Trembling in fear, I scooted up and sat in the middle of the bed. "Everything stops right now. We need to talk." His words were calm and soothing, but I could still see the worry in his eyes.

"I'm sorry," I whispered, drawing up my knees and lowering my head.

"There's nothing to be sorry for. You've done nothing wrong, my love." His broad hand soothed my back as he edged closer. "We need to talk about this. I've obviously pushed a button you're uncomfortable with. We need to work this out."

He lifted my chin with his fingers, forcing me to look at him.

"What does the term 'slave' mean to you?" he asked.

I wanted to look away from his compassion, hide from the understanding and patience resonating in his voice. I wanted to run away from my damn stupid insecurities.

"It's just a term." I sighed, angry with myself for allowing a word to wrap me in a brutal stranglehold of fear.

"But?" he pressed patiently.

"But to me, slave means I lose everything. I lose myself. I don't have a say in anything that happens to me anymore. I can't be in control of me if I need to. And it terrifies the living crap out of me. I gave up everything once before, and I vowed never to do that again." I closed my eyes to hide my shame.

"When you first began to learn about the lifestyle, yes, I know." Shock that he knew about my past must have reflected in my eyes as

178

they flew open wide. "Drake and I have no secrets, love. I know about Nelson."

I wanted to find a hole that would swallow me up. I jerked my chin from his fingers at the sound of Nelson's name. I wanted a safe place to hide from my humiliation. Mika knew what a fool I'd been, knew how stupid I was in giving all my power to a wannabe Dominant. It had been years ago, but the damage Nelson inflicted on my psyche felt like it was only yesterday.

"Drake's disclosure was not meant as a breach of confidence toward you. I needed, no I demanded, to know everything about you. So I know your first Master, Nelson, was a miserable excuse for a Dominant. He was uneducated and inept. My love, he wasn't ever a real Dominant. That is not your fault. I know he hurt you physically and emotionally. The stupid bastard nearly turned you away from the lifestyle entirely. Baby, I can't take your negative experience away. As much as I'd like to, sweetheart, I can't."

"I know that. It was a long time ago, and I've healed from it," I lied.

"No, I don't think you have. I think you still carry a negative opinion of Master/slave relationships."

"I do not. There are lots of Master/slave couples at the club who I admire and love," I huffed, refuting his allegation.

"Do you trust me yet?"

"Yes. I trust you."

"You shouldn't, you know."

Even though his eyes were warm and loving, his edgy comment made my blood turn cold. Fear permeated my core as a shudder of panic raced through my body. Even knowing it was a knee-jerk reaction, I still wanted to grab my clothes and race from the room. Instead, I defiantly raised my chin and stared into his eyes.

"Why not?" I brazenly asked.

"Because you don't know me yet. You don't know personal things about me. You know them peripherally, but not first hand. I'm not a Dominant, Julianna."

I blinked in confusion. He was lying to me, lying straight to my face. "Bullshit."

"It's not bullshit, love. I'm a Master. I don't require a submissive. I require a slave."

179

Slave.

My heart hammered in my chest as my throat constricted. Even the walls of the room seemed to close in on me.

"And I can see by the fear in your eyes that term terrifies you."

I didn't answer him, well aware he knew my sentiment and the reason for it. I was struggling with swarming feelings of betrayal. I'd been betrayed by Drake for divulging my secrets, even to Mika. Sammie knew about my past because I had been the one to tell her. But Drake telling Mika? It was a bitter pill to swallow. Drake had betrayed my vulnerabilities, ones I'd never wanted exposed to Mika.

"We're not going to play in the dungeon today."

I opened my mouth to speak, but Mika raised his brows and held up his hand, shutting off my words before they could leave my lips.

"Not because I'm unhappy with you, but because the newness of our relationship isn't solidified yet. I'm pushing you. I don't want to do that, well, not in this way. I want to train you, guide you, show you that being a slave doesn't include stripping your identity."

I felt as if I'd failed him. I wanted to believe him, believe that he could get me past my fears. But why would he? There was no doubt in my mind that he was already second guessing why he'd chosen to be in a relationship with me in the first place, especially now. The poor man had a certifiable basket case on his hands. A woman so fucked up that she'd allowed a complete douchebag to manipulate her to the point that she'd lost her identity. She couldn't stand up for herself and had let the prick abuse her over and over again.

Of course, he was pushing, that's what Dominants do. They push the limits of their submissive. I wasn't a slave! Dammit. I was a submissive. I'd never be a slave. That alone would be a deal breaker for him, I was sure. Why would he invest his time and energy in me if I could never be what he needed? This was never going to work. It couldn't, no matter how he tried to candy coat it.

"Make no mistake, I'm here for the duration, girl, however long it takes for you to be comfortable with everything I ask of you."

Shit! Why did he have to read me like an open book? Was I that transparent?

"You may not believe me, but I'm proud of you, proud of how far you've grown since your first days at the club. I want you to listen to me, really listen."

Rising from the bed, he plucked a cotton robe from the closet
and held it open for me. Standing, I slid my arms through the sleeves
as he wrapped his arms around me.

"Love has no pride. Love is open, honest, and given freely
without bonds or secrets or inhibitions. I love you. You have all of
me. The good, the bad, and the sometimes ugly parts of me. I'm not
a God. I'm human. I guarantee I will make mistakes, but never
intentionally. Neither of us are prefect. When I claim you, I claim all
of you, not just the parts of you that you want to dole out. I won't
allow there to be a wall between us in any sense of the meaning."

Without uttering a word, I listened, absorbing the depth of his
words.

"This is all moving much too quickly for you. I'm painfully
aware of that. I'm asking for something that terrifies you, something
you'll want to fight me for. I'm asking you to be vulnerable. Not just
sexually. You've already opened yourself up to me without
reservation. It's been a stunning, mind-altering gift that you give.
What I'm asking for now is far more precious to you than your
sexual delights. I'm asking you to give me your defenseless and
fragile heart."

I lowered my head and rubbed my fingers over my forehead. I
thought about my dream and the brick wall. In a way, he was asking
me to knock the damn thing down again, but with a different
meaning. He wanted me to decimate the walls around my heart. The
cast iron walls I'd erected with far more fortification. The ones I
swore no man would ever breech again. Tipping my head back with
his fingers, he looked into my eyes.

"I want you to do something for me. It's not painful, I promise.
It may be a bit awkward, but I'll be here to help you through it."

He smiled and turned me to face him, tying the sash in a knot at
my waist. "For the next two weeks, I want you to refer to me as
Master. Can you do that for me, love?"

"I think so," I whispered, feeling small and vulnerable.

"Good. Let's go make some breakfast."

"Now?" I asked, bewildered that we weren't going to finish
what we'd started.

"Now, who?"

"Now, Master?" I whispered tentatively.

"Yes, now, girl. We'll have time to resume where we left off later." A smirk curled on his lips. "Come. I'll cook for you."

"You already make me cook like a Master chef!" I grinned.

He placed a firm kiss on my lips then pulled on a pair of well-worn jeans. As we made our way to the opulent kitchen, I wondered how I was going to manage to eat. Mika sans a shirt was a decadent, delicious sight to behold. Breakfast was sure to challenge my libido.

CHAPTER FIFTEEN

The Master/slave topic was put to rest as we danced around each other, cooking in the kitchen. More times than I could count, I caught myself watching Mika's muscles bunch as he flipped the bacon.

My body hummed in need. Glowing embers smoldered just below the surface, threatening to erupt into a raging inferno. I found myself focusing on tamping down my lust, over and again.

Of course Mika was no help, whatsoever. As I whisked the eggs, he took full advantage of my giggling breasts by slipping his broad hands beneath my robe, teasing and plucking my aching nipples while his teeth nipped the column of my neck. He found it quite humorous that I whimpered as he ignited every nerve ending, ratcheting my desire to an almost decimating level and then walking away.

The evil man.

The pungent scent of my arousal was thick in the air, and it brought a smile to my lips knowing the tempting and teasing was taking its toll on Mika as well. Standing by the stove, I suddenly felt the heat of his hard shaft pressed up against my ass. Purring low, I arched, pushing my ass back to meet him. Rolling my hips, I ground my buns against his turgid erection. My purrs turned into needful moans as his warm hands caressed my breasts. Thick, hot honey slipped from my empty pussy as I bent over the sink in offering.

Mika hissed and smacked my ass, then led me to the table. He pulled out a chair, instructing me to sit while he dished up breakfast. It was more than obvious we both needed a few minutes to calm the scalding hunger boiling within.

It was nearly impossible to eat seated across from Mika's half-dressed savage hot body. Gazing at me, his eyelids were heavy with promise. My appetite for food waned but my appetite for him continued to grow voracious.

"You're doing exceptionally well addressing me as Master, pet.

You make me proud."

My heart soared, and his praise warmed my soul. "Thank you, Master."

At first, it felt awkward addressing him as Master, but by the end of the meal, the term rolled off my tongue as if I'd employed the honorific my whole life.

While we cleaned up the dishes, Mika eased up behind me, pinning me to the counter. His warm breath wafted over my neck. Pressing against me, his irresistible erection snuggled between the cheeks of my ass and his devilish lips nuzzled my throat. Peeling the robe from my shoulders, his mouth and tongue trailed fervent kisses over every inch of flesh revealed.

"It's time to finish what we started earlier, pet. I need to feel your sweet, hot pussy gripping this." His steely erection cried in demand as his smooth, silky voice lulled me with promise.

"Yes. Please, Master." I gasped as I turned, gliding my tongue across his luscious caramel-colored chest. The smoldering embers flared, engulfing me in a wild firestorm.

Mika's hand slid to the small of my back and the other upon the nape of my neck as his mouth devoured mine. Our tongues dueled as he lifted me from the floor. Wrapping my arms and legs around his rippling hard body, he carried me to the kitchen table. Easing me onto the long wooden surface, he opened my robe as his eyes sparkled and danced over my ivory flesh.

"All through breakfast I've thought about laying you out like this and feasting on your lush body. I'll be damned if I'll wait another second." Trailing one finger from between my breasts down to my pubic bone, a predatory grin spread across his lips. "Raise your hands above your head and don't move, precious."

Trembling with excitement, I did as he instructed. Walking to the end of the table, he began wrapping my wrists to the sturdy legs of the table with soft cotton dish towels. Once satisfied that my arms were secured, he moved between my legs. Grasping beneath my knees, he pulled my ass to the table's edge. My arms stretched tightly against the binding, and I shivered knowing I was at his mercy.

He seated himself on a chair between my open legs, reminding me of my yearly gynecological exam, and I almost giggled. I'd never been turned on for that little adventure. Lifting my legs, he draped them over his broad, sculpted shoulders. Blowing a stream of air over my simmering flesh, his cool breath teased my wet folds.

"Breakfast was good, but this is going to taste so much better." The hungry growl had barely left his lips when his tongue took a long languid slide up my center. I jerked and moaned, arching my hips higher, desperate for more of his wicked tongue.

White lights of raw pleasure flashed behind my eyes as he ravenously assaulted my pussy. His lips surrounded my labia, and his teeth scraped over my clit. Helpless and soaring, I abandoned all my control over to him.

"I could stay here all day, feasting on your sweet, hot cunt. You're addicting, pet, and spread out like this, like my own private buffet, you look simply fuckable." He drove his tongue deep inside my quivering core.

My cries of delight echoed through the room as I bucked and writhed beneath his gifted mouth. Shafting two fingers deep inside, he concentrated on that sensitive bundle of nerves deep within, and in no time had me poised on the cusp of release. Primed by his previous enticements in the bedroom, I hovered dangerously close to losing control of my orgasm.

"Please," I gasped as a tingle of warning slithered up my limbs. "Oh God, Mika. I can't hold this back. It's too much. Please!" I screamed.

"Who are you?" His goading words vibrated over my clit, sending a shock wave rippling down my spine, melding with the electricity already surging through my veins.

"I'm yours," I cried in a voice full of panic.

"Tell me, Julianna. I want to hear it from your lips."

Panting and grinding my cunt on his face, desperate to hear him roar the magic word "come," I would have confessed to being Santa Clause, the Easter Bunny, and the Tooth Fairy all combined.

"Yours." I whimpered.

"My what?"

"Your slave."

His mouth left my throbbing, screaming cunt, but his submerged fingers still worked their devilish magic inside my clenching tunnel. He stood and leaned over me, his eyes locked onto mine.

"Yes, you are precious. Indeed you are my slave. I know you want to come so desperately, don't you my sweet, wet, succulent slave?"

"Yes, Sir," I whined in a loud, pitiful wail.

"I'm not your Sir, girl. I'm your Master. Your salvation. I'm the one who will make all your naughty dreams come true. The one who will keep you safe. Treasure you. Push you to the brink of all you can endure and savor every frantic cry. Every tear. Every precious gift you shower upon me. And by God, I'll give them back to you tenfold."

I didn't doubt his vow for one second. Surging with anticipation of every promise he made, every limit he would push, my heart filled with joy. His fingers stretched my tender tissue as he twisted them deeper, burnishing my G-spot. His other digits honed in on my pulsating clit, feathering and taunting my screaming bud.

He narrowed his lust-filled eyes and stared down at me. "Who am I?" he growled as he pinched my clit between his fingers, rubbing with just the right amount of pressure.

"My Master!" I shrieked as my hips arched off the table, grinding upon his able hands.

"Yes. Come for your Master. Come hard for me, slave," he bellowed as he slid another finger deep inside me, stretching my already clenching tunnel.

As I sailed over the crest, my screams of deliverance filled the room. Wave after wave crashed through me, and then suddenly I felt Mika's massive, thick cock thrust inside me.

"You. Are. Mine," he grunted with each powerful lunge of his cock. "You. Belong. To. Me. I am your Master. You are my slave. My treasure. My love. My. Whole. Fucking. Life."

As he emphasized his declaration with unyielding, feral thrusts, tears streamed from my eyes. His affirmation ripped my heart, mind, body, and soul apart. He was claiming me, confirming ownership of every fiber of my being. Never again would I have to dream about finding my "one." He had finally found me.

Wrapping my legs around his waist, I arched my hips, meeting each brutal stab of his cock. Grunting and panting, I looked into his turbulent, lust-glazed eyes.

"I love you, Master. I love you," I cried out uninhibitedly.

Mika's amber pools darkened and narrowed. His jaw ticked as his massive hands savagely gripped my hips.

"Say it again, Julianna. Tell me. Again," he roared as a wild, untamed expression converged across his face.

"I love you, Master. I love you. I am *your* slave, forever," I sobbed.

Lowering his body over mine, surrounding me in his fiery heat, he buried his face in my neck as he furiously pounded into me.

"I'm yours now, too, my love," he grunted against my neck. He released inside me, unleashing a feral, thunderous growl that resonated in my ears. His hot seed erupted, splattering against my quivering walls.

Marking me not only as a woman, but as his slave.

Slave.

I waited for the panic of that word to course through me, but oddly enough the dark, terrifying sensation never blossomed. As we both gasped in completion, my mind reeled. How had he wiped away years of fear in such a short time? Why wasn't my blood turning to ice at the realization that I was, once again, a slave? A tiny voice inside my head answered the perplexing questions. *Because it's different this time, just like he said it would be.*

Clutching Mika's sweat-slickened shoulders, I knew the magic of his Dominance and fulfillment of my submission lay within him. I would find my serenity through him. And by his command, I would finally be free.

Mika's heated body rested upon me, and his ragged breathing matched mine as we slowly ebbed from our euphoric release.

While I should have felt wonderfully sated, boneless and blank, I couldn't turn off my brain. I wondered how I could be a slave and with absolute surety maintain a sense of self, like he'd promised. How? How would he do that? How could I retain my independence while handing all of my power unto his care? But, he was already doing it. He'd taken one of my darkest fears away, replaced it with a feeling of absolute serenity, and I was helpless to stop him. I didn't want to stop him. I *wanted* to give him everything.

Suddenly a dark foreboding sensation began to bloom.

Adrenaline teeming with anxiety and doubt pumped through my veins.

"Mika," I whimpered fearfully as I began jerking frantically against my restraints.

"What's wrong?" Mika pulled back in alarm, searching my eyes. I knew he was startled by my sudden change of demeanor.

There were too many emotions zinging through me to pinpoint just one. A new depth of my submission had been brought to life. It was overwhelming and exciting and beyond frightening.

"Julianna? Talk to me, love." His brows knitted together in concern.

"I...I'm scared," I confessed, sounding too much like a frightened child.

"I'm sorry baby. I lost my head. You're on the pill, right?" He slid from my tunnel and quickly released my wrists. Pulling me to his chest, he wrapped me in his strong arms, and I clung to him as if he were a buoy in a churning, rolling sea.

"No, I'm not. That's not it. I don't care about the condom." My words stumbled as I clung in fear against his slick chest. "I mean I do, but that's not it. I'm..."

"You felt the depth of the exchange, didn't you?" He tenderly brushed a strand of hair from my cheek to behind my ear.

"Yes." A tear slipped from my eye.

"Shhh. It's okay. Please don't be afraid. It won't be like before. I swear on my mother's life it will be nothing like before. He wasn't a Dominant, baby. This time it will be everything you need, I promise."

Like before. I hadn't been thinking about Nelson, but Mika's words brought the memories rushing back, an icy blast of fear. My blood ran cold, and my body tensed.

He was right. Nelson had been a miserable excuse for a Master. He'd possessed just enough knowledge to be dangerous. He enticed unsuspecting newbies, like me at the time, to believe he was an experienced Dominant, a lie he manipulated to suit his own desires. He didn't know whit about the lifestyle or the true meaning of being a Dominant.

Nelson wasn't at all concerned about the mental, emotional, or physical well-being of his slave. He was only interested in fulfilling his greedy, self-centered, and horrifically sadistic desires all under the guise of being an "Old School Master." Nelson was slimy, calculating, and manipulative. He exercised his influence in heinously dangerous and damaging ways.

At his insistence, I had moved in with him, sold all my possessions, and quit my job. He wanted a "total power exchange" and wove dreams of our future into a tapestry of glorious perfection. It was far too enticing to refuse.

My being solely dependent upon him was the only way, in his eyes, that I could prove I was serious about my submission. What a crock of shit! I found out later what a horrible, soul-shattering mistake I'd made.

At first, life with Nelson was nearly a storybook existence. He didn't want sex—wasn't interested at all in making love to me—and while I thought that was strange, he'd brainwashed me by claiming that giving him my power was more potent than giving him my body. And that he could "fuck any hole out there, but he wasn't that callous." No, he was far more evil than callous.

I took care of him every way possible, and he doled out praise, delicious heartwarming praise. But the fairy tale soon grew into a nightmare from hell, a horror story void of any opportunity for a happy ending.

Soon my tasks were never good enough. I would try harder, but it never mattered. He continued to be critical and scornful. Then the reprimands began. Verbal at first, they quickly escalated into corporal punishment and numerous rapes. For a man who claimed to have no interest in sex, he certainly had no compunction when it came to forcing himself on me. Control, not Dominance, drove his ego.

I was allotted forty-five minutes for grocery shopping and seventeen minutes to drop off or retrieve his suits from the cleaners. If I was late because of heavy traffic, having to wait in long lines, or any other reason I was powerless to control, I was beaten. The memories enveloped me in a black, oily slime. I couldn't breathe. The room was suddenly spinning and sweat dripped from my temple.

"Julianna. Julianna!" Mika's voice splintered my wretched memories.

I blinked and looked into his concerned eyes, trying to reel my mind back to the present.

"Where did you go just now?" he asked, stroking his fingers along my cheek.

"The past."

Mika nodded in solemn understanding. "He still lives here. Nelson's attempted to join the club numerous times."

A gasp of terror escaped my throat as I tried to pull away. Mika wouldn't let go. He only clutched me tighter.

"Don't worry. He's not getting inside Genesis. He's been consistently rejected and always will be. He'll never gain access to become a member. He's a player, Julianna. An imposter. I've known about him long before I knew you. You're not the first woman, and sadly probably not the last, that's succumbed to his charade."

My mind spun in a riot of concern for the other women he'd abused.

"You got away from him and rebuilt your life. You're a strong woman, and I'm proud you had that courage inside you. There's another submissive at the club that unfortunately was tangled up with him. And sadly she knows of other women he has preyed upon." He paused and sighed heavily. "The night Dennis abused you, you told Moses that there were monsters using our community to fulfill their own distorted view of what we really are. You couldn't be more right, sweetheart."

"How did you know I told him that?" I pulled back slightly and looked into his concerned face, surprised he knew what I'd said to Drake. We were alone in Mika's office. He wasn't even there. He was back in Drake's private room dealing with Dennis.

"Headset. My office was wired to my headset. I knew the minute Moses had you safely stowed away." A roguish smile curled on his erotic lips. "Once you were locked up tight, I dealt with Dennis on my own terms."

"Well unfortunately for you, but fortunately for the rest of us, you ended up dealing with him in an ultimately decisive way."

Mika rolled his good shoulder in a shrug. "Yes. And I would gladly put a bullet through Nelson's head if it would wipe the ghost of his abuse from your memory."

"No you won't," I argued indignantly, jerking from his chest. "First of all, he's not worth it, and second of all, I want no more blood on your hands because of *my* nightmares."

"So," he stated as he slowly slid his fingertips over my nipples, "the panic that grabbed you wasn't because you were thinking about Nelson?"

He pulled away from me and picked up one of the dish towels used to tie my wrists, gently wiping our combined fluids from between my thighs.

"Something had you spooked to lead you down the path of your past. Tell me what it was, Julianna. What made you go there?"

I gently pulled the towel from his fingers, thinking how cute he looked with his jeans still bunched at his knees and smiled.

"You look like you were in an awful big rush, Master. You didn't even take your jeans off," I teased as I gently cleansed his glistening shaft, paying special attention to the glossy juices still clinging atop his tight black curls.

"You're stalling pet. Tell me what you felt. What made you suddenly turn to ice beneath me?" He slid his fingers around my wrist and removed the towel from my hand.

Stalling? Hell yes I was stalling. How in the world was I going to put into words the feelings that ripped through my soul as he claimed me with such command? Dammit, he probably already knew. Of course he knew. This wasn't unchartered territory for him, just me. I'd never been "claimed" by Nelson, not in the way Mika claimed me. Good God! Could it get any more convoluted? I sighed heavily and lowered my head.

"No. Look at me, love." Mika lifted my chin, grazing his knuckles over my lips. "Put your emotions into words and tell me what you felt."

"You marked me...inside," I said shyly.

"Indeed I did." He chuckled with a sublime, satisfied smile. "I plan on doing it over and over again, too. As soon as we get you on the pill."

Suddenly I saw that mischievous twinkle in his shimmering butterscotch eyes, the same glimmer he wore in my dreams. I shivered with déjà vu.

"When you told me to come for my Master, it was heavenly. It felt right. Well, it felt better than right." I felt my face burn in embarrassment. "It felt fantastic. Then when you started driving into me, your words were like a hot iron branding me, marking me, claiming me."

"Yes, pet. That's exactly what I was doing, and I'm glad you understand." His smile was filled with warmth, and his words of praise were slathered in pride.

"And when you came, I felt like your slave. It was exhilarating, and it was so...I'm having a hard time putting all this into words. I...I felt complete."

"But..." he prodded.

"But then I started worrying about losing myself, wondering how you're so damn certain that I won't lose myself again. How can you be so sure? I have no idea how I'm going to keep that from happening. Then you mentioned Nelson, and that's when I got scared. I'm sorry. I know that's not fair to do to you."

"No apologies for that, love. It's human nature to expect what you've experienced. Our past dictates our present. The only thing I ask is for you to keep an open mind. Let me show you that the role of a slave isn't like what you've experienced before. Nothing remotely close. I guarantee it's not the preconceived notion you carry in your mind. Try and keep an open mind for me, will you?"

I nodded and nibbled on my bottom lip.

"Do you want to keep working?" His question seemed to come out of left field, and I gave him a puzzled look. "I know you shuffled your clients to another accountant when I got shot. Moses told me that you cleared your work schedule indefinitely."

"Yes, I did. I haven't taken back any of my clients yet."

"Do you want to take them back?"

"Yes. Of course."

"Fine. You want to continue working. I have no problem with that. But I want you to understand that I'm financially secure, and if you don't want to work, you don't have to. But, if you need that lifeline to feel secure with us, then I'm more than willing to allow that. For you."

I nodded as I issued a weak smile. It really was sweet of him to be so worried about my peace of mind. Foreign, actually. I was taken aback that he would do whatever necessary to ensure my emotional level of comfort remain secure.

"The title of slave doesn't mean you are without options. It means we, me as your Master and you as my slave, discuss and communicate all aspects of your life. Rest assured I will determine what's best for you." He wrapped his thick hand around my wrist. "Now, before you go running out of the room screaming in fear at my statement, let me explain so there's no miscommunication."

Fear clutched my heart until Mika winked and grinned. I was struck with the realization that I would be a fool if I allowed my fears from the past to tarnish the Master/slave relationship he and I were now forging. There was no real reason for me to be scared, not with Mika caring for me.

"I am responsible for your emotional well-being. I would never take away anything that defines who you are in your heart, mind, and soul. However, if you take on more clients than you can handle, it's my responsibility to demand that you cut back. I won't allow you to stress yourself out or become sick. I'm responsible for your physical well-being, too."

"I understand."

"Your mental welfare is also my job. I would never expose you to any type of mental abuse. Ever. It's beyond the realm of a consensual relationship. Master/slave is a power exchange. You know that. And while a total power exchange is synonymous with Master/slave relationships, I would never tell you how to feel or how to think. You are still in command of the you inside, girl. However, it is paramount that you share with me all that goes on in that gorgeous head of yours. I won't allow you to leave me out in the cold in regard to your emotions. I am the one who decides what is best for you. And that is what I think sends you to the dark side, that someone other than you is making that determination. Am I right?"

Of course he was right. The idea of him taking control over my every decision, taking over my life, really did make me want to run from the kitchen screaming in fear.

"Yes. You hit the nail on the head."

"Remember this above all else, you hold all the power. Submissives, slaves, whatever label you want to put on bottoms, hold all the power. Without giving that power over, we Dominants, Masters, Tops, would have no one to control."

I nodded as the dynamics of the lifestyle took on a whole new meaning.

"I'm not Superman. While I'd like to think I'll always know

what's best for you, in reality, that's simply impossible. Even we Masters have our limits, occasionally." He flashed a teasing wink. "What I'm trying to say, is that I won't allow you to lose yourself. I won't take that liberty. That would be a huge waste of what makes you my perfect slave. I don't want you to change. I happen to love you just the way you are, my sassy, mouthy little wench."

My heart melted as he tenderly caressed my cheek.

"Above all else, we are individuals, and no matter how close we grow together, we will remain separate entities. My dream is that we will choose to mesh ourselves as one as best we can. I guarantee I'll want things my own way, but I will never disregard your feelings or your desires. I will always take them into consideration to determine what is best all around for you."

I blinked in disbelief, disbelief that his ideals of Master/slave were so similar to what I'd always envisioned them to be.

"So, do you think you can live with that, pet?"

"Yes, Master. I think I can. Wait, no." I nodded with confidence. "I know I can."

Mika's strong arms wrapped me tight against his chest. "Always tell me your fears. I'm here to ease them, to work through them with you. You can count on me, Julianna. And I promise that I'll strive damn hard to never let you down."

"I'll do my best never to let you down either, Master. Thank you." I laved my tongue across his bronze chest and felt his cock jerk back to life against my belly. Unable to resist a tease, I ground my crotch against him.

"Insatiable, much?"

"Only when you're around," I mumbled, latching onto that tantalizing lip of his, tugging and purring.

"Show me," he growled, palming his engorged erection.

CHAPTER SIXTEEN

Easing off the table, I sank to his feet, kneeling before him in proper submissive form. With a provocative gaze, I savored his majestic body. He allowed me to admire his ample cock, rippling abs, broad chest, and chiseled shoulders. Imploring him with my eyes, an urgent whimper of need escaped my throat.

"Yes, pet, all of it's for you. Take me into that sinfully hot mouth of yours. Make love to my cock. Worship me with your tongue, your lips. Worship me from your heart."

I'd never felt so free, so naturally uninhibited. His shaft was mine to adore, to bathe with my reverence, to lavish with unrestrained adoration.

This new level of submission was like a rebirth, a powerful awakening. I poured every ounce of that magnificent emotion into my lips, tongue, and fingers. My hands cupped and coveted his tightened shaft and slid like silk up and down the pulsating veins. Immersed in giving him pleasure, I was bathed in a golden warmth of serenity.

"Your mouth feels like molten silk."

His hands clenched my mane as I groaned in delight around his cock.

"Yes, like that. Keep sucking me just like that. Touch your clit. I want to feel you explode with me, feel you come with my cock in your throat. Take yourself to the edge, love. I'll tell you when to fly."

Sweet Jesus! The idea of coming apart with his shaft deep in my throat was enough to catapult me to the brink. Emitting desperate muffled whimpers of gratitude, my fingers snaked down past my stomach and began strumming my clit.

"Rub it hard for me, pet. Imagine my tongue batting that tight knot of nerves back and forth." He hissed as he adjusted his fingers in my hair. Gathering even more curls into his fist, he tugged persuasively. "Look at you. You look so goddamn beautiful.

Stunning. Your eyes are glazed in desire. Your lips are stretched so tight, stuffed full of my cock."

His coaxing words were a potent aphrodisiac, intensifying every sensation to a staggering level. I could feel each engorged vein rippling over my lips. My fingers dripped in my own sultry dew as I kneaded my slippery bud. I flicked the tip of my tongue along each contour of his cock and then sucked him deep and hard. Mika strengthened his claim on my hair, spiraling me up so fast, the fear of succumbing too quickly had me crying out to him in a muffled warning. I was close.

"Wait for permission, girl. Don't come," he growled. "Just a few more minutes bathed in your heavenly throat. Then I'll let you scream for me, pet. Christ, I love the way you look right now. So needy. Holding on by a thread. Your mouth is like a slick, sinful vise, and it's mine, Julianna. Your mouth, your cunt, your ass, your very soul belongs to me." His voice was like smooth scotch.

I was slipping, sliding over the edge. Panicked cries vibrated over his shaft as I lunged forward, taking him as far down my throat as I could. Robbing myself of oxygen, I swallowed upon his crest as tears spilled from my eyes.

"Fuck! Come my sweet slave. Now!" Mika cried as he released my hair and wrapped his hands around my throat, forcibly face fucking me upon his expanding shaft. His screams thundered and vibrated through my body as his hot seed blistered my throat.

Swallowing rapidly, I inhaled a deep breath and joined him, shattering as I sucked him in a ravenous frenzy. His sweet cream exploded again, leaking out the sides of my straining lips. I was sucking and coming, screaming and swallowing in a crazed fervor. My pussy contracted forcefully, and I continued to guzzle his slippery, scalding seed.

Whimpering as my own storm subsided, I eased the torrid suction of my mouth around his shaft. I fostered the last remnants of his come, lapping every last trickle from his twitching cock. My core spasmed in aftershocks as I cleansed him with my tongue.

Forcefully pulling me to my feet, I swore there were tears in Mika's eyes as he kissed me with an intense urgency. His arms held me in a desperate grip as he trailed his lips to my cheeks, over my jaw, and down my throat. Burying his face against my neck, his broad hand cradled my nape.

"I love you, Julianna."

"I love you too, Mika." Awestruck by the powerful sensations cascading through me, tears leaked from my eyes.

Lying in bed after numerous rounds of exhilarating and exhausting sex, Mika's fingers played with my curls as they spilled over his chest. My pussy was swollen and sore. It was obvious I'd not had sex in...forever. Thank goodness my jaws weren't sore.

"I'm so damn anxious to take you to the dungeon," he whispered.

Looking up at him, I smirked. "Impatient are we?"

"Where you're concerned? Always. You force me to struggle for patience, girl. I'm not sure I like that." A serious expression fell across his face as my heart clutched with fear, fear that I wasn't what he'd wanted after all. "I've been waiting for what feels like a lifetime. I need you to keep communicating with me. I don't want anything to spoil what we have together. I won't lose you, pet. I'm never going to let you go."

"I pray you never do." Trying to chase away my insecurities and block the scary thought of losing him someday, I snuggled tightly against his chest.

"Not happening," he promised, squeezing me against him.

After a long pause, Mika pulled me on top of his body and looked into my eyes. "I've been cooped up too long. Let's go out for dinner and then stop by the club. Besides, even though you've not said so, I know your pussy is sore. I'll beat your ass later for not telling me."

There was a wicked promise in his words.

"Why would I have to tell you? You already know." I bit my lips together, but couldn't hide the rueful smile tugging the corners of my mouth.

His hand landed soundly on my ass. "Communication, wench. Just because you think I might know...it's your job to make sure I know. Got it?"

"Yes, Sir. But you're not supposed to drive for another week," I reminded him, raising my brows.

"I'm not supposed to be having marathon sex sessions with you, but that hasn't stopped me now, has it?"

"Stubborn man. I swear!"

"I'm probably not supposed to take you over my knee and blister your ass, but I can do that too if you keep it up, pet," he warned with an evil grin.

"Look at the time. Where has the day gone? I think I'll just go hop in the shower now!" I giggled and jumped out of bed.

"You can run, but trust me girl, you can't hide." He laughed.

~*~

Seated at a romantic table in the far corner of Maurizio's, I picked at my veal, nervous and anxious about going to the club. I'd not been back since the night of the shooting. A million questions swirled through my brain. Was Mika planning on taking me up the back stairs to his private office, or was he going to reveal himself to the members? Were they still buzzing about the shooting? What kinds of questions would they ask me? What was I supposed to say about my absence? About the shooting? Only a select few from Mika's inner circle even knew we were together.

As the mixture of worry and fear fluttered in my stomach, I secretly wanted to go back to Mika's, curl up on the couch with him, and watch a movie. I'd be safe from scrutiny there and wouldn't feel as if I were under a microscope.

"Julianna, look at me." Mika voice was low but commanding. Jerking my head to meet his gaze, I could tell by his expression I'd done a pisspoor job of masking my worries. "What's bothering you?"

"It's nothing. I'm okay," I lied, determined not to spoil our first real date.

A staid expression lined his face as he slowly placed his fork on the table. "Totally unacceptable, my pet. Not now or any day forward, will you keep secrets or omissions from me. I won't tolerate it. Do you understand?" His voice was quiet but his words were clipped and terse.

"Yes, Si...Master," I mumbled.

Easing back in his chair, his shoulders tensed. Crossing his thick arms over his broad chest, he narrowed his eyes as his lips set in a tight line. Saying nothing, it was clear he was pissed and patiently waiting for me to speak. It unnerved me something fierce.

"You may begin."

I knew what he was doing, but dammit, I didn't want to confess that my insecurities were getting the best of me again. But like a dog with a bone, I knew he wasn't going to let me off the hook until I spilled my guts. "I'm worried about going to the club."

"Worried about what?"

"I don't know what to expect. How will we be accepted? Are you going to scene with me in public? Are we going to your office so you can keep your identity secret still?"

"So instead of asking me, you allowed all these questions to swirl in your head, thus shutting me out completely. Correct?"

Guilt drowned out my anxiety. I'd let him down. And damn it, this is why I didn't say anything. I didn't want to ruin our romantic dinner with my stupid fears. I nodded yes.

"So instead of being in the here and now with me, sharing this lovely dinner, you've trapped yourself inside your mind with fears and insecurities, never bothering to share them with me or allowing me to help you work through them. You've taken on the onus of trying to deal with them all yourself. Is that right, pet?"

Feeling like a chastised child, I exhaled, frowning and nodding.

"So tell me. What purpose has it served, besides excluding me from important worries concerning you?"

I lowered my head in shame. "They're not important worries. They're stupid."

"Look at me," he whispered in an urgent tone.

I raised my tear-filled eyes, and he blinked in surprise.

"Whoa, girl. I'm not mad. You're not in trouble," he reassured me. "I'm not upset with you in the least. I'm simply trying to make a point. Anything that worries you or makes you feel unsure is important to me. You're not alone anymore. You don't have to handle uncomfortable issues or situations by yourself. The point I'm trying to make is a very simple one. This is a perfect example of what I've been saying to you. I won't allow you to shut me out of anything concerning you. Do you understand?"

"Yes," I mumbled.

"Yes, what?"

"Yes, Master."

"Good. Now, you have questions. Ask me, precious." He smiled and leaned in, wrapping his warm, soothing hand in mine.

I exhaled a deep sigh of gratitude. Sharing every thought and worry was going to take some getting used to, but my heart soared once I realized he wasn't mad, that I hadn't failed him.

"What is it going to be like at the club tonight, Master? What if they ask me about Dennis?" I asked in a low, soft whisper.

"Very nice, girl. Okay, when we arrive at the club, we are going to enter through the front door. We're not going to skulk through the back. We're going to sign in like all the other members. We will find a couple of empty stools at the bar and visit with Sammie, Drake, Trevor, and whoever else wants to chat. As for the gossip mongers? We both know they're going to talk no matter what. I'm fairly certain once my identity is revealed there'll be more than enough fodder to keep the attention away from you and the shooting. It might very well keep them busy gossiping for weeks on end." He smiled and gave me a reassuring wink. "And if you find yourself too uncomfortable, you tell me. Immediately. I'll remove you from any awkwardness or prying questions that make you uneasy. We'll simply retire to my office upstairs."

A twinkle of security danced in his erotic eyes and in an instant, I felt a sense of relief. A strange confidence filled me.

"Thank you." I sighed gratefully.

"Baby steps, love. Baby steps." He smiled broadly.

~*~

When we walked into the club, all eyes turned toward the door. I felt like I was on display and eased back trying to shield myself behind Mika. A low buzz of murmurs filled the lobby. He gave my hand a reassuring squeeze then slid a protective arm around my waist.

Drake and Trevor stood at the familiar scarred podium. Trevor issued a squeal of delight that made me giggle. He began dramatically begging Drake for something, and while I couldn't hear what Trevor was saying, I surmised he was asking permission to leave his post and come to me.

My heart fell to my stomach when I saw Drake glare at him and give a stern shake of his head no. Trevor's eyes took on a pained expression, and Drake's jaw twitched as he flashed a harsh, almost searing silent reprimand. Trevor looked at me once again and then lowered his eyes.

I leaned in to Mika's warm, broad chest and whispered in his ear. "I think Drake's angry with me."

Bending his head to my ear, his hot breath caressed the shell. "No girl. He's simply keeping Trevor from making a spectacle of our arrival. Drake is not the least bit angry with you. Trust me." Gently nuzzling his cheek against mine, he dragged his tongue over my ear. "Relax beautiful. Everything is fine."

A shudder of need thundered through my veins. I wanted to tug Mika out the door and race back to his house, to beg him to put out the fire that just standing next to him conjured. I swallowed tightly, trying to reign in my lust, and raised my eyes to Drake. A slow little smile pulled at his lips, and he issued an almost imperceptible nod. Exhaling a deep breath, relief flooded me, and I nodded to him ever so slightly. My heart soared when a broad smile flashed over Drake's mouth.

"Told you so," Mika growled in my ear.

I wanted so badly to stick my tongue out at him and say "neener neener," but that would only serve to bring down a serious wrath on my ass, one he'd make sure I would *not* enjoy. Choosing the smartest avenue, I just smiled and bit my tongue.

"Emerald. It's so good to see you back. We've missed you." I turned to see Carnation standing with Master Stephen. A big curious smile adorned her face.

I looked up at Mika, seeking his permission to speak, and he smiled with pride and nodded. "I've missed you too, Carnation, and you as well, Master Stephen. It's wonderful to be back."

Stephen extended his hand, introducing himself to Mika. "Mika."

"It's a pleasure to meet you, Mika. I see you've been lucky enough to discover our little gem of Genesis." Stephen grinned, looking directly at me.

"Indeed I have." He beamed with visible pride.

I'm not sure how I kept from bursting out laughing. It was surreal that a member of the club was introducing himself to the owner without a clue in hell who he was talking to. I swallowed the laugh that bubbled in my throat. Mika once again squeezed my hand, only this time I knew it was in warning.

"Emerald is a pure delight, to be sure. Even though I've only enjoyed her submission for a short time, she's brought me more joy than I've experienced in years," Mika boasted, and I felt my cheeks burning as I lowered my eyes. The attention being drawn to me was unnerving.

"Is this your first visit to Genesis?" Stephen asked.

My body began to shake as I held in my laughter. Mika pinched my fingers together beneath his hand and I stiffened.

"No, Stephen. I own Genesis." Mika said with a respectful smile.

Oh, it wouldn't take long now. The entire club would know exactly who Mika was as soon as Carnation and Stephen breeched the thick velvet curtain. Carnation was a sweet girl, but hands down she was the hub of the wheel of every tale of gossip in the club. I was certain that half the members, no nix that, *all* of the members would know who Mika was in a matter of seconds.

"Well, it's truly an honor to meet you, and may I give a heartfelt thank you for supplying us kinksters such a spectacular venue," Stephen praised.

"I'm more than happy to provide an outlet we all can enjoy." He humbly nodded.

Carnation's eyes grew to the size of dinner plates at Mika's admission. She remained uncharacteristically silent as the men talked. I could almost see the wheels in her head spinning and smoking. Finally, she looked at me and mouthed "wow" then gave me a subtle thumbs-up sign. I smiled, winked, and gently nodded. I couldn't agree with her more. Mika blew the needle off the "wow chart," and I couldn't help that I beamed with pride.

As the two men talked about the club, the lifestyle, and other Domly topics, I was anxious for the line to move faster. I wanted Drake's reassurance and Trevor's sweet kisses, provided Drake and Mika would allow it, of course.

More members trickled in behind us, and Stephen took great pride in introducing Mika to practically everyone in the lobby. While many approached me and welcomed me back, their attention to Mika outweighed my return. It was a welcomed relief to my fears and precisely as he'd predicted.

After what seemed an eternity, which was more like five minutes, Mika and I were standing at the podium. The delight dancing in Trevor's eyes made me feel like I was home.

It wasn't as if I hadn't seen the two during Mika's recovery. Both Drake and Trevor came by almost every day. But being back at the club was like my sanctuary, and I was centered and filled with contentment.

"May I *now*, Daddy? Please? Please? May I?" Trevor whined like a child.

"After me, boy," Drake growled in a perturbed tone.

"Shit!" Trevor mumbled under his breath then slapped his hands over his mouth.

"Oh, slut, you try my patience to the nth degree!" Drake admonished Trevor with narrowed eyes.

"I'm sorry, Daddy. I didn't mean to curse. It just slipped out," Trevor apologized, stumbling all over himself in an attempt to make amends.

"I'll be filling your mouth with something later. Something so big you can't possibly swear, at least out loud." Drake gave him an evil smile.

"Lucky slut," I giggled, winking at Trevor.

Mika arched a brow and glanced at me from the corner of his eye. "The very same can be arranged for you too, girl."

"Oh, God. I hope so," I gushed in a breathless sigh.

Drake and Mika wrapped each other in a warm, brotherly hug. "Seems you and I managed to get the two most insolent slaves in the universe." Drake laughed as he gave Mika a sound pat on the back.

"Would we have it any other way?" A pride-filled chuckle rumbled deep in his chest.

"Not in this lifetime," Drake flashed a wolfish grin. "May I?" he asked Mika, nodding at me.

"You never need ask, my friend."

"Come here, girl," he demanded as he wrapped his big warm arms around me. "It's damn good to see you here, sweetheart. It's not been the same without you."

"I've missed you Moses," I whispered in his ear as a lump

formed in my throat.

The stark realization that I was no longer Drake's responsibility hit me like a truck. I would no longer be running to him with my worries, fears, or enlightenment, and it caught me completely off guard. Like an anvil, comprehension that I had to give up Drake's protection, give up my rock, slammed me hard.

Tears slid down my cheeks as Drake held me in a near death-grip against his chest.

"Are you happy Julianna?"

I choked on my response and managed to nod my head.

"He's waited a long time for you, girl. I know you can make him happy, and I know without a shadow of a doubt he can handle your smart mouth and sexy little ass. He's the one, the only one I know that can." There was a mixture of pride and sadness in his voice. "I release you from my care now, sweetheart. You've finally found the one that can provide you with everything I couldn't."

The floor dropped out from under me. I was falling down a black, empty chasm into a realm of unknown. Drake had always been my lifeline, my security blanket, and now he was gone. My gut tightened as my heart pounded and panic consumed me.

"No. No." I sobbed as I buried my face against his warm, soft leather vest, uncaring that Mika or any other members in the lobby witnessed my irrational behavior.

"Trevor. Continue, boy," Drake directed as he pulled me toward a quiet section of the lobby. Pressing my back to the wall, he pinned me into the corner, his broad chest concealing me from curious eyes.

"Look at me," he demanded in a loving but stern voice.

I shook my head as fear continued to drag me under.

"Damn it, Emerald, I said look at me," he whispered in an urgent tone.

I raised my eyes slowly, expecting to encounter his malevolent gray glare. I was even more unsettled when I saw a sympathetic and loving expression on his face.

"You know I can't continue to protect and guide you anymore, baby. That's Mika's job. Just as it's your job to honor and respect him as best you can. You didn't sit outside his office those nights for me. You did it for him and yourself. You didn't spend all that time at the hospital, never leaving his side, for me. You did it for him.

You've already handed over your power to him. There's not a shred of doubt in my mind, in yours, or in his. I see how you look at him with so much adoration, so much love. It's the way you're supposed to. He owns you now. And you're allowing him that honor. It's the beauty of this glorious exchange, sweetheart."

His reassuring words hit me hard. I'd not realized the depth in which I'd given myself to Mika showed outwardly.

"It's time for you to bestow everything I've taught you, everything you've learned from your family here, and grant all of it to Mika. Make him as proud of you as I've been of you all these years. I'm not walking out of your life." A soft chuckle rumbled in his massive chest. "You'll be seeing me more now than you ever did before."

Drake wiped my tears with the broad pads of his thumbs and kissed my cheek. "I'm still your friend, Julianna. And I always will be. Nothing will ever change that."

I inhaled a deep breath then nodded with determination. As Drake turned, I saw Mika standing directly behind him. His amber eyes held an expression of concerned understanding.

"Are you all right?" he asked, reaching for my hand. I nodded and sucked in a deep breath. "Change isn't easy, pet. Even when it's something you want with all your heart. It can still be a little scary. But I vow to make the journey spectacular, beyond your wildest dreams." That mischievous little twinkle danced in his eyes.

"I know you will, Master. Yes, I'm very much all right." I nodded with resolve.

"That's my girl," he praised. "Drake, we'll be at the bar. Will you and Trevor please join us when the doors are locked up?"

"Hell, yes. We'll be there shortly." Drake grinned, giving me a reassuring wink.

"Walk beside me tonight, pet," Mika instructed as he wrapped his arm around my waist and parted the heavy, velvet drapes.

CHAPTER SEVENTEEN

A hush fell over the room as we stepped into the dungeon. From the back of the room, someone began to applaud. Clapping spread like an ocean wave, growing louder and stronger. A smile spread across my lips as I looked at Mika, my heart swelling with pride.

"I think they're glad you're back, pet," he murmured in my ear.

Throwing my head back, I laughed. "None of this is for me, Master. This is *all* for you."

Mika raised his hand and gave a humble wave, smiling at the members as we tried to make our way toward the bar. It seemed to take forever. Nearly every step we tried to take, members approached and stopped us.

Most thanked Mika for allowing them such a wonderful place to fulfill their desires, and some who knew about the shooting inquired about his health. I was welcomed back with open arms, and not one hint or question was raised about my involvement with Dennis. Most of the attention, thankfully, was centered on Mika. Still, it was all a bit daunting.

Reined in tight against Mika's side, his strong arm was comfort in itself. There wasn't another Dominant on the planet I wanted to be next to.

By his side was where I belonged.

Sammie beamed like a ray of sunshine as we approached. She raced from behind the bar and threw her tiny body straight into Mika's arms, giggling like a schoolgirl. I couldn't help but laugh.

"It's so good to see you up and about, boss." She grinned.

"It's good to be back home." Mika laughed. "I've missed you, woman."

He lifted her petite body off the ground and kissed her cheek. She looked like a frail pixie in his strong, broad arms. Only I knew better. That little pixie could pack a punch and did so without compunction when she had to.

"How are you feeling?" Serious concern replaced her impish

grin as she placed her small hand against his cheek.

"Fantastic." Mika nodded. "Emerald's taking exceptionally good care of me."

"Of course she is." Sammie laughed and gave me a wink. "What can I get you, two?"

"Cranberry juice for me, and a cola for Emerald, please."

"Coming right up." Sammie nodded as she trotted on her high heels, resuming her duties behind the bar.

Mika sat on a barstool and pulled my back against his chest, wedging my hips between his thighs. With my butt resting on the edge of the stool, I felt the warmth of his crotch against my butt and his strong muscles grip my hips. I melted against his hard chest and looked out over the dungeon.

"I want you to watch, pet. I want you to look at your submissive brothers and sisters. Pay close attention to the way their Dominants care for them."

I nodded, scanning the room, taking in the sights and sounds of home. Lady Ivory was standing at one of the crosses attaching cuffs to her longtime slave, Dark Desires. His bronze-skinned body rippled as he ceded beneath her loving hands. I smiled as I watched their exchange.

The Domme's blood-red fingernails slithered over her boys flesh as he squirmed beneath the sensation. Reaching between his ass cheeks, she grabbed his dangling balls in the palm of her hand and squeezed without mercy. His shorn orbs protruded bulbously from her hand, taking on a purple hue as she compressed them in a tight grip.

Rising up on his tiptoes, Dark Desires tossed his head back and released a mighty roar. She gave a terse tug on his scrotal sac then released it before raking her glossy fingernails over his back as she whispered in his ear, soothing his pain.

"You like to watch, don't you pet?" Mika beguiled.

"Mmmmm, yes Master," I purred.

"It looks like Nick, Dylan, and Savannah are having a fun night."

Scanning the dungeon for the ménage couple, I spotted them in a dark corner. Savannah sat on a low padded bench with her arms secured high above her head. Her bare legs tangled with Nick, her

Master, whose jeans were shoved to a heap around his ankles. Dylan, her other Master, stood behind her plucking and pinching her swollen nipples as he whispered in her ear. Even in the dim light, it was obvious Savannah's mouth was busy worshiping Nick's cock. His hips rocked back and forth in deliberately long and slow strokes. I smiled broadly. Savannah was new to the lifestyle. She'd only been a member for about six months. Nick and Dylan had patiently trained her, and I was happy to see she was at last breaking free of her shyness. When she'd first come to Genesis, both Dom's sought me out to help her understand the dynamics of the lifestyle. Her appetite to learn and to please them was voracious.

Like many of us at first, she didn't understand the driving need to please inside her. She'd confided in me that within the first week of meeting the Dom's, she'd run away from them. Her feelings for each one combined with the new experiences they had exposed her to were too intense. She'd fallen head over heels in love with them both but was scared and confused by their domineering seduction. It didn't take long for her to realize that with their absence, a vital part was missing inside her. Like a romance novel, they eventually got back together, and with Nick and Dylan's patience and love, they continued to grow and satisfy their darkest cravings.

It was evident she loved and yearned to please them, but revealing her adoration intimately in public was testament to how much she'd grown in her submission. It warmed my heart that both Dom's, always cognizant of her modesty, had concealed Savannah in such a way. They were undoubtedly protecting her and reassuring her courage while enjoying her submissive surrender.

I sighed heavily and licked my lips, wishing I was perched on that low bench with Mika's thick, hard cock sliding in and out my mouth.

"Problem, pet?" Mika asked as I continued to watch Nick, Dylan, and Savannah.

"Hungry." I moaned.

"But we just had dinner."

"Not for food, Master."

"Well, I'll have to fill you up...everywhere," he growled as his lips and teeth teased my earlobe.

"Please!" I moaned in a desperate whimper.

Mika bunched his fingers in my curls and slowly drew my head back. Tiny, needful gasps escaped my lips as I closed my eyes and ground my ass against his sturdy erection.

"I love to hear you beg, my sweet insatiable slut." His deep voice purred in my ear as his tongue swiped a languid trail down my throat. Shivering, I tilted my head, trying to steal a kiss from his sinful lips. He shook his head and exerted a tiny tug on my hair, then guided my head back to observe the sessions being played out. "Watch, sweet girl. Watch and simmer for me."

Dahlia was suspended in the air, her limbs in chains. Master George's firm hands held her hips as his mouth devoured her pussy. The chains clanked and clattered as she bucked beneath his ministrations. I squirmed, watching and wishing Mika would slide his fingers beneath my skirt and stroke my aching, wet clit.

"Would you like to be suspended with my tongue buried deep inside your center?"

Drawing in a needful gasp, I nodded and squeezed Mika's strong thighs.

"You're wet, love. I can smell the spice of your sweet cunt and almost taste your flavor on my tongue."

"Mika," I lamented as I tried to turn toward him.

He placed his hands upon my head and forced me to continue watching. "It's Master to you, girl. Don't forget that."

Frustrated and edgy, I arched my butt against him, rumbling in a low growl. His guttural laugh at my lamenting made me ache for him all the more.

Observing the interactions had never affected me the way it now did. Before my focus was centered on finding my contentment, to a small extent, by watching as others fulfilled their needs. But now I wanted, no, I smoldered to receive every conceivable torture-filled pleasure I watched unfolding before my eyes. And I was certain Mika could conjure a few more interesting scenarios in his sadistic mind.

My nipples ached, my clit throbbed, and my folds were thoroughly saturated. No wonder he could smell me—I was flowing like a damn river.

I jerked my head in the direction of a snapping whip. Lady Ivory was arching the leather tail high into the air, flicking it with a delicate but demanding snap of the wrist. The repercussion cut through the air in a sizzling declaration of power. Dark Desire's buttocks were nicely reddened, and a shiver rippled down my spine as she snapped the popper over his crimson ass. Tiny red welts appeared with each swipe of the whip's tip. Moaning, I could almost feel every delicious bite. More nectar spilled from my folds, moistening the tops of my thighs. The image of Mika lashing me as I stood stretched upon the cross filled me with savage longing. I was so focused on the pair, I hadn't realized Nick, Dylan, and Savannah were standing next to us.

"Nick! Good to see you again, man." Mika's deep, jovial voice brought me back from the fringes of fantasy. "Dylan, how are you doing, brother?"

"I can't tell you how glad I am to see you up and about, dude." Nick smiled as Dylan nodded in agreement, and the men shook hands. "And Emerald, you look delicious as always."

"Doesn't she though?" Dylan piped in with a warm smile.

"Thank you Sirs." I smiled nervously then quickly looked at Savannah.

"May I, Sir's?" Savannah asked with a timid arch of her brow.

"You may ask Mika's permission, my love." Dylan nodded.

"May I please have permission to give Emerald a hug, Mika, Sir?" she asked in a shy voice.

"Of course, dear." Mika gently rolled his hips forward, grinding his hardness against me as if I needed any reminders that his incredible cock was hard, hot, and ready. It was all I could fantasize about. As I began to stand, he gripped my hips, holding me tightly to the barstool.

"You'll stay right where you are, girl," Mika whispered. "Savannah can reach you just fine."

Of course Mika didn't want me to move. My ass was shielding his wicked thick erection. I wanted to laugh, but smiled instead and opened my arms, accepting the warm tight hug Savannah offered. Her soft breasts pressed against my painful nipples. Her innocent caress was blessed heaven. She had no idea she was sending shards of delight down my spine and centering them on the blazing knot between my dripping folds. Grudgingly I released her, wishing I could focus on something other than my own gnawing hunger.

"I'm so glad you're back, sis. I can't begin to tell you how much I missed you," Savannah confessed as she pulled away.

"It's wonderful to be back. I've missed our girl talks *so* much." Suddenly it dawned on me. Nick and Dylan already knew Mika. I looked at Mika and then back at Nick and Dylan. "So you already knew Mika owned Genesis, Sirs?"

"Yes." Nick smiled broadly. Damn, but he was a gorgeous man. He was a tall Native American with long, blue-black hair that hung past his shoulders. Of course he wasn't as handsome as Mika, but he was definitely easy on the eyes. And Dylan was no slouch either. He was shorter with sandy-blond hair and warm blue eyes. Savannah couldn't want for sexier, more rugged men. The lucky wench had two.

"We're in construction," Dylan announced with pride.

"They built my house, love." Mika smiled. "I designed the plans, and Nick and Dylan built it. Or rather their company did."

"It's phenomenal."

"Thank you." Nick smiled with a hint of pride.

"Hey, when you feel up to it, we'd love to have you both over for dinner," Dylan chimed in. "Savannah is an awesome cook."

"We'd like that very much." Mika nodded as Savannah blushed.

"Just let us know what night works for you. We're going to head on home now and finish what we started here," Nick announced with a wolfish grin. Savannah's eyes lit up in delight as her cheeks flushed a deep crimson. Dylan growled and smacked her on the butt.

"You guys have a fun night." Mika chuckled.

"Thanks. You, too." The matching smiles on Nick's and Dylan's mouths were almost comical.

As they walked away, I turned to Mika. "When can we go home, Master?"

Mika laughed, rich and deep. "When I say we can, girl. Why? You're not enjoying yourself here tonight?"

His eyes twinkled, adding to my torment. Raising my brows and pursing my lips in stubborn rebellion, I shook my head.

"Oh precious, that look will get you nowhere. Weren't you begging moments ago? I much prefer that over such a disgruntled look. Besides, once you find out what I have in store for you when we get home, you might decide sitting here simmering isn't a bad

211

choice."

"What do you have planned, Master?" I asked, looking at the feral gleam in his sexy eyes.

Moving his mouth close to my ear, I shivered as he lightly outlined the shell with his warm, slick tongue. "I'm going to claim your virgin ass tonight, love." His tone was so carnal and sinfully decadent, I gasped and my eyes flew open wide.

Before I could respond, Drake and Trevor appeared. I swallowed multiple times before I could even think of speaking. My face blazed, and I knew I was like a blushing virgin on her wedding night. Well, in a way I was that virgin, or at least my ass was. Lowering my head, I inhaled several deep breaths, attempting to calm my racing heart. I had no intention of confessing to Drake, my brotherly former mentor, that Mika planned to deflower my ass. Okay, so confessing that tidbit to a gay man was no big deal, at least not to him, but for me it was far more information than I wanted to share.

"Still so anxious to leave pet?" Mika taunted.

"No. I'm fine." I choked out.

"Really? Are you sure?"

"You're not leaving already are you, Sir?" Trevor gasped.

"Well, actually Emerald's been dying to go home but has suddenly changed her mind. For some strange reason she's not quite as anxious, are you, love?"

"No," I growled unsubmissively.

Mika's brows raised in warning. "Tone? You give me that tone after I told you what I have planned for you later?"

"What are you getting later, sis?" Trevor giggled. "Is it something I'd enjoy?"

I couldn't help but laugh wildly and nod my head.

"Oh no doubt you'd enjoy it, Trevor my boy." Mika chuckled. "In fact, I've seen you receive that particular pleasure on many occasions, and you don't enjoy it, you fucking love it."

"Oh, sis. You're gonna get some nasty butt lovin' tonight, aren't you?"

"Trevor!" I hissed in mortification.

"What?" he asked with a mimicked tone and wide, innocent eyes.

"Daddy Drake, don't you have a ball gag for this mouthy boy of yours?" I asked in exasperation.

"I think Mika will agree that Trevor's not the only one who desperately needs a ball gag, my sweet." Drake grinned with a wicked smile.

"Oh, do you need any help, Mika, Sir? I'd gladly help, or hell, just watching would be fun too." Trevor giggled, licking his lips.

"Trevor, I swear to God, I'm going to pinch your balls off," I threatened.

"I'm sure you'd enjoy watching dear boy, but no. I'm keeping her all to myself. Forever." He turned and looked at me with a look of warning. "And you, my pet. You'll do no such thing to Trevor. I remember how sweet your delicate wrists looked that night outside my office, locked up in those shiny cuffs," Mika growled against my neck. His lips nibbled on my erratic throbbing pulse point.

"Master," I whimpered, in a pitiful mewl.

"Want the keys to my room?" Drake offered with a sly wink.

"No. I'm going to deflower her sweet virgin ass at home." Mika spoke nonchalantly as if his plans were an everyday occurrence. Didn't he realize I was scared half out of my mind? His enormous cock was going to split me in two.

"Deflower?" Drake asked with confusion as his smile instantly faded.

"Yes."

"But didn't Nelson..." Drake didn't finish his thought. He simply swore under his breath.

"No. He didn't. And I don't want to talk about him or the other thing anymore." In bold feigned courage, I set my chin, attempting to shield my embarrassment of not been worthy to be claimed in the usual slave fashion.

"Inept, fucker!" Drake muttered.

"Thankfully, he left me a very special gift," Mika boasted with pride. "And whether you want to discuss it or not, your ass will be properly claimed tonight, girl." His voice held a hint of reprimand, but more so, a promise of tenderness and love. Suddenly I wasn't *as* afraid of his big, thick cock invading my tiny virgin orifice.

"Well, I intend to deliver a hard, thick reminder straight down Trevor's throat for cursing earlier," Drake announced, his voice thick with lust.

"Mmmm," Trevor purred.

"You think that now, boy. Trust me. I can make it less than enjoyable for you."

"You never do, Daddy. Even fast, hard, and rough, I love the taste and the feel of your cock," Trevor gushed with a hungry look in his eyes.

"Why don't you come by tomorrow? We'll throw some steaks on the grill and then adjourn to the dungeon for a nice long night of play with our respective slaves." Mika grinned at Drake.

"Will do, man. Thanks." The two men shook hands then Drake softly kissed my cheek.

"Make sure you take a video, Master Mika. I'd love to see Emerald lose her virginity!" Trevor giggled.

"Trevor," I cried in a terse whisper. "Shut. Up."

"You'll do just fine, baby," Drake whispered in my ear then wrapped his burly fist in Trevor's silky blond mane. "Don't get too excited yet, boy. You have no idea what I plan to do before I make you gag on my cock."

Drake led a whimpering Trevor toward his private room.

"I'm sorry, love," Mika confessed.

Jerking my head back to look at him, my brows drew together in confusion. "For what?"

"For what, girl?"

"What are you sorry for, Master?" I amended in quick order.

"For announcing to Drake and Trevor that your ass had not been claimed. That was something I should have kept between us. I assumed Drake knew."

"It's okay, Master. Drake never asked, and I never volunteered. I should have, but it wasn't something Drake was going to claim, well not personally, anyway. But thank you for being concerned about my feelings, Master."

"I'm always concerned, girl. Don't ever forget that." Slanting his velvety full lips over mine, he consumed me in a fervent claim. His hot slick tongue plunged deep into my mouth. I whimpered and opened for him as our tongues swirled in urgency.

His cock jerked against my ass as his hand caressed the column of my throat. Pulling away from me, his teeth captured my lower lip and tugged. "We're leaving now."

Within minutes, Mika's big black Escalade was racing down the street. My mind filled with questions and fears. I swallowed my growing anxiety and nibbled my bottom lip. Neither of us said a word. Mika seemed focused on the road while my mind flittered with burgeoning anxiety.

"Is it going to hurt, Master?" I whispered softly.

Mika smiled then slowed the Escalade to the shoulder of the road.

"Come here," he ordered as he unfastened his seat belt and turned semi-sideways in his seat, his arms held open wide for me.

Following his directive, I unbuckled and slid onto his lap.

"Do you know what you just did?"

I shook my head as I looked at the proud smile curled on his full lips.

"You just made me the happiest man on the planet," he beamed as he kissed me soundly. "You stopped stewing on your worry and shared it with me. Thank you, precious."

He brushed his thumb over my lips as a smile full of love spread upon his mouth. I wanted to bury my face in his chest and cry.

"Don't be afraid. I'll prepare you so thoroughly you'll beg me to fuck your tight little asshole."

I shivered not with fear, but with longing at his feral words.

"First you'll take my seed in your mouth. I'm so ready to burst right now I wouldn't be able to keep from pounding into your ass."

I gasped and he chuckled.

"Your introduction to anal sex will be slow and careful. Even though I'll be claiming you, I'll prepare you thoroughly. There'll be no condoms since we are both free of disease. Martin ran a full screen on your blood the night of Dennis's attack. I was tested after Vanessa passed and am clean. So no condoms, no barriers. You'll feel every drop as I mark your rectum in a boiling shower of come. We'll get cleaned up when you're able, then I plan to bury my cock deep in your pussy, claiming it as well."

A groan escaped my throat.

"Are you ready to be mine for eternity, Julianna?" he asked, brushing his lips over my ear.

"Yes, Master," I answered in a breathless whisper.

"Back in your seat, pet. Buckle up."

Mika whipped the vehicle back on the road and sped toward home. Sexual vibrations burned in my veins. I could already taste his tangy essence on my tongue. Licking my lips, I yearned to launch my mouth on his cock and suck him deep down my throat as he drove.

"More questions, pet?"

Giving a throaty chuckle, I shyly smiled. "Not really a question, Master. More like a need. A clawing, aching need."

"Do tell." He tore his gaze from the road, assessing me in a quick glance.

"I want to worship your cock right now," I confessed with an impish grin.

"You're going to be the death of me, woman," he growled as he unzipped his jeans, extending his hand in invitation.

"Really?" I squealed with delight. Clamoring between the seats, I knelt and eased his engorged shaft from the confines of his jeans. Thick and hot, he pulsed in my palm. I could see the blunt crest seeping beads of expectant liquid beneath the passing street lamps. Licking my lips, I opened wide and plunged my mouth over his blistering hot column.

My taste buds rejoiced. Sliding my lips over his throbbing veins, I raised slightly, sipping his essence from the purple, swollen tip.

"Christ Julianna. I'm going to wreck the damn car!"

I tried to grin, but my lips were stretched far beyond the flexibility.

Mika's strong hand gripped my hair. "Just don't stop, girl," he hissed.

As his fingers threaded through my curls, I groaned on his shaft as it nudged the back of my throat. Quivering, I rubbed my mound against his seat.

"Fuck," Mika snarled between clenched teeth. "I can't drive. You keep making me cross-eyed."

I released his cock with an audible pop. "Do you want me to stop, Master?" I asked with feigned innocence.

"Do you want me to spank your ass raw?" A stern look of retribution flared in his eyes.

"I'll take that as a no." I giggled.

Without waiting for any further threats, I swirled my tongue over his slick bulbous crest and seated my lips to the base of his shaft.

"Sweet fucking Jesus," he snarled, tugging my hair unmercifully.

Thinking I couldn't possibly get any wetter, hot cream slid upon the inside of my thighs. The throbbing knot of nerves on my clit screamed for relief. Tugging my skirt up with one hand, I slid my fingers over my distended clit, furiously batting it back and forth.

"Don't you dare come. You don't even have permission to touch yourself, let alone release *my* orgasm. Do you understand me?" Mika's tone was infuriated and untamed.

Issuing an affirmative grunt and a nod of my head, I slurped relentlessly upon his shaft. Half out of my mind in lust, I moaned as I rubbed my pebbled clit.

Suddenly Mika stopped the SUV and snapped on the dome light. I didn't know where we were, but it didn't matter. We could have been in the middle of Grand Central Station. I wasn't stopping. Determined to compel his treasure come hell or high water, nothing would stop me, except, of course, his command.

"Your mouth is a hot slice of heaven, baby," Mika purred as he twisted his fist in my hair and pulled my head back.

I growled, dipping two fingers into my weeping tunnel and thrusted them in and out, wishing it was his cock. "I'm going to scald your fucking throat to hell and back. Goddammit."

Shoving my head down, his expanding cock blocked my airway. His thunderous cries reverberated in the vehicle as blistering streams of come exploded down my throat. Jerking my head back long enough to gasp in a breath, I swallowed every decadent blast of his tangy seed as it painted my tongue and throat.

The familiar tingling of release raced down my legs as I began to unravel. Finding the strength somehow, I jerked my fingers from my sodden channel. Lifting my mouth from Mika's cock, I raised my face toward the heavens and cried out in a mournful wail of denial. The flames of release licked at the fringes of my core, threatening to swallow me in its fiery explosion.

Mika snatched my wrist, guiding my cream-covered fingers to his mouth. Sucking and licking my glistening nectar from each finger, he shushed me. "Save that explosion for me, pet. I want to feel it when I'm balls deep in your ass."

A wild cry of desperation filled the vehicle. I was out of control, lost in a fog of demand and solely focused on gaining relief. My other hand plunged into my dripping core, and Mika seized my other wrist then pulled me to his chest. My body quaked uncontrollably, and my nipples burned like hot coals as they brushed against his chest.

"Mika," I screamed. "Please. Please. Please let me come." Tears of denial streamed down my cheeks.

"My God, Julianna. You are so fucking gorgeous. I've never seen you so desperate. My cock is hard again just watching you like this. So fucking free and untamed. Get out of the car." He cocked his head and issued a wary look as if he couldn't trust that I'd not resume masturbating. "Keep your hands were I can see them." He leapt from the driver's seat and raced around the front of the Escalade.

Still kneeling between the seats, both arms raised high in the air, I trembled and panted like an animal snared in a hunter's trap. I was trapped all right, trapped in my submission. Trapped in Mika's Dominance. Caught and controlled, every nerve ending sang in elation.

CHAPTER EIGHTEEN

Wrapped in Mika's warm embrace, I opened my eyes and blinked. He was holding me tight to his chest, whispering soft words in my ear. I felt as if I were coming out of some foreign fugue as I realized we were in the dungeon, yet I had no concept of how we'd gotten there.

"Mika. What happened?" I gasped in fear.

"It's okay baby. I'm right here. You're safe. Everything is fine," he reassured as he rocked me in a slow rhythm on his lap. "That was amazing."

"I'm so embarrassed." I moaned, feeling shamed.

"That's the last thing I want you to feel. You were so far gone, I thought I was going to have to allow you to orgasm before I'd get you back." He smiled in delight. "But you held on. I've got you, precious. You're safe."

"I've never had that happen before. What the hell was that?" I asked in a combination of wonder and awe.

"You totally let go, sweetheart. You let go of all your inhibitions and control. It was truly the most amazing thing I've ever witnessed in my life. I want to see it again. I want to get you so damn needy that you lose your mind and fall apart around me. That was spectacular."

Shooting him a weary glance, he smiled. "Don't worry. I'll be here to pull you back together. I'll always be here."

Still cradled safely in his arms, he stood and carried me to a large bed in the corner of the dungeon. Gliding me down to the soft mattress, he began peeling off my clothes, trailing his lips, teeth, and tongue in a beleaguered path over my tingling flesh. I arched to meet his every touch. Mewling and rocking my hips as he released my black lace bra, my ultra-sensitive nipples ached in time with my throbbing clit.

"Please, Master."

"What is it my love? What do you need?"

219

"Touch me. I need to feel your strong hands on me."

"In time, pet. In my time," he assured as he continued trailing his tormenting kisses. "I want to hear more of your sweet, pitiful pleas, precious."

His mouth covered my breast, and his teeth bit into my burning flesh. Arching my back from the bed, a scream tore from my throat. His dark peach-tinted lips fed upon my skin while his teeth and tongue prevailed upon my nipples. I felt myself falling faster and further than before.

Unconsciously, my fingers found their way to my clit. Before I could begin to bring some blessed relief to my inflamed bud, Mika's hand encased both my wrists and pulled my arms high over my head.

"That belongs to me. It's no longer yours, and you don't have permission to play with it yet."

"Help me," I pleaded.

"Soon, pet," he growled. "On your hands and knees in the center of the bed. Now."

His terse, demanding tone sent a ripple of fear down my spine. With quick obedience, I complied with his instructions.

"Head down, ass up," he snarled.

Open and vulnerable, a feeling of déjà vu washed over me. This was the exact position I was in the fateful morning that Mika stormed from my bedroom. The same morning I mistakenly convinced myself I was not a submissive. I was never so glad to be wrong about anything in my life.

Then his hands were gone. I felt the bed sway and heard him move across the room. Raising my head, I turned and watched as he stripped off his shirt. His muscles bunched as he pulled several items off a low shelf near the opposite wall.

"Head down. Don't look up again unless I instruct you to."

Not even realizing that I'd disobeyed him, I jerked at his command and lowered my head.

"Much better," he praised.

Listening intently, I heard him release the zipper of his jeans. The urge to sneak a peek was overwhelming. Wanting to gaze upon his mouthwatering cock, his sculpted body, and hypnotic eyes was a brutal mindfuck. But the urge to please him won out as I kept my forehead pressed to the bed.

The incessant throbbing of my clit was maddening, and the orgasm bubbling inside me was so enormous, I seriously thought I might spontaneously combust. Reminding myself he would *eventually* sanction my release, I wondered how long I could last before losing my mind. *You can do this. You will do this...for him.*

Feeling the warm glory of my submission eased my blistering demand, and I knew without a shadow of a doubt I would not fail him.

Sucking in a deep breath, I continued to calm my anxiety, reminding myself that Mika's pleasure was my reward. And it was working well until I felt him climb onto the bed. All the self-talk on the planet couldn't candy coat the fact that his massive cock was going to somehow squeeze into my tiny virgin asshole.

Drawing in a ragged breath, I pinched my eyes shut and clenched my butt cheeks, readying myself for the onslaught of blistering pain. But it wasn't his cock stabbing, it was his warm body draped across my back.

"What are you doing, my pet?" he asked with a hint of amusement.

"Preparing for you to claim me, Master," I squeaked in fear.

His warm tongue brushed the shell of my ear. "Wrong. *I'm* the one who will prepare you pet, not the other way around."

Lifting from my body, his tongue traced a slow indecipherable pattern down my spine. All the tension sagged from my body as his broad thumbs spread my ass open, and he began to lick my puckered rim. A low moan escaped my throat as tiny pulses of tingling pleasure arced outward from my sensitive opening.

"Mika," I gasped.

"Who?"

"Master."

"Yes, precious. Your Master has you. You're safe. You'll always be safe." His words vibrated against my virgin opening nearly sending me to the stars.

"I can't take this. I...please, Master. Please."

"You *will* take it. For me. You'll take everything I give you and beg for more."

He was right. I *would* take it all. Every pain. Every pleasure. Every mind-bending frustration. I would take everything if it pleased him, if it made him proud.

Yielding every ounce of my control, I knew he would never abuse or break me. I trusted Mika. Fully. Without reservation. Trusted him with my submission, my body, my heart, my life.

With a final flick of the tongue, his warm mouth vanished. Caught in a torrid tango of demand and compliance, a pitiful groan of denial rumbled in my throat.

"I have a feeling this is going to be exceptionally hard for you to manage, pet."

"I know. Your cock is huge." I whimpered in fear.

Mika's rich, deep laughter filled the room. "I'm not talking about you accommodating my cock. Trust me girl, I'll manage to fit every fucking inch balls deep in your hot virgin ass. I was actually talking about you maintaining control. It's going to be hard for you to keep from coming. You seem exceptionally primed to orgasm. Why is that?" His words were slathered in sarcasm.

"Oh, gee, Master. I can't imagine why. It's not like you've been teasing the piss out of me for hours or anything," I responded in a sarcastic tone.

Mika's response was a sharp, stinging slap upon my ass. "That just earned you a nice long session with my whip, pet."

"I'm sorry, Master." I tried to sound contrite, I really did, but the thought of his whip kissing my flesh cheeks was enticing beyond words.

"For the love of..." His exasperated sigh confirmed my apology wasn't the least bit convincing. "You know that orgasm you're clinging to by a thread, pet?"

"Yes."

"I can make sure you don't get to release it."

"No, Master." I panicked at the thought of being suspended in a pre-orgasmic prison. It would kill me. "I'm sorry. I'm scared, and I know it's going to hurt."

"Trust me, pet. I'll make it feel so good for you. But I need your trust. Will you give it to me, my love?"

"Yes, Master. I trust you. I do." I nodded then focused on his promise. He would make it feel so good. He already had with his tongue. The sensation of his tongue on my asshole sent a spasm of pleasure through my core. "I give you all of me. Please, take it."

"Good girl. I'll remind you only once, pet. You do *not* have permission to come. Don't let go. Don't lose control until I tell you."

"Yes, Master. I won't fail you." I acknowledged his directive, but still worried how he could fit his massive dick into my tiny ass and how the hell I was going to stave off the enormous orgasm already screaming to be set free.

"Reach back and spread your ass cheeks apart. Hold yourself open for me. Don't move your hands and don't even think about touching your clit. Oh, and remember to breathe, pet."

With my forehead pressed to the mattress, I reached behind me and held my cheeks open for him. I heard the snick of the lid as he opened a tube of lube. Holding my cheeks open, exposing myself to him, felt lurid. I felt small and defenseless. Any other time I would have automatically hid behind my walls, cordoning off my feelings of vulnerability, but the undeniable need to please Mika was in control now. The scared, insecure woman was gone, replaced by a submissive slave, unequivocally granting all to her Master.

"Remember to breathe, pet," Mika instructed as a cold glob of lube plopped against my puckered anus. His thick finger gently massaged the gel along my gathered rim.

Sucking in a deep breath, my body seemed to melt as I relaxed beneath a myriad of delightful explosions pulsating from the brim. My clit throbbed in a relentless thrum and more cream spilled from my pussy. I gasped as the tip of his finger breached the tender opening, and he rimmed me with the slick gel. I rocked my hips, aching for him to glide his finger in deeper as he swirled and opened the sensitized tissue. It was blissful euphoria. Speeding toward orgasm at an alarming rate, shallow gasps of delight cooled my throat as I fought to maintain control.

Soft mewling whimpers slid free as he slowly introduced another finger. My hips stilled and I inhaled a deep breath as the blissful burning sensation crawled up my spine.

"That's it, precious. Just relax. Let me stretch you. Your soft little whimpers are so fucking sexy, and your ass is like a heavenly seething inferno. You've got my cock dripping like a goddamn faucet. I can't wait to be balls deep inside your ass, love." Hissing out the words, his knuckles passed through the resistant ring as I groaned loudly. "Hang on to it, girl."

His fingertips glanced over my clit.

"Mika," I screamed as I dipped my hips, driving my ass toward him. I tried to press my clit against his fingers and force him to sink deeper inside my ass.

"Who?" he growled with a firm pinch to my clit.

"Master," I screamed in a panicked tone, fighting the powerful surge threatening to drag me under.

"Don't do it," Mika warned with a bellicose tone.

"Help me," I wailed in distress.

His hand landed a brutal slap against the inside of my slickened thigh. Searing pain radiated through my flesh, taking with it all desire to orgasm. I screamed and panted, trying to rise above the fire. My mind reeled, confused on which sensation to focus, the pain or the pleasure.

Desperately craving the gratification of release, I knew it wasn't time. He'd not given permission. If I allowed myself to topple over the edge, I would disappoint him. Failing him was not an option. So I concentrated on absorbing the pain. It was my only salvation.

"Are you under control now, girl?" he asked with a hint of humor in his voice.

"Yes, Master." I gasped, welcoming the engulfing pain.

"That's a good girl," he praised and eased yet another finger into my burning, stretched ass. "Three fingers, now pet. You're doing excellent."

Another cold burst of lube slid over my stinging tissue. The burning sensation cooled for a split second before he began driving all three fingers in and out of my ass with a slow, steady rhythm. My thigh stung, but the waning pain was no longer potent enough to override the mounting demand of my clit.

"Please," I begged as tears stung my eyes.

"Oh, girl. You're trying my patience tonight," Mika hissed in a tone of warning.

"Please, Master. I need to come," I whined.

"Much better, girl, but no. This is for me, not for you. This is for my pleasure." Plunging his fingers through my throbbing ring, his other hand captured my curls and gave a firm yank. "You've not suffered enough for me, pet."

"Fuck me," I cried as my body trembled. My swollen clit

224

pounded like a jackhammer.

"Already begging, love?" A small chuckle bubbled from the back of his throat.

"No."

"No what?"

"No, Master," I choked, panting like a porn star while concentrating on a strand of my hair that jostled on the mattress. I was desperate to focus on anything to take my mind off my screaming demand.

With one final, brutal push, his fingers were lodged to the hilt. Surges of lightning zipped through my body and gathered like a fireball beneath my clit. Gasping and moaning, I shook my head, willing away the unrelenting demand to come.

Mika removed his fingers and within seconds, I felt the hot, thick crest of his cock positioned at the entrance of my undefiled anus. I squeezed my eyes shut while mentally imploring myself to relax. It wasn't happening.

"Stop fighting this, pet," Mika barked in a bellicose tone. "Breathe. Focus on my voice and relax my fuck hole. It's mine! What are you?"

"I am your slave, Master," I whimpered.

Releasing my hair, I felt the wide tip of his cock press inward, invading my virgin opening. I cried out in shock. Immediately his fingers began to caress my forlorn clit, melding the pain into pleasure. The cool lube coupled with the fiery heat of his cock was a chaotic blend of blissful torture.

Unable to process the combined sensations, my mind shut down. Mika ruled every cell in my body. I was helpless, at his mercy, and I realized with startling clarity that I would always crave his possession of me.

"Yes. You *are* my gorgeous slave, girl." His words were strained, as if he too were struggling to maintain control. Feeding inch after painstakingly slow inch of his cock into my diminutive tunnel, I cried, not in pain but in glorious surrender.

"Do you relegate your body to me to use as I wish?"

"Yes, Master."

"Do you relinquish your control to me, to mold and bestow back to you as I see fit?"

"Yes, Master." I sobbed as he thrust further into my narrow passage, stretching me with a fire so blistering I wanted to explode from the heat and pressure.

"Do you resign your will to me, to hold in my hands like fragile glass, to nurture and protect?"

"Yes, Master. Oh God, yes."

"Do you release your heart, mind, and soul for me to treasure with my tender mercies?"

"Yes, Master. All of me. You have all of me." My body shook as sobs of renunciation echoed through the room.

"I love you, Julianna." His voice suddenly changed to a soft, compassionate plea. "I promise to honor you. Protect you. Love you. I will hold every precious gift you grant me with fragile wings. Lock them safely within my heart, mind, body, and soul...till my dying breath."

I couldn't speak. My heart felt like it was ripping in two. His tender words, his promise, split me open. Raw. Vulnerable. Unprotected. So many terrifying emotions detonated within, yet his crushing vow of unconditional love filled every exposed part of me with a salve of trust.

Protection.

Promise.

Refuge.

Salvation.

I was releasing every part of me unto his care, and he was claiming himself my anchor. My shield. My redeemer. My strength. My comfort. My guide. My love.

My Master.

My Master!

Hammering into my searing ass with unmerciful thrusts, his fingers plucked upon my clit like a fine-honed violin. My sobs soon turned to cries of rapture as he drew me to a height I'd never thought possible. Grunting with each thrust, his fractured words of praise tangled with my screams, a haunting melody of confirmation. Validation. Ownership.

Pain swirled into pleasure so enormous I was powerless to stop it. Pleasure mixed with panic threatened to swallow me whole.

"Please, Master! I can't..." I screamed as my limbs tingled and

226

grew numb, terrified, knowing I was only a matter of seconds away from shattering.

"Now. Come hard for me slave," he roared in command. Fingers dug into my hips as he launched his cock like a piston, in and out of my quivering hole.

Bursts of multi-colored lights blinded me as I plunged headlong into the swelling abyss. Tumbling and falling in a spectacular prism of color, I splintered.

Ripped apart at the seams, I disintegrated.

Screaming at the top of my lungs, my pussy and ass contracted and seized around his cock. I succumbed to the blinding explosion. Spasms wracked my body as I thrust back against him, matching in ruthless abandon his every lunge.

"Mine!" Mika screamed in feral declaration as his molten seed erupted.

His scalding shower singed my virgin walls while his ferocious cries melded with mine. As he emptied into me, I could feel the unconditional love of his heart and soul thread through me, weaving me to him for all time.

My body hummed with a palpable current. My pussy and ass continued to flutter and contract in powerful aftershocks. With his cock still buried deep in my ass, he stilled his hips as his fingers lovingly danced down my spine.

An unfamiliar warmth filled my soul, much different from the usual sated exhaustion following sex. A languid peacefulness, like a blanket of serenity, settled over me. No chaos cluttered my mind. No fears seeped into the recesses. Just a placid tranquility enveloping me.

I had been claimed.

The gnawing ache inside to be owned had at last been sated. Filled. Tears stung my eyes. I felt complete and safe with him surrounding me.

Mika slowly withdrew from my quivering passage. My shoulders slumped to the bed as I sobbed. My ass was still posed in the air with my hands still spreading my cheeks open for him as I buried my face in the sheet and wept.

Mika moved my hands away from my ass and gently tugged my legs from under me. Lying flat on the bed, his hot body covered me

227

and with a gentle touch, his fingers brushed the ringlet curls from my face.

"Talk to me, pet. Did I hurt you?" There was a note of fear in his voice.

"No, Master." I sniffed as I tried to stem the flow of tears. "You were loving, like you said. You...you...prepared me. It didn't hur...hurt. I just feel small and fragile."

"Awww, pet. Come. Let me hold you."

He wrapped me in his steely arms, repositioned himself and lifted me onto his lap as he sat upon the bed. "You were spectacular, love, far more than I could have imagined. I love you. I love you so much. We are bound together now, precious, for all time. You've made all my dreams come true, Julianna."

"I love you Master. I love you Mika. Dreams," I nodded with a slow, sated smile. "They really do come true."

After long minutes wrapped safely in his arms, he stood. My head lolled against his hard chest as he made his way toward the spacious bathroom opposite the bed.

"Come, let's get you cleaned up."

"I thought I was supposed to care for you," I murmured as the delicious warm water cascaded over my still-throbbing flesh. Clutching the loofa and citrus shower gel, Mika began slathering suds over my breasts.

"Not yet, pet. My job isn't done yet. I need to take care of you. Then after you're totally spent and near coma from all the demands I plan to make on your succulent body, I'll shroud you in even more aftercare."

Issuing a soft sigh, I closed my eyes and savored the touch of his broad, strong hands sliding effortlessly over my body.

"Mmm, that feels so good. I love you, Mika." I moaned when his fingers massaged shampoo into my scalp.

With a feral growl, he tightly gripped my hair. Slanting his lips over mine, he plunged his tongue into my mouth with an urgent, demanding kiss. I took everything he gave with a greedy moan. His hot cock was hard and ardent, pressing against my stomach. The man was a machine, not that I was complaining. His kiss alone rekindled a carnal fire and my clit throbbed, yet again, in need. How was it possible? He'd just given me the most explosive orgasm of my life, yet I craved more. Mika was an irresistible drug, and I was a strung-out junkie so addicted I would forever reject detox.

Ending the kiss, a wicked smile curled on his swollen lips as his hand eased between my thighs and his fingers circled my well-used asshole. "Are you sore?"

"A little," I confessed in a shy voice.

"Good. Let the pain remind you who you belong to, pet."

"As if I could forget," I taunted, raising my brows.

"Wash me. I can already tell you need the sass fucked out of you, and I plan on doing that right now."

His hand cinched tight in my curls, and he forced me to my knees. Reaching up, I plucked the soft loofa from his hand and coated my fingers in its thick, rich suds. Dropping the sponge, I washed his dark, ridged cock with my fist. His angry, pulsating veins made my mouth water, and I licked my lips, whimpering as I slid my tightly squeezed hand up and down his shaft.

"Insatiable much, love?" he asked with a hint of amusement.

"With you, Master? Always," I confessed as I teased his seeping crest with my thumb.

"Keep it up my sweet slut and you'll be begging for mercy." His growled words weren't a threat but a promise. A shiver of anticipation shook my body as I gripped his stalk, fist fucking his bubble-coated hot shaft. "Rise and fuck me, girl."

"Is that a command, Sir?" I giggled.

Without another word, he pulled me to my feet. My giggles were quickly replaced by gasps, then a long sultry moan when he quickly rinsed the suds from his cock and pushed my back against the cool, tiled wall. With one demanding thrust, he was buried balls deep in my pussy. Crying out in a combination of pleasure and pain, my narrow opening clutched around his shaft working furiously to accommodate it.

"What are you?" he growled with his mouth pressed against my ear.

"Your slave."

"Show me, girl. Fuck me like a slave."

Rolling my hips, I wiggled back from his warmth, just dislodging his cock a slight bit. Biting my lip to contain my cries of pain mixed ecstasy, I slammed my fluttering tunnel onto his shaft.

229

Over and again I fucked him like a wild animal, humping and grinding upon his turgid, thick cock. Unrestrained. Uncontrolled. Unbridled.

Mika's low grunts of approval bred a newfound freedom within. I lost all inhibitions.

His pleasure was my purpose.

My fingers dug into his marbled shoulders as I pounded upon his cock with a crazed frenzy. His broad crest scraped over my G-spot with a vengeance, and the mounting pressure built like a giant tsunami. My growls of need fused with his grunts of pleasure. An erotic song of power filled my ears.

"Beg for it, precious. You know you want it. I want to hear your desperation," his husky lust-filled voice beckoned.

"Please, Master. I can't hold it back. It's going to..."

"Now, girl. Give it to me. Now!" he barked as his fingers pinched my nipples while his other hand yanked my hair with savage demand.

"Master!" The cry slashed from my throat as a thunderous wave of ecstasy pulled me under, and I screamed loud and long as the orgasm ripped through me. Mika's hot seed jettisoned deep into my spasming womb. Filling me. Marking me. Once again, claiming me as *his*.

Limp and sated, I sagged against his hot chest, gasping the steam-filled air into my lungs. He loosened his fingers from my hair. Pulling me from the wall, he adjusted the water temperature then embraced me in a powerful hold. As the cool water pelted my blazing flesh, I clung to him, floating in a delirious, sated haze.

Neither of us said anything for a long time. As the water became cold, he turned off the shower and handed me a towel. I dried the droplets of water from his chocolate flesh, paying special attention to his half-limp cock and heavy sac.

Unable to resist the temptation, I leaned down and planted a kiss on the tip of his cock. Without a word, he clutched my hair and pulled me upright.

"Did you have permission for that girl?" he asked with a twinkle in his eyes and a small smile on his exotic lips.

"No Master," I whispered in mock shame.

"Brat," he growled with a much broader smile. "You need to

work on subterfuge, pet. Your remorse was nowhere near convincing."

A guilty giggle vibrated in the back of my throat, and I gave him a playful wink.

"Back to the bed, girl. I think you need to feel some leather upon your ass cheeks."

With a gleeful squeal of delight, I snagged another towel and dried myself in record time. Running to the bed, I jumped into the air and landed with a whoosh upon the mattress. Clamoring onto my hands and knees, I wiggled my ass in invitation.

Mika's laughter made me smile. Seconds later, a broad leather paddle landed a burning slap against my butt.

"Thank you, Master," I hissed in delight. "May I have another?"

"For now, your safe word is 'mercy,' my love. Soon you'll have no safe word and will be totally at my mercy."

"I can't wait," I purred as my heart soared in absolute bliss.

EPILOGUE

Three Weeks Later

"Julianna. Come on, we're going to be late," Mika called from the hallway.

I danced on one foot, trying to slide into my shoe while I attempted to secure the back of my earring.

Drake, Sammie, and Trevor had pulled out all the stops at Genesis in preparation for our collaring ceremony. Well, mostly Trevor. From what Sammie had told me, Trevor had gone "gay-zerk" on decorations alone.

I looked up. Mika was standing in the doorway, his brow arched as I continued to hop on one foot. Flopping to the bed, I gazed upon him with hunger gripping my core. He was dressed in a formal tux. His bronzed skin glowed against the crisp cotton shirt. Broad shoulders filled out the black tapered jacket, drawing attention to his narrow waist.

"Master, you look decadent. I want to stay home and undress you with my teeth. Please? I don't want to be put on display in front of everyone at the club," I whined in a pitiful moan.

"Tough shit, girl. I'm claiming your tight ass tonight in front of God and everyone. Now get that sexy ass of *mine* moving. We're late."

My lips formed an exaggerated pout. "Yeah, yeah. I'm coming." I huffed as I yanked the strap of my shoe over my heel.

In three long strides, Mika ate up the hardwood floor then cupped my chin. Lifting me from the bed, his eyes narrowed.

"Who am I?"

A sly smile curled on my lips as I smoothed my fingers over the lapels of his jacket. "Why, you're the great and powerful Oz, Master." I smiled with a shameless, wicked grin. Then slanting my lips over his, I took one last liberty and kissed him. Kissed him with all the passion, love, devotion, and submission I held in my heart.

ABOUT THE AUTHOR

Jenna Jacob is married and lives in Kansas. She loves music, cooking, camping, and riding Harley's in the country. At thirteen she began writing short stories and poetry and dreamed of one day becoming an author.

Now that her four children are grown, she has time to paint with words, the pictures in her twisted mind. Outgoing with a warped sense of humor, she's never once been accused of being shy or introverted. With close to twenty years of experience in the dynamics of the BDSM lifestyle, she strives to portray Dominance and submission with a passionate and comprehensive voice.

COMING SOON

ONE DOM TO LOVE - Is the first in a brand new BDSM Erotic Romance Series titled: *The Doms of Her Life* and will be available soon.

Jenna is co-author with New York Times Bestselling Author Shayla Black and Isabella LaPearl. The three have created a toe-curling, knock-you-off-your-feet erotic treat. Here's a peek:

Raine Kendall has been in love with her boss, Macen Hammerman, for years. Determined to make the man notice that she's a grown woman with desires and needs, she pours out her heart and offers her body to him—only to be crushingly rejected. But when his friend, very single, very sexy Liam O'Neill, watches the other Dom refuse to act on his obvious feelings for Raine, he resolves to step in and do whatever it takes to help Hammer find happiness again, even rousing his friend's possessive instincts by making the girl a proposition too tempting to refuse. But he never imagines that he'll end up falling for her himself.

Hammer has buried his lust for Raine for years. After rescuing the budding runaway from an alley behind his exclusive BDSM dungeon, he has come to covet the pretty submissive. But tragedy has taught him that he can never be what she needs. So he watches over her while struggling to keep his distance. Liam's crafty plan blindsides Hammer, especially when he sees how determined his friend is to possess Raine for his own. Hammer isn't ready to give the lovely submissive over to any other Dom, but can he heal from his past and fight for her? Or will he lose Raine if she truly gives herself—heart, body, and soul—to Liam?

MASTERS OF MY DESIRE—The second book in *The Doms of Genesis* series will be available in early 2013.

Two Dominant men and one unsuspecting submissive make for

a lurid, luscious ménage. *Master of My Desire* is guaranteed to keep you hot in the coming winter months. Just take a look:

Watching two big burly men walk toward the patrol car, I couldn't decide which one to focus on. Both were equally scrumptious, and I'd been void of a good dose of eye candy for what seemed like forever. They were the most mouthwatering, gorgeous, virile men I'd ever seen. Startlingly aware of my contracting nipples, I tried to swallow but suddenly my mouth was dry and my throat seemed to close up. A warm slippery release wept from between the folds of my sex as the tall, Native American-looking man captured my gaze with a commanding hold.

A lusty tremor rippled through my body as the sheriff turned to me. "Do you know these boys?" he asked, concern wrinkling his brow.

"No sir," I whispered in a shy voice as I shook my head.

I didn't know them, but I sure as hell wanted to. Know them up close and personal. The tall Native American man continued to grip me with his erotic and dangerous eyes. A shiver slithered down my spine. No man had ever made me physically squirm before, but this guy evoked an agonizing flurry within me.

"Can I help you boys?" the sheriff asked after lowering his window.

"We're here to pick up Savannah. We're supposed to take her to Kit's place," the shorter one smiled. His voice was warm and soothing. Bending his head, he raised his beautiful baby blues, captivating me with his intense gaze. My heart leapt in my chest. His eyes were so penetrating I could almost feel him invading my soul. Something wicked flashed over his cerulean pools as he continued to stare at me. "Kit told me to tell you that we're safer than Merlot...whatever the hell that means."

Yeah, you look about as safe as a baby rattlesnake, Mister. With a nervous chuckle, I nodded. "It's okay, I know what she means."

With a nonchalant roll of his shoulders, his blue eyes softened. At least he was attempting to put me at ease while the big Native American man's eyes continued to penetrate me in an uncomfortably appraising way. Oh hell. No, he wasn't reassuring at all. He looked like danger and sin all rolled up into one hot, orgasm-inducing package.

35828113R00142

Made in the USA
Middletown, DE
16 October 2016